Savage Birthright

Clay Warrior Stories
Book #18

J. Clifton Slater

Savage Birthright is a work of fiction. Any resemblance to persons living or dead is purely coincidental. I am not an historian although, I do extensive research. This book is set in the time of the levied, seasonal Legion of the mid-Republic and not the fulltime Imperial Legion. There are huge differences.

The large events in this tale are taken from history, while the dialogue and close action sequences are my inventions. Some of the elements in the story are from reverse engineering mid-Republic era techniques and procedures. No matter how many sources I consult, history always has holes between events. Hopefully, you will see the logic in my methods of filling in the blanks.

The manuscript for *Savage Birthright* has been dissected, beaten, and straightened by the eagle-eyed Hollis Jones. With each correction and red penned note, she has removed extra verbiage and tweaked the story. Her editing notes are the reason the tale makes sense and flows. For her work and guidance, I am grateful.

If you have comments, please e-mail me.

E-mail: GalacticCouncilRealm@gmail.com

To get the latest information about my books, visit my website. There you can sign up for my newsletter and read blogs about ancient history.

Website: www.JCliftonSlater.com

Thank you for being a part of Alerio's stories.

Euge! Bravo!

Savage Birthright

Act 1

Two years earlier, Consuls Scipio and Calatinus rebuilt the Roman fleet, sailed Legions to Sicilia, and captured Palermo. Balancing the win, Qart Hadasht forces captured the fortress and farms of Agrigento on the west coast of Sicilia.

The next year, the fleet under Consuls Caepio and Blaesus lost one hundred and fifty of their new warships to a storm. Hoping for a different response from the Gods, the first plebeian was elected Pontifex Maximus of Rome. Tiberius Coruncanius, a new man and the first non-noble to hold the position, took office as the Republic's Chief Priest. From then until part of the following year, the Senate hunkered down to wait for answers to their prayers.

Taking advantage of Rome's crippled fleet, raiders preyed on unprotected merchant ships. Tons of merchandise and numbers of transports were captured, their cargo and vessels sold, and the crews condemned to a life of slavery.

Unlike the Roman and Greek Gods, the deities of the raiders didn't meddle in human affairs. The Cult of the Serpent left the pirates to their own fate. For the men of the Illyrian Tribes, success and promotion came from an individual's aggression and ambition, and not from actions of the Gods or birthrights from their fathers.

Therefore, while the Roman Republic sacrificed and read entrails seeking signs, the Kings on the east coast of the Adriatic Sea prepared their nations for conquests.

Welcome to 252 B.C.

Chapter 1 – Raiders in the Fog

Visibility dropped to nothing when the white mist appeared over the waves. Before Captain Orsini could order a change in course, the transport sailed into the cloud.

"Cafatia, get on the bow and, for whatever good it'll do us, keep your eyes open," Orsini directed his First Mate. Once his second in command was moving to the foredeck, the Captain instructed the other three crewmen. "Roll the sails and man the oars. We need to keep forward momentum and stay off the rocks."

"Skipper, I didn't see any rocks," a sailor responded as he tied off one side of the midship sail.

"You can't see anything in this soup," another said while tying off the port side. "Let alone rocks along the coast."

"When the Goddess Achlys places her hands over your eyes, death can't be far away," Orsini warned.

"Do you think this is her mist-of-death, Captain?" the third sailor inquired.

"Not if we stay off the rocks," Orsini answered.

The oarsmen walked fifty strokes with the oars before the merchantman, *Juno's Grip*, rowed out of the fog.

"Ah, Hades," Cafatia swore from the foredeck.

Moments later, Orsini mirrored the sentiment of his First Mate. Their concerns provoked by an approaching ship.

The liburnian style vessel ripped across the clear water with both levels of oars rising and falling rapidly. In addition to the sixty oarsmen, fifty pirates stood between the rowing stations.

"Dashed on rocks or dashed by Illyrians," Orsini complained, "it seems the Goddess was waiting for us in the fog after all."

The raider ship lined up with the side of *Juno's Grip*. As the bows passed, three pirates jumped from the low-profile ship to the deck of the transport.

"I'd suggest you stop rowing," one stated. He glanced from side to side at the men accompanying him and, with a smile, added. "If you make my oarsmen row after you, they'll demand that I feed your crew to the fish."

"Hold water," Orsini instructed. One of his crewmen reached for a knife. To prevent bloodshed, the Captain added, "and hold your weapons."

The sailor's hand dropped from the hilt and his shoulders drooped. When stopped by Illyrians, the crews of transports and their boats sometimes vanished. And while the vessels would resurface under new ownership, the crews were sold as slaves.

"Very wise," the pirate leader exclaimed.

"You've chosen the wrong transport," Orsini informed the Illyrian. "We're hauling dirt for ballast to balance the boat. Nothing of value to you."

The pirate waved at the deck boards. His two men grabbed an end and lifted a plank. He peered into the cargo hold.

"Dirt? Not valuable, you say?" the pirate laughed. "Captain, we've been watching you since you took on the load of ore at Caorle."

Noricum iron ore made excellent steel. However, it wasn't rare enough to warrant being targeted by Illyrian raiders.

"It is Noricum," Orsini admitted, "but it is just iron dirt."

"That's better. Now that we've established trust, who owns this transport? And please don't lie to me."

Along with the caution, the pirate rested a hand on his sword. Orsini nodded his understanding.

"Why do I suspect you already know the answer?" the skipper of *Juno's Grip* questioned. The pirate's face remained impassive, but his fingers wrapped around the hilt of his weapon. Even without the threat, Orsini couldn't think of a reason to hide it, so he told the Illyrian. "This merchantman is owned by Senator Spurius Maximus. I don't think you want to steal from one of Rome's most powerful citizens."

"Under other circumstances, I would disagree with you," the pirate leader remarked. Facing in the direction of his ship, he raised a hand and mimicked a catching motion. In response, a scroll flew from the liburnian. The pirate snatched it out of the air, looked at Orsini, and winked. "But today is your lucky day. I'm on a mission for my King."

He handed Orsini the scroll along with instructions.

"When *Juno's Grip* returns to the Adriatic Sea," the pirate informed Orsini, "you better be hauling an answer."

"And if I don't?" Orsini asked.

"Then you'll need a big sack of silver," the pirate leader replied. "Or I'll take your cargo, your boat, and your bodies."

The three Illyrians jumped down to the deck of the two-banker. Using their oars, the rowers pushed the raider away from the sideboards of the transport and moved off with powerful strokes.

At eighty feet, the liburnian was longer than *Juno's Grip* but not as wide or as deep. Yet, the raider ship with the low profile had enough width to accommodate rowers and fifty warriors. Without a ram, the soldiers provided the ship's offensive weapons. Its speed and maneuverability came from the sixty rowers. Together, the soldiers and oarsmen made an excellent weapon's system for overtaking and seizing merchant vessels.

"I thought we were done for," Cafatia commented. He walked from the bow to the steering deck on shaky legs. "When we land, I'm making a sacrifice to the Goddess Juno for her protection."

"You might want to include prayers to Bia," Orsini suggested.

"Why the winged Goddess of Force?" the head rower asked.

"Because that's Senator Maximus' household deity. And Spurius Maximus had as much to do with saving us as the Goddess Juno did," the Captain proposed. Then, realizing he might have spoken blasphemy, he rushed out. "I'll be joining you in the sacrifice. We'll make it a grand one to honor both Bia and Juno, the Goddess of Protection."

***

Arching through the air, the heavy sword cracked when it impacted the shield. The shock passed through the hardwood, the small amount of padding, and raced up the victim's arm and shoulder. Most swordfighters would shuffle back seeking recovery time from the mighty blow.

Alerio Sisera wasn't most fighters. He dropped as if the strike had driven him to his knees. Immediately, he swung his practice gladius under his shield and that of Merula Mancini. Before the wooden blade impacted with his legs, the household guard hopped back five paces.

The first four hops were to get out of range from a roll and stab by the villa's Master. Alerio had done that on more than one occasion. And the final jump took Merula out of the sand pit and clear of the fight.

"You are about to be attacked, sir," Merula advised with a smile.

Still on his knees, Alerio pivoted, shook off the shield, and tossed the wooden gladius aside. A heartbeat after the tools of war were discarded, two small bodies crashed into his chest. Alerio Carvilius Sisera, noted swordsman and Legion officer, was knocked over. Landing on his back, he cried out in mock pain while hugging his children. The sound and gentle squeezes brought laughter from Olivia and Tarquin.

"They've been standing on the patio jumping around and waiting for me to release them," Gabriella explained while strolling to the sand pit. The gold flecks in her brown eyes danced and a smile graced her face. "It's almost bath time, so I turned the demons loose."

"Your timing was perfect," Alerio assured her. "I feared that Mancini was about to get the better of me."

The household guard picked up Alerio's shield and creased his forehead before grabbing the practice gladius.

"It's not good to lie to children or infantrymen, Battle Commander," he scolded. "You were in control for the entire session."

Alerio stared at the household guard for a beat before instructing, "Put the weapons away. And thank you for the workout."

"My pleasure, sir," Merula Mancini responded. "It helps keep me sharp."

He marched to the weapons' shed and vanished through the doorway.

"I need to give the babies a bath," Gabriella said while holding out her arms. Then she sniffed and advised. "And you need one as well."

Before Alerio could sit up and hand over the twins, Hektor Nicanor raced from the patio. Halfway across the yard, he stopped.

"Colonel Sisera. Lady DeMarco. Senator Maximus has come to visit," the Greek youth announced.

Gabriella and Alerio peered towards the patio.

"Where is he?" she questioned. "Usually, he heads right for his grandchildren."

"The Senator went directly to Colonel Sisera's office," Hektor answered. "I've ordered refreshments for him."

Alerio stood and held out the little ones. When Gabriella reached for them, Alerio pulled them back, leaned froward, and kissed her. Only then did he hand over Olivia and Tarquin.

"What was that for?" she challenged.

"My father wouldn't snub his grandchildren unless it was urgent," Alerio told her.

"What does that mean?"

"It means trouble," Alerio replied. "Hektor, fetch a clean tunic and bring it to my office."

***

Unlike the office at Villa Maximus, at Villa Sisera the walls were empty of memorabilia.

"You should put up trophies," Spurius Maximus suggested. He indicated the unadorned walls with his glass of vino. Then noticing Alerio dressed only in underwear, he added. "And put on proper clothes. An outfit befitting a member of society, I would think."

"You're babbling, General," Alerio remarked. "That means one of two things. You have a problem with no obvious solution. Or you can't decide on a course of action for a difficulty."

Hektor stepped in and handed Alerio a fresh tunic. After dropping it over his head, Alerio walked behind his desk and sat.

"But I have a clue," he continued. "You went straight to my office and ignored your grandchildren. That tells me, there's a problem."

Spurius Maximus had changed since Alerio first met his adopted father. Then, he was a robust man with mass and muscles. Now, the Senator had shrunken until he was thin, and his bones poked at the underside of his flesh.

"Were I a younger man, I would put together a squadron of warships and a couple of Centuries and fix this," Spurius Maximus boasted. Then he glanced at the noticeable tendons of his hands, the slight tremor, and deflated. "But at eighty, I'm afraid my days of charging off to war are long past."

"Maybe if I knew the situation, I could offer options to war," Alerio proposed.

Spurius Maximus reached into a pouch and tugged. Then, he tugged again before managing to extract a scroll. With his arm shaking from the exertion, the old Senator slid it across the desk. Alerio noticed the frailty but refrained from mentioning it.

"Nice artwork," Alerio commented. The wooden end caps of the scroll were carved into the likenesses of serpent's heads. After admiring the engraving, he unknotted a piece of twine and freed a length of animal hide. Where the back remained dark, the underside had been bleached to create a surface for ink. Although the leather wasn't proper parchment, the lettering was readable. And the message elicited a question from Alerio. "How did they get my name?"

***

Spurius Carvilius Maximus, Senator of the Republic, slayer of Samnites, and trespasser on our sea.

The Ardiaein Nation salutes your audacity. However, General Maximus, your free passage has ended. Henceforth, your transports and any merchant vessels carrying cargo for you will be seized. The boats taken, and the crews sold to mining operations where they will certainly perish. I can imagine that it will only take a few instances before captains and sailors curse your name and refuse your commissions.

To have your economic foundation stripped away and your legacy destroyed will give me immense pleasure. That stated, I have a need and a name. To prevent this just punishment, send me Lance Corporal Alerio Sisera. I have a task he is suited for, and, in return, I will not pursue your merchant vessels or your cargo. If one or two vessels are taken, you can rest assured they were simply business and not targeted assaults.

I expect the Legionary or your reply on the next voyage of the transport, Juno's Grip.

King Pleuratus II, the Constrictor of Ardiaein Kingdom and Servant of the Ardiaean People.

***

"There're a number of oddities in this message," Alerio noted. "My rank and the assumption that shipping is the sole source of the family's fortune."

"If a foe only reacts to the obvious, he hasn't done an investigation," Maximus lectured. "Apparently the pirate from Ardiaean is acting on superficial knowledge. I'll, of course, suspend our trading ships until the Republic's Navy is back to full strength. In the meanwhile, should we need funds, the travertine quarry and farm can produce more."

Alerio rolled and unrolled the leather in nervous motions. After a few cycles, he placed it on the center of his desk and admired the snake heads.

"We can't allow an impudent ruler of a pirate town to dictate our future," Alerio exclaimed. "Besides, I'm curious. The last time I had contact with the Illyrians was thirteen years ago at Bovesia on the Kaikinos river."

"That explains the rank disparity," Maximus proposed. "But what skill is he talking about?"

"Back then, it could only be swordsmanship," Alerio answered. "Do you mind if I keep the message?"

"Why would you want that piece of vexed leather?" Senator Maximus inquired.

"I'm going to mount it on the wall of my office."

Chapter 2 – The Journey into Illyria

The shoreline slid by making trees and beaches a blur. With the midship sail full of air and the foredeck straining on the shorter mast, *Juno's Grip* appeared ready to leave the swells and fly. Then a huge, ungainly pelican flapped by showing the real speed of the transport.

"She's a decent ship," Hektor said, "and sort of fast."

"It's a good sailing day and our hold is half empty," Captain Orsini remarked. "I don't know what the scroll said, but Senator Maximus only allowed us a partial load."

"Should we be nervous?" Cafatia asked.

"The Senator has his reasons," Alerio offered from where he sat. While his legs dangled off the steering platform, his face was turned to the afternoon sun. In a lazy manner, he assured the crew. "You don't need cargo to pay ransom. I'm here to fulfill the demand."

"I hope you're worth more than you look," Cafatia observed.

Hektor pivoted to face the First Mate. Before he could challenge the crewman, Alerio called to him.

"Hektor, if you don't mind. Please, hand me my hat."

Distracted from correcting the offensive tone with a knife blade, Hektor pulled a felt petasos from a bundle, crossed the deck, and handed it to Alerio.

"Remember, the Captain does, but the crew doesn't know who I am," Alerio whispered to Hektor.

"Having the Senator's adopted son turn himself over to pirates isn't a clever idea," Hektor uttered. "And putting up with a sailor's disrespect is maddening."

"Let's assume we'll hear worse before we're finished in Ardiaein," Alerio told him. "For now, relax and enjoy the ride."

Hektor blew out hard to show his dissatisfaction.

"The Port of Bari isn't far," Orsini announced. "We'll put in, do some trading, and relaunch in the morning."

They hadn't seen any Illyrian vessels which, under normal circumstances, would be a good thing. But the pirate leader had threatened the crew if they didn't come back with an answer to the scroll. Hopefully, docking at Bari would give the Illyrian a chance to find them.

When Orsini leaned on the rear oar to angle the transport closer to shore, Cafatia strolled to the bow section. The First Mate had already forgotten about the poor Legionary and the medic.

On the aft platform, Alerio sat quietly watching the wind fill the sails. In the threadbare woolen pants and shirt and a pair of old hobnailed boots with cracked leather bindings, he appeared to be a poor soldier-of-fortune. And worthy of the First Mate's scorn.

***

In the morning, the crew of *Juno's Grip* finished loading new cargo and setting the deck boards. Then they hurried to the dock and clustered around a vendor. Smoke from a grill filled the air with an alluring aroma.

"Other than the crew eating honey coated pork," Alerio questioned, "why aren't we launching?"

"The wind at mid-morning blows to the northeast," Orsini explained. "If we left now, we'd row against the tide trying to reach the point at Vieste. By waiting, we'll reach there with less wear on my crew. Unless you think otherwise."

"You're the Captain," Alerio granted. He sniffed and added. "The pork smells delicious."

"Usually, the vendor is set up near the market," Orsini told him. "We got lucky, he's at the dock today."

Alerio glanced around until spotting Hektor standing near the grill. He held up two fingers. A short while later, Alerio, Hektor, and the crew munched on grilled pork encrusted with honey and waited for the wind to rise.

Thirty-three miles up the coast, an Illyrian vessel slid from the beach at Barletta. For the sleek two-banker, the tide didn't present a problem. Plus, the early start would let the crew fish in deep water until the Republic transport happened along.

The night before, a rider reported that *Juno's Grip* had docked at Bari. Along with the message, the spy assured the pirates that his brother, the vendor, would fire up the grill. The grilling pork was a guarantee that the transport would be late leaving the harbor.

***

The sweet spot across the Bay of Manfredonia was sixteen miles. Sixteen from the mainland and the same distance from where the land reached far out into the Adriatic Sea. And, as predetermined by the Illyrian raiders, the perfect area to intercept *Juno's Grip*.

"How did they find us out here?" Orsini questioned.

From over the horizon, the Illyrian raider rowed on a direct course to the merchantman. What the Captain couldn't see were the warriors putting away the fishing nets and stowing the catch in baskets. At a rapid closing rate, the two vessels soon came abreast, then slid side to side.

"I told you we'd be here when you returned," the pirate leader exclaimed from the rail of his ship. After jumping onboard the *Juno*, he inquired. "Do you have the reply to my King's message or my bag of silver?"

Alerio stood, touched the brim of his cap in greeting, and dropped both hands outward as if dumping something on the deck.

"You asked for Lance Corporal Alerio Sisera, and you get Legionary Alerio Sisera," he declared. "Easy tasks done in a timely manner, the difficult may take me a little longer."

"You're pretty brash for a destitute vagabond," the pirate said, noting the rough clothing and barely held together hobnailed boots.

"Pull that sica off your belt, and we'll see who's the poorer man," Alerio challenged. Looking at the Illyrian crew, he called out. "Anybody want to put coins on your Navarch?"

The crew laughed at the title. Their Captain wasn't even a squadron leader, let alone an Admiral. A few touched their coin purses. Then they remembered their purpose was to transport the man not to bet against him.

"If you're Sisera, grab your gear and come with me."

Alerio picked up a bundle, then twisted his neck in Hektor's direction.

"You wanted adventure," he said to the youth. "Here's your opportunity."

Hektor hesitated as if he couldn't decide. Finally, he picked up a bundle and crossed the deck to Alerio.

"Wait, I'm here to pick up Sisera," the pirate complained. "Not a Latian delegation."

"Hektor is my medic," Alerio responded. Dropping his bundle, he crossed his arms. "If he doesn't go, neither do I. Besides, he's Greek, not Latian."

"We can pull you off this tub," the pirate leader threatened.

Alerio squatted and reached into his bundle. In a smooth series of motions, he pulled out a pair of short swords and rose. Then with a flourish, he spun both blades into the air.

The sharp steel reflected the midday light in flashes before coming down. He caught both swords and rested them on his shoulders.

"How many of your crew are you willing to sacrifice to the Goddess Nenia?" Alerio inquired.

Leaders of war bands, be they raiders on foot, on horseback, or afloat needed to be brave and the best among their fighters. Another requirement was to protect their men by avoiding dangerous engagements. And the Legionary, although poor, certainly qualified as a hazard to the Illyrian crewmen.

"Fine, he can come with us. Step lively, we've a long way to go."

"How far?" Alerio questioned. He stowed the blades and picked up the bundle.

"If the God Redon allows, we'll make the coast before dark," the pirate skipper replied. "If the God who protects travelers doesn't, then we may never reach home."

"That's a harsh God," Alerio observed.

He jumped to the two-banker followed by Hektor.

"Redon doesn't usually meddle in the affairs of men," the pirate Captain explained. "None of the Illyrian Gods do, unless they're motivated by revenge or debt."

"Have you offended Redon?" Alerio inquired.

"I haven't but he wears a petasos like yours to signify traveling. I'm not sure if that offends the God or not."

"I'm not taking off my hat," Alerio remarked. "So, I guess we'll find out by the end of the day."

The oarsmen powered the liburnian to the east, away from *Juno's Grip* and the coast of the Republic.

***

Alerio had crossed the Ionian Sea, but each time in slow-moving merchant vessels. The cargo boats required a night's sailing on the open sea to reach the other coast. To transit the Adriatic, the Illyrian two-banker had sixty oars to aid the sail. Even with that many rowers, mostly, the wind pushed the raider swiftly through the water.

Alerio sat on the steering platform beside the pirate leader.

"What's your name?" Alerio inquired. "And the name of your vessel."

"I command the *Boria*, a ship as sturdy as the mountain God its named for," he replied. After pounding his chest with a fist, he bragged. "I am Epulon, feared by lesser men from north to south and on either coast. And a lover of beautiful women from north to south and on either coast."

"They all weren't so beautiful," one of the warriors tossed out.

Epulon leaped to his feet and drew his blade.

"Do you challenge me?" he demanded.

"No Captain. It was a joke," the warrior responded. He lifted both hands away from his blades to show he wasn't willing to draw.

"Then keep your opinions to yourself," Epulon advised. He sheathed the sica and dropped onto the platform. Then he whispered to Alerio. "I'll admit, they weren't all like the Goddess Prende."

"I take it she's your Goddess of Beauty," Alerio guessed. He received a smile and a nod of confirmation. "Do you take the *Boria* across the sea often?"

"Whenever the mood strikes me or my purse is light," Epulon told Alerio.

"Aren't you afraid of the Republic Navy?" Alerio inquired before pointing out. "Your ship doesn't have a ram for offense."

"A ram would only slow us down. We take what the sea has to offer," Epulon exclaimed. "Whether from beneath the waves or from boats sailing over them. It's all there for us. And no waddling warship can catch the *Boria*."

Alerio noticed an empty rowing station at midship.

"Do you mind if I get my hands on an oar?" he asked.

"As long as you don't disrupt the rhythm of my oarsmen."

Alerio dropped the wide brimmed felt hat on the platform next to his bundle.

Several pirates eyed the nice petasos. However, when the Legionary pulled his woolen shirt over his head, battle scars from prior fights became visible. Considering the signs of an experienced fighter, none would touch the hat.

"I'll do my best not to interrupt," Alerio promised before marching to the empty rower's bench.

***

Late in the day, the sun hung low, and light washed down the length of the two-banker, creating shadows. But the sky darkened, and the long shadows vanished when cloud moved overhead. Soon after, a light rain fell forcing Epulon to call for the sails to be rolled.

"This can't be good," Alerio offered. He glanced at the rowers who now provided all the power for the ship. Lifting his face to the sky, Alerio let rain drops splatter off his forehead. "How far to the coast?"

The question wasn't an off-the-cuff inquiry. Memories of waves washing across the deck boards of a transport sent shivers down Alerio's spine.

"About as long as I want," Epulon stated by pointing at the bow.

"Are you a wizard?" Alerio asked. He gazed ahead of the ship and into the curtain of rain. "I don't see anything except a wall of wet."

"Look closely, that's not sheets of rain. Those are cliffs of stone," Epulon told him. "My choice is to seek shelter under the cliffs or make for a beach."

"When will you decide?"

"When we're close enough for me to recognize our location."

***

The *Boria* rowed through the haze and rain. As it drew closer, the wall of damp rock took shape until it towered over the water.

"It looks dangerous," Alerio observed while staring upward, trying to find the top of the cliff.

"Only if you don't know the area," Epulon boasted. "I know exactly where we are. First Mate, bring us around, back it down, and let the boat drift in."

While the first officer issued the orders, Epulon grabbed Alerio's arm and guided him to one side of the steering platform. Hektor tagged along.

"This is one of the blue caves," the pirate Captain explained. From racing across the water, the two-banker drifted into a small bay. Epulon instructed. "First Mate, bring us closer. Starboard oars, keep us off the rocks until the anchors are set."

As the *Boria* maneuvered in the bay, Alerio could see a spot where the surface of the water vanished under the cliff. Through the drizzle and the little light that seeped through the clouds, he made out a sea cave. By the time the ship finished swiveling, the cave was off the stern and lost to Alerio.

"What's a blue cave?" he asked.

"You'll see in the morning," Epulon promised.

Crewmen pulled out leather tarps, raw fish, iron skillets, sticks, kindling, and logs. A few men jumped into the water and swam for the flat part of a rocky protuberance. After they climbed up, others on the ship tossed them the items. The flipping of the axes to the men on the rock provoked the most laughter. Second was the humor derived from men trying to stop the logs from skipping into the water on the far side of the rock. After fires were built under rainproof covers, the rowers and soldiers on the ship stripped down and dove over the side.

"The cliff walls protect the bay, and the caves pass the tides through the sea vents," Epulon described. "Without the slapping of waves against the granite, the water here is always calm."

"Making it a good place to spend the night," Alerio submitted.

"And the rock, a good place for the cooking fires."

Hektor pulled his shirt and pants off, climbed to the rail, and vaulted into the sea. When he splashed down, the Greek went under but quickly reappeared.

"It's not as salty as the Mediterranean," he observed.

"We have a lot of rivers feeding the Adriatic," Epulon explained. "Now, Lance Corporal, come swim with me to the rock. We have things to discuss."

Moments later, Alerio and Epulon climbed out of the water. They didn't stop at any of the fires where cooks were cleaning fish but climbed higher on the rock. Once out of hearing range from the crew, they selected flat areas and sat.

"This is very curious," Alerio mentioned. "What do we have to discuss that requires secrecy?"

"King Pleuratus didn't send the scroll."

"If your King didn't, who authored the threat to Senator Maximus?"

"It was sent on behest of Queen Jeta," Epulon replied. "She requires…"

An Illyrian cried out in pain. Blood gushed from between his fingers as he attempted to stem the bleeding by clamping his hand over a wounded wrist.

"In my bundle is a leather satchel," Hektor shouted while climbing out of the water. "Throw it to me."

A pirate holding an ax stood over the injured man stammering, "I'm sorry. So, very sorry."

A partially split log lay on its side. Hektor put a foot on the log and shoved it away. Then he reached for the wounded wrist.

"Don't touch me," the injured man screamed.

Other Illyrians shoved the youth away.

"Master Sisera, a little help?" Hektor pleaded.

From high on the rock, Alerio and Epulon watched the drama unfold.

"Captain Epulon. Are any of your oarsmen or soldiers trained medics?" Alerio inquired.

"The best I have can scarcely sew a sail," Epulon admitted. "Why?"

"Hektor Nicanor, although young, is a combat medic," Alerio offered. "He can treat your man. Or we can wait and chance him losing the hand."

"He's a good oarsman," Epulon remarked. Then to the group gawking at the wounded man but not doing anything else, he ordered. "Let the Greek see the wrist."

Hektor peeled the fingers back and studied a piece of bone sticking through the cut. Around him, crewmen pressed in to be sure the Greek did nothing more than study the wound.

"What have you got Hektor?" Alerio called down.

"The ax glanced off the bone and cut a splinter loose," he reported. "Painful, but I can save the hand if he lets me."

"Captain?" Alerio questioned.

"We're a hardy people, Sisera. It's a rough land and going to sea isn't much easier. Our Gods and the serpent demand strength from us," Epulon said. Then he shouted down to the crew. "A one-handed man can't farm, learn a trade, or go to sea. Let the youth treat him."

The crewmen separated and Hektor's medical kit was placed within reach. While the medic worked, Alerio turned to Epulon.

"The Gods, I honor and understand," the Legion officer granted. "But you said the Gods and the serpent demand strength. What did you mean by serpent?"

"The snake is sacred to all Illyrian tribes," Epulon replied. "I told you the Gods don't mettle in our everyday lives. While they don't, the serpent does."

"The God Asclepius has snakes in his temple. They assist in healing," Alerio recounted. Seeking understanding, he asked. "Do you mean serpents in a temple?"

"We worship serpents in temples, under rocks, in trees, in water, and on land. It's against the law to kill a snake. And to prove the power of the serpent," Epulon informed Alerio, "the Cleric of the Snake authored the scroll that brought you and the medic to us."

On the flat part of the rock, Hektor cut away the splinter of bone, and washed the wound with vinegar. Although rough men, the crew cringed while the injured oarsman screamed.

Chapter 3 - Cleric of the Snake

The fires turned to ash, the sky filled with fading stars, and sunlight beamed over the top of the cliff.

"It's Lady Prende's Belt," several sailors called out.

Alerio tossed off his blanket, sat up, and looked in the direction they pointed.

"It's a rainbow," Hektor observed.

In the sky, a multicolored arch bridged over the sea.

"Prende is the Goddess of Love and Beauty," Epulon explained. "While her display is magnificent, walk aft and gaze on the cave."

Alerio and Hektor crossed to the steering platform, stopped, and gawked. In the rain the day before, the mouth of the cave had been gray and black. In the morning sun, the water in the sea cave radiated a bright blue.

"With a smaller boat, you can row in," the pirate Captain told them, "and get the full impression. It's equally as glorious as the Lady's display. But we haven't time for exploration."

"So much beauty for such a harsh land," Alerio remarked.

"The flatland is rich, the rivers teem with fish, and the mountains are filled with game," Epulon uttered while signaling the First Mate. "It's a good place for serpents and the strong. For the weak, Ardiaei is not so pleasant."

In a few strokes, the *Boria* glided from the inlet and out onto the sea.

***

Three miles to the north, the ship left the Adriatic Sea via a channel. At the end of the watercourse, they rowed into the lower chamber of Kotor Bay. After a long sweeping curve to the left, the vessel exited the lower chamber. Tracking northward they followed a narrow stretch of water to the upper chambers of the bay. Resembling two apples hanging from the same stem, the upper part of the bay had two nodes of water. Taking the one on the left, the raider ship rowed around a mountain and a short while later a town came into view.

"Your capital?" Alerio questioned.

Nestled on the shore of the upper reaches of Kotor Bay, the settlement occupied the only flatland along miles of rocky coastline.

"No, this is Risan, a prominent town," Epulon answered. He scanned the Illyrian ships in the water and the forest along the coast. "Although, it should be the residence of King Pleuratus. But he prefers Shkodër on Lake Shkodra."

"Better defenses there?" Alerio inquired.

"You saw the twists and turns needed to navigate the bay," Epulon replied. "Imagine attacking from the sea. If you made it this far, where would you land your army?"

The ship nosed to a beach and crewmen jumped to the rocky shore and pushed the *Boria* out of the water. Less than a mile of curved beach was available for landing and beyond the shoreline, mountains rose above Risan.

"I'd land the Legion right here," Alerio described. His eyes shifted to a rushing river that cut the beach in two. "Or, if it was too well defended, I'd land them on the other side and build a bridge over the river."

"Your men would build a bridge while under attack?" Epulon questioned.

"Of course, Legionaries are capable builders as well as talented fighters."

"Now I understand why the Cleric wanted you," the pirate leader offered. He jumped to the beach before telling Alerio. "Leave your bags."

Alerio leaped then turned to look for Hektor. Bent over the crewman with the wrist wound, the youth wrapped a fresh bandage over the injury.

"I told you, no rowing for at least eight days," he scolded. "It's not magic. Your body requires rest to heal properly."

Once done, Hektor pulled the strap of his medical kit over his head, walked to the rail, and jumped to the rocky beach.

"Is this the capital?" he asked.

"No, it's their fortress," Alerio stated while pivoting and scanning the high peaks above the town. "Trouble with your patient?"

"Bone injuries are painful, and men think they can work through the pain," Hektor complained. "What they miss is the bone and skin need to stitch together. If they put too much pressure on the wound, they'll delay the healing."

"I'll have a talk with him," Epulon offered. "Now, follow me."

They took a set of steps off the beach. The houses of Risan were built of thigh sized stones and hefty beams of lumber. It made sense as they were the two most common building materials in the area. After a particular steep incline, they came upon a flat expanse.

Rocks with flat tops and sloping sides dotted a yard of grass and sand. Based on the shapes and placement, they had been purposely placed in a pattern. A two-story stone building occupied the center of the yard. Leading to an upper floor, a rock staircase wrapped around the back of the building. Where the staircase reappeared on the other side, the final steps went to the roof.

"From the top, you can see the lower chamber of Kotor Bay," Epulon pointed out. "Enemy ships rowing in will be sighted before they reach the upper bay."

"Fortress Risan," Alerio acknowledged.

"Snakes," Hektor warned. "Several of the rocks have serpents on them."

A man dressed in a robe with a hood pulled down low on his face strolled slowly from the building. He held out his hands as if walking through a wheat field caressing the stalks. But here, he motioned gently to the snakes stretched out on the flat rocks.

"They are sunning themselves," he whispered. "Do you not enjoy absorbing the warmth of the sun? Note the rocks are in concentric circles to draw the sun's power. Can you not feel the energy of the sun here in our serpent garden?"

Epulon bowed to the man and took a step back.

"Monk, a good day to you," he said. Then the pirate Captain advised while backing away from the garden. "I'll meet you at the ship, Sisera."

"I thought you people revered snakes," Alerio commented.

"Honoring them is one side of the coin," Epulon replied. "Respecting their territory is another."

"You're afraid of snakes," Alerio guessed.

The brash pirate leader didn't respond. Instead, he hurried down the steps and soon vanished from view.

"What happened to being feared north and south and from coast to coast?" Alerio called after him.

"Would you like to hold a living facsimile of the great God Boa?" the monk inquired. "It will put you closer to the Divine Snake."

"Look priest," Alerio told him, "I'm here to speak with the Cleric of the Snake, not to join your cult."

"Then I shall select a gentle one for you."

"I didn't agree to holding a snake," Alerio protested.

"Boa's Temple is a place of harmony, undefended by steel or staff," the monk reported. "To maintain the peace, everyone entering the temple holds a poisonous serpent. You see, if you make a sudden or aggressive move, the Divine Snake will strike you down through its intermediary."

Alerio glanced at the sleeping snakes, swallowed nervously, and questioned, "You did say a gentle one?"

***

The eyes with the vertical slits didn't look at Alerio. But the coils of the long muscular body on his neck and down his arms made him aware that the snake knew it was in contact.

"Serpents don't care if you are a friend or a foe," the monk advised when he placed the snake across Alerio's shoulders. "Your thoughts and intentions mean nothing to them. They recognize movement for hunting and self-preservation."

"In short, don't startle the reptile," Alerio offered.

"It is the only rule you need in Boa's Temple."

Alerio slowly climbed the stairs. They wrapped around to the back of the building and ended at a second-floor patio. Curtains at a doorway blew in the morning breeze.

"Enter visitor," a man's voice called from inside.

Using the back of his arm to push aside the material, Alerio passed through the curtain without disturbing his snake.

Once inside, the door closed behind him. Alerio stood blinking and trying to adjust his eyes to the darkness.

"Bright light hurts my eyes," the voice informed him. "We will speak in shadows and the half-light of candles."

Across the room, a highbacked chair with arms that came up and over as if fangs of a snake were only partially lit by candles. The light didn't reach the seat or the occupant.

"Are you the Cleric of the Snake?' Alerio inquired.

"I am. And who are you?"

"Alerio Sisera," he answered.

The sharp inhalation by the man sounded like the hiss of a snake.

"Say, *making sport*," the Cleric instructed. "Then say, *for throwing the babies' bodies in with the women and children*."

A shiver ran down Alerio's spine. Those words didn't sound familiar but the orders to repeat the phrases had an ominous tone.

"Is this a test?" Alerio asked.

Without thinking, he raised an arm and braced for an attack. His snake hissed and the head lifted from the back of his hand.

"Temper, temper," the Cleric warned. "My babies are sensitive to threats."

"Why am I repeating nonsense?" Alerio questioned. "Is this a ritual?"

"A ritual? Oh, bless me no," the Cleric chuckled. Except there was no humor in the laughter. It came out dry and brittle as burnt leather. "It's a test of identity, if you must know."

"Making sport. And for throwing the babies' bodies in with the women and children," Alerio repeated the phrases. Then his knees grew weak, and memories flashed in his mind.

Thirteen years ago, Navarch Martinus Cetea fought Alerio when the Lance Corporal of heavy infantry intruded into the Illyrian commander's tent. Outside, Legion archers and a madman dressed in a snake's head caused a riot, while inside, Alerio got revenge for a farming community terrorized by the Admiral. But rather than killing Martinus, Alerio crippled the man at his ankles, cut the tendons in his wrists, and blinded him by drawing a blade across the Navarch's eyes.

The requested phrases were the last things Alerio said before the acts of carnage. Although unsatisfactory for avenging the farmers, the actions allowed Cetea to live. And that left the Illyrian boats crews with a wounded Admiral and a problem. Their leader was alive but incapacitated.

No Illyrian Captain could claim the leadership position while Martinus Cetea lived. The siege of the coastal town ended when the ships rowed for home to select a new Navarch.

"I remember now," Alerio spit out. "Why aren't you dead?"

"Harsh words for a man locked in my chamber, and holding one of my pets," Martinus Cetea pointed out.

"Confident words for a blind cripple," Alerio shot back. "Are we going to fight again? This time, I will kill you."

"Just as I desire to end your life, Lance Corporal Alerio Sisera," Cleric Cetea replied.

There was the old rank, as the scroll had used it. Other than the poisonous snakes in his hands, the temple wasn't guarded. And Alerio had a gladius and a dagger on his hips. Something beyond the obvious was happening.

"We aren't going to fight, are we?" Alerio suggested. "If you only wanted revenge, Captain Epulon would have delivered me squirming and thrashing in a fishing net. But he didn't."

"As much as I would relish seeing... Wait, I can't see anything except shadows in a blue fog," Martinus stated. Then he chuckled, making the ugly sound again. "I want you dead from the depths of my soul."

The two men were silent. Only the hint of slithering serpents on the floor reached their ears. But in the quiet, Alerio's snake rested its head on the back of his hand. Somehow, the tension in the room had drifted away.

"But I love my tribe more than I love the idea of revenge," Cleric Martinus Cetea admitted. "I need your help, Lance Corporal Sisera. Or rather, the Ardiaean Kingdom needs your help."

His hands rose into the candlelight. Snakeskin gloves with the fingertips cut away covered from the back of his hands to his elbows. Using the little finger and the finger next to it, he gripped the high arms of the chair, and pulled. The Cleric of the Snake stood, allowing the light to hit his features.

Snake like, he moved his face from side to side as if sampling the air. Adding to the resemblance of a reptile, courtesy of Alerio's blade from more than a decade before, his eyeballs displayed horizontal slits.

"Why would I help you?" Alerio challenged.

"I can stand and, although slowly, I can hobble around. Only two fingers on each hand works. But I've learned to use what I have," Cetea listed. "Strong light hurts my eyes, but in muted light, I see shapes in vibrant blue. Do I miss the color of a woman's hair in the sunlight and the glint of moonlight in her eyes at night? Of course. I am a man. But I've aged and taken on responsibilities and gained wisdom."

"What wisdom had you bring an enemy into your midst? Could it be suicide by Legionary?" Alerio asked. "If so, I'll gladly fulfill your wish, butcher of farm children. My personal Goddess is Nenia. I'll call her to collect your rotten soul if you like."

"In my fevered dreams, after we fought, I woke in fear that the swift, agile, and angry Lance Corporal had come for me," Cetea stated. "I had as much as given up on living. But Queen Jeta brought a brother of the snake to me each day.

They bathed me and wrapped my wounds in fresh bandages. Then they sat and talked of ancestors, the potency of life, and the need for intelligent guidance to balance strength and might."

"Am I supposed to forgive you, now that you've acquired the ability to feel?" Alerio questioned. "The fire in my belly remains unquenched."

"Queen Jetta warned me that this was a bad idea," the Cleric reported. "But I had to try. So here goes. Our leaders are selected by challenges. No birthright title is passed down from father to son. To ascend to an office, requires the candidate to fight and gather the support of tribal Chieftains."

"You want me to train someone to become King of your people?" Alerio guessed.

"If only it was that straight forward."

"How complicated can it be?" Alerio stated. "What do I get in return?"

"A sack of silver for you. And for your Senator Maximus, his transports will have two years of pardon from our pirate ships," Cleric Cetea responded. "Plus, I grant you, your life. Unless you're killed during the mission. Then, I will take immense joy in your demise."

"And where do I find your hero?" Alerio inquired. "Here or in Shkodër?"

"Your quest starts at Lezhë Castle," Martinus Cetea corrected him. "It's home to the Taulantii tribe, Queen Jeta's people. Through them, you'll make introductions to King Pleuratus and his court at the Capital."

"Who is this tender lad I'm going to instruct in the use of weapons?"

"Prince Agron. He's nineteen years old and a brute by training," the Cleric of the Snake replied. "We need him to learn to win with grace."

"Like crippling, and blinding, but not killing?" Alerio mocked.

Martinus Cetea leaned back, then dropped. The fang like arms of the chair remained in the candlelight. But the Cleric himself was lost in the darkness.

"If that's what it takes to win without creating a blood feud. Then yes, crippling and blinding are acceptable."

Act 2

Chapter 4 - Queen Jeta's Brother

The fort at Lezhë loomed over the river Drin. Even from the bay more than two miles away, Alerio could see the power of the Taulantii Tribe. And it wasn't from the stone walls on top of the steep hill. While the fort projected might, the real power came from the miles of cultivated land under the watchful eye of the fortification.

In addition to the farms, a hoard of fishing boats worked the bay, and a fleet of raider ships rested on the beach. The economic wealth allowed for a large population as displayed by multiple villages along the shoreline. It all pointed to a good supply of well-fed men to staff an army and a navy.

"It's no wonder the Ardiaeins want a strong King," Alerio submitted. "The Taulantii are so prosperous, they have to be a threat."

"Years ago, the Taulantii controlled land for hundreds of miles around," Epulon responded. "But the Ardiaein Tribe and others beat them back. If not for the fort, they would have been annihilated. Now, they hold to their territory and thrive."

"If the Taulantii are no threat," Alerio inquired, "why am I here and not at Shkodër?"

"The Ardiaein King was a fishing fleet Chieftain before challenging for the crown. With help from his wife, Jeta, he maneuvered ahead of wealthier men and fought for the title.

When he became king, he took the name Pleuratus the Second," Epulon answered. "Ninety years ago, Pleuratus the First fought King Philip of Macedonia. The storytellers relate that Pleuratus lost land but he and his Taulantii warriors managed to wound the Macedonian King and kill many of his elite soldiers. To this day, he is a hero to the tribe. For an Ardiaein King to take the name Pleuratus and have a Taulantii wife, means the border is secure."

"And the border will continue to be safe as long as the kingship remains with a Pleuratus," Alerio summed up. "That still doesn't explain why I'm here and not at the Ardiaein capital."

"Because you need a reason to be in Shkodër."

"I'm going there to train Prince Agron," Alerio submitted. "Isn't that reason enough?"

"Unfortunately, it isn't. There are factions, both traditional and rebellious, who want the transition to be left to chance," the pirate Captain informed him. "Which brings us to your problem. Neither faction wants you since Prince Agron already has a trainer. But Queen Jeta needs her son to be the next King and will not leave it to fate."

Alerio glanced up and down the beach as the *Boria* rowed closer to the shoreline.

"I'd expect a welcoming committee by their Navy," Alerio suggested. "So far, no one seems alarmed with the appearance of an Ardiaein warship. Or, is bothered by it rowing towards their coast."

"Why would they?" Epulon proposed. "Half my crew are Taulantii. We are, after all, a Queen Jeta ship."

Tingling as if a snake slithered down his spine, caused Alerio to stiffen. The warning sensation, honed over years of combat, alerted him to trouble.

"Those factions against getting Agron trained properly," he inquired, "is one of them King Pleuratus?"

"I'll let the Queen's brother answer that," Epulon said pushing the question aside. "He should be along shortly after we beach."

"Will Agron's uncle know the inclination of the King?"

"He should," Epulon told Alerio. "Admiral Driton is the commander of the Taulantii fleet. From what I hear, he has spies in the court of every Illyrian King."

***

The keel of the Queen's raider ground into the sand. Men jumped down, placed their palms on the hull, bent their backs, and shoved it up and out of the water.

"They don't park stern first," Hektor observed.

"I guess without the ram out front, the Illyrian warships can go to ground in either direction," Alerio responded.

"Is there an advantage to that?" Hektor asked.

"Only if they're being chased to shore by a Republic warship," Alerio described. "While the Legion vessel would waste moments backstroking to shore, the Illyrian raider could beach, and the crew be in battle lines before the Marines reach land."

Hektor went to collect their bundles, and Epulon took his place at the rail.

"Thank you for the ride, Captain," Alerio offered. "And the information."

"The outcome is important," Epulon replied, "and the result depends on you surviving. The Cleric of the Snake says you are a great fighter."

"Over a lot of years and even more battles," Alerio asserted, "I've found ways to stay alive."

Epulon let his eyes roam from Alerio's hat to his hobnailed boots.

"Personally, I can't see what the Cleric sees in you."

Hektor dropped the bundles containing their gear beside Alerio's leg. Then the youth jumped to the ground, turned around, and held out his arms.

"That's all right," Alerio comforted the pirate Captain while tossing one of the bundles to Hektor, "the Cleric is blind."

He threw the other bundle and jumped from the liburnian.

"Where to now, sir?" Hektor inquired.

Alerio glanced at the nearest village. There was no one coming to greet them from that location. But movement at a group of fishing huts caught his eyes. Scanning from the village to the huts, he watched three men march from between fishing nets.

"Weapons, sir?" Hector inquired. He squatted, pulled his medical kit from one bundle, and placed a hand on the other package. "Or will you stay with the gladius?"

The men carried far more muscles than men who rowed out to sea and cast nets all day. That work left fishermen sunburned, and the diet of fish made them sinewy with little bulk. The trio shuffling through the sand had thick thighs and wide shoulders. Their physical development resulted from marching long distances and practicing with a shield and a spear.

"Captain Epulon, what's the fine for dueling on the beach?" Alerio called to the raider ship.

"No fine for fighting anywhere."

"And the punishment for killing a man in a fight?"

"This is Illyria," Epulon noted. "The worst case is relatives of the dead man coming for revenge."

"And the penalty for crippling a man?"

"If he's alive, the family will expect him to extract his own revenge."

"What are you thinking, sir?" Hektor whispered.

The three stopped two body lengths away.

"I think this is a test," Alerio replied. He untied his sword belt and let it drop to the sand. "Throw the matched set of blades when I move. Let's see if they'll be satisfied with a little show."

Hektor reached out and scooped the belt with the gladius and Legion dagger to his side. Then he peeled back a fold and placed both hands in the bundle.

"Ready, sir," he exclaimed.

"Gentlemen, good day to you," Alerio greeted the three soldiers. "Would one of you be Admiral Driton?"

"What are you doing on my beach?" the biggest one challenged.

"We don't like it when Latians wash up on our shore," the smallest bellowed.

Alerio placed them in order of which one was more dangerous. The smaller because he was already hyped for a fight and the hilt on his sica was rubbed smooth from use. Next came the big one. It would take warmup strikes and punches before he committed himself to the fight. But when he did, it would take a lot to bring him down.

"How about you?" Alerio asked the third man.

"I don't like you," he blurted.

The unimaginative response put him at the bottom of the list.

"Hektor, the little one," Alerio said to the side. Then, he squared his shoulders and addressed the third man. "I meant are you, Admiral Driton?"

The three exchanged glances. Maybe they questioned how the stranger knew the Navarch was involved. Or, the thugs thought it odd the man assumed one of them was the Admiral. But neither choice mattered. Alerio Sisera sprinted at the smaller man. Lowering a shoulder, he rammed the man, pushed through, and tossed him to the ground. The other two turned to their fallen comrade and offered their hands to help him up.

"Get away from me," he stammered while vaulting to his feet. "Get him."

The three pivoted to face Alerio.

***

A pair of sharp blades whistled and spun over the heads of the assailants. The whoop-whoop sounds caused them to duck. With little momentum, the weapons flew above them, then fell just beyond. Despite the rotation, the Latian snatched the hilts of the swords out of the air.

Only when the swords were stationary and pointed in their direction did the trio see the blades. On average, a sica blade measured thirteen inches. The Latian held a pair of sica swords seven inches longer than average.

"That's the free show," the stranger stated. "Stepping forward for more fun has a price. Are you ready to pay it?"

In a bar fight, if they knew they were up against a swordsman, they would call in more of their unit. But they knew the Latian was a swordsman before they started. But he'd been unarmed a moment ago.

"He dropped his sword belt," the dullard mumbled. "Where did he get the blades?"

"Don't worry about his blades," the short man ordered. He pulled his sica and reminded the other two. "We have blades, as well."

A knifeman will draw his blade without looking at the sheath. The short man did. But he needed to check and see if his men also pull their sicas. In the beat where the leader looked to the side and the big man glanced down to the grip of his knife, the Latian jumped forward.

The pommel of the right sword hammered into the big man's forehead. And a swipe with the left blade forced the other two to move away. After dropping the big man to the beach, the swordsman hopped back two paces.

"The price goes up from here," he warned.

The short assailant crouched and etched the air with his blade. From any of the positions, he could stab or slash. All it would take was a quick shuffle forward and...

Flying above the knife, the toes of the hobnailed boot hooked behind his shoulder and spun him to the side. Anticipating the arrival of a steel tip, the soldier danced away from the path of the sword. The move saved the knifeman but put him out of striking distance.

***

Alerio swung the sword but turned the blade at the last moment. The steel smacked the slow soldier in the side of his head. He crumpled to the beach, ending up draped over the legs of the big man. Left with one adversary, the Legion officer shuffled sideways to line up with the short soldier.

"Your two friends are going to wake up with headaches," Alerio commented. Then he shouted. "Hektor. Which is easier to stitch up, an arm or a shoulder wound?"

"The arm is messier and takes longer to stitch. But after treatment he can hold it immobilized and sleep with it," the Greek replied. "The shoulder is quick to treat. Unless you cut him to the bone. In any case, he'll sleep sitting up for a month. Shoulder wounds are painful, and the patient can't get comfortable laying down."

The soldier rushed at Alerio. Sica extended, he drove for the Legionary's gut. One sword came up while the other chopped downward. They caught the man's sica in a scissor's movement. The short blade snapped in half.

"Your arm or your shoulder?" Alerio asked the man holding the broken knife.

"Look, Latian, I was just supposed to find out if you could fight," he explained.

He took a step backward.

"I know that," Alerio acknowledged. He mimicked the step except he moved forward. "Your arm or your shoulder?"

"But you've proven yourself," the man pleaded.

"You see, I'm not just a good fighter," Alerio stated while keeping pace with the retreating soldier. "I'm a man who demands retribution for those who offend me. Arm or shoulder?"

"Epulon, get him off me," the short assailant begged.

"I'm not sending any of my crew into that meat grinder," the pirate Captain responded. "Maybe you should run."

As if the idea was a new concept, the soldier paused. He took a breath, spun from Alerio, and sprinted away.

"Hektor, pack these but not too deep," Alerio instructed.

He dropped the matched set of swords and picked up his weapons belt. While strapping it on, he peered up at Epulon.

"Is that the best you have?" he asked.

"Probably not. But to be honest, he's usually a dangerous man."

"I figured," Alerio stated. "Now what?"

Epulon pointed in the direction of the village. Six men, including the knifeman, strutted from between houses.

"Is this another test?" Alerio questioned. "Or is one of them Admiral Driton?"

"The Navarch is the tall man in the front," Epulon responded. Then he shouted to his crew. "Launch us. It's time we reported to our Admiral."

The *Boria* slid off the beach, splashed into the swells, and headed for deep water.

***

The six stopped four paces from Alerio, and the man at the head of the group raised his hands to show they were empty.

"I am Admiral Driton, and you must be Legionary Alerio Sisera," the Navarch announced. "Welcome to Lezhë."

"That man owes me blood," Alerio barked. He indicated the short knifeman.

The Admiral rocked back on his heels as if punched.

"It was just a test," he informed Alerio. "And I might add you passed…"

"Do you think this is a game? He pulled a knife on me with the intention of slicing open my stomach and spilling my guts on the sand."

"Let me understand. You want to continue the fight with Sergeant Gezim?" Driton questioned. "But you have your man bandaging the heads of the other two soldiers and giving them herbs."

"Hektor, what are you doing?"

"Sir, head injuries usually cause dizziness and vomiting," the medic reported. "I'm giving them spearmint to settle their stomachs and apple vinegar with honey to help with the wooziness. Should I stop?"

"No, you're doing fine," Alerio replied. He faced the Admiral. "Those men stood and fought. Not well but they fell in combat. Your Sergeant Gezim ran. For that alone, I want him to bleed."

At the insult, the short man marched to the front. Using the end of the broken blade, he sliced deeply into his forearm.

"Satisfied?" Gezim sneered.

Alerio cocked his head to the side, smiled at the drops of blood dripping from the wound, and called to Hektor.

"Bring your kit," he directed. "I'll speak with the Admiral while you stitch up his Sergeant."

"Yes, sir."

"You aren't just a Legion infantryman, are you?" Driton inquired.

"No, sir," Alerio stated. "But for the purposes of this mission, that's all I am. A hardnosed Legion weapon's instructor."

At the description, the Illyrian Sergeant nodded his head before closing his eyes against the pain.

"The vinegar only burns for a few moments," Hektor assured Gezim. "I like to clean a wound before stitching it closed. It prevents the rot."

Chapter 5 – Reasons for Arguing

The two-story stone and lumber building sat back from the coast at the halfway point between the beach and the Drin River. It wasn't the only building with a second story in the town, but it was the only one with a tower on the roof. Three men stood at rails on a platform, peering off into the distance.

"We keep an eye on the shoreline and the river, both upstream and downstream," Admiral Driton explained.

The watchers knew when the *Boria* hit the beach. Alerio was tempted to bring it up. But the test of his martial skills told him, why he wasn't met by Driton, when he landed. Instead of questioning the Admiral, he probed, "I thought you were friendly with your neighbors."

"We are for the most. But ever since King Pleuratus began adding raider ships and increasing his army, we've grown cautious."

A watcher lifted a flag and waved it. Across the river, and high on a hill, another flag signaled a reply.

"You communicate with soldiers in the fort," Alerio noted.

"The Taulantii was once the most powerful tribe in Illyria," Driton boasted. "Now, we guard what we have and remain vigil for invasion. Especially from the north."

"Are Ardiaeins assembling at the boarder?" Alerio inquired.

Driton and Sisera marched through the town while Hektor, his three patients, and the Navarch's entourage followed. The Admiral glanced back to be sure none of his people were close.

"Pleuratus has his troops on the Dardani border chasing bandits," Driton informed Alerio. "But, in three days, he could bring them from the west and be on my doorstep. So, we keep watch and remain ready to defend our property."

"I thought the whole purpose of the Agron mission was to maintain cordial relations between your tribes," Alerio submitted. "You make it sound adversarial."

"Shkodër is only twenty-two miles from here," Driton responded while pushing open the door to the building. "My sister can only do so much. The rest is up to me and my King."

They entered a large room and Alerio smiled. Military headquarters were the same everywhere he went. Clerks at desks scratched ink on scrolls, then passed them to another clerk to make more marks. Junior officers jumped to their feet when the Admiral entered.

"We'll have lunch and discuss getting us to Shkodër," Driton directed. Responding to waves for his attention, the Navarch pointed Alerio to a door at the back of the room. "Go through there and stack your equipment out of the way. I'll meet you in the dining room when I've finished with these issues."

"I understand, sir," Alerio replied.

He and Hektor walked through the busy administration area. On the far side of the doorway, they saw a table with place settings. Alerio guided Hektor to a side wall where they dropped the bundles.

"Good throw back on the beach," Alerio complimented the youth. "You didn't hit any of the soldiers in the back of the head or me in the chest."

"It's because you suggested I throw axes with both hands at the range," Hektor responded. "Before that, neither sword would have reached you. Colonel Sisera, do you mind if I make a couple of observations."

"You're the only confidante I have in the vicinity," Alerio told him. "I would hope you'd speak your mind."

"For a tribe that is simply holding their territory, the Taulantii seem to be very organized," the youth asserted. "The other room is not full of scribes doing an accounting of the harvest, sir."

"I caught that," Alerio remarked. "Keep your eyes and ears open. What else?"

"Why did you want the Sergeant to bleed?" Hektor inquired. "The fight was over, and you had won."

"The Illyrians are warriors," Alerio replied. "To prevent them from trying me again, they need to know there is a cost for challenging me. They still might, but they'll think twice before acting on the impulse. Besides, the Admiral had to take us seriously for whatever reason."

"You don't think he's earnest about getting Agron trained?"

"I think he wants Agron on the throne," Alerio surmised. "If not, then why the elaborate scheme. But I question if we're part of his plan. We may have been dumped on him by his sister and the Cleric."

"From what I've heard, Queen Jeta sounds capable," Hektor commented.

"I was thinking along the same lines," Alerio agreed. "Except, formidable was the word that came to me."

They left the bundles against the wall and walked to a table holding a carafe of wine, a pitcher of beer, and a collection of pretty glass cups.

"Fresh off an Egyptian transport," Hektor suggested while picking up a cup and admiring the workmanship.

He poured wine for Alerio and a glass of beer for himself.

"The vino is from the Isle of Rhodes, if memory serves me," Alerio declared after a sip. "Probably taken off an unfortunate Athenian trader."

"You're wrong about the source," Navarch Driton corrected. He strutted through the doorway. "The Isle of Rhodes wine came off a Qart Hadasht merchant ship. My raiders were very proud of themselves when they presented the casks to me."

Alerio lifted the glass in salute but held the vessel aloft. Peering at the cup, he inquired, "Is King Pleuratus adding to his army and fleet because he's aggressive? Or, is he responding to your actions?"

"An excellent observation," Driton allowed. A junior officer reached for the carafe and a glass. Moments later, he handed the Admiral the beverage. "Let me shortcut that for you, Sisera. I could put my nephew on the throne. But that would mean war and blood feuds. My King and I much prefer a peaceful transition."

"If there's contention between your people, how am I supposed to go from here to there and complete the mission?" Alerio questioned. "Won't I be seen as an agent of Taulantii?"

"That won't be a problem once we have our falling out," Driton replied.

"What falling out?"

"The one we'll have at my nephew's birthday gala," the Admiral responded. He ushered Alerio and Hektor towards the table. "I'll explain while we eat."

Alerio took a step forward, but a hand pulled him back.

"If they can't murder each other for fear of a blood feud," Hector whispered. "Who can they kill?"

"Us," Alerio answered. He placed a hand on Hektor's shoulder and shoved the youth in the direction of the table. "But that's for later. Right now, let's eat."

***

Hot pork with a mint sauce and baked turnips were served to the four men. The center of the table held stacks of flat barley bread and a platter of roasted chestnuts. Servants refilled the glasses with beer, wine, or spring water. Always an enthusiastic eater, Alerio relished the meal.

"In six days, my nephew will celebrate his twentieth birthday," Driton explained. "The Ardiaeins are planning a grand party for their Prince Agron. We'll be attending. Me as his uncle. And you, as a mercenary hired to train my soldiers."

"What will we argue about?" Alerio questioned while peeling a chestnut. His fingers paused and he thought for a moment before suggesting. "My training methods?"

"I thought we'd fall out over your compensation. It's too high," Driton teased. "Once our relationship ends, my sister will take over."

Taulantii officers filed through the doorway and took seats around the table. While they were being served, the Admiral addressed them.

During the new conversation, Alerio felt a tug at his sleeve. Turning to his valet and medic, he started to ask if there was a problem.

The Greek youth mouthed a warning, "blood feud."

Much later, the occupants around the table were relaxed and stuffed.

"In the morning, we'll run drills and Commander Sisera will give us the benefit of his experience," Driton exclaimed. He stood and told the gathering. "I'm sure it will be instructive."

"For whom," Alerio asked, "your officers or me?"

Driton chuckled but didn't answer. He marched from the table. A junior officer collected Alerio and Hektor and took them to their quarters.

"When King Alexander' Silver Shields were broken up into small units," Hektor described while unpacking their bedding, "it allowed their enemies to finally defeat them."

"You think we'll be separated?" Alerio questioned.

"You already are, Colonel Sisera," Hektor replied. "The closest Legion is across the sea while you are here. We should return home, sir."

"Not yet. I need to know if we can strike a deal with these Illyrians."

***

In the morning, a stableman brought Hektor a mule. Once the bundles were secured to the animal, the Greek and several officers hiked after Alerio and the Admiral.

"The fort is impressive," Alerio told the Navarch.

Even from two miles away, the stone walls of Fort Lezhë against the sky created a majestic scene.

"Wait until you see the view from the top of the hill," Driton replied.

After leaving the settlement, they marched across farmland, before entering a forest.

"You've a nice mixture of trees," Alerio observed. "Just from the road, I can see oak, pine, chestnut, ash, and maple. Everything needed to build a merchant fleet. It's a wonder you Illyrians don't have more transports for trading."

"Why build merchant ships only to have your neighbors steal the cargo," Driton responded. "We find it better to build raider ships. They protect our beaches and waterways. And when not defending what's ours, we harvest from the sea."

"You mean, your raiders seize cargo from honest merchants," Alerio said challenging the farming reference. "It's hardly a harvest."

"Maybe not to you, Latian. But to us, the merchants use our seas. We are simply collecting taxes. It's the reason you're here. To pay the fee, isn't it?"

"Call it what you like," Alerio said defensively. Senator Maximus had disagreed, but Alerio thought the scroll provided an opportunity to forge a trading treaty with the Illyrians. Now he could see the Taulantii weren't likely partners. He still held out hope for an agreement with King

Pleuratus. With nothing to lose, he accused the Admiral. "What you're doing is theft."

"Theft?" the Navarch repeated as if confused. "Theft would be illegal. In Illyria, we believe anything from the sea is ours for the taking. If it were theft, someone would stop us."

"The Republic Navy will, someday," Alerio promised.

"Maybe, maybe not. Until that day, we'll harvest what we please," the Admiral told Alerio. Then he indicated a wide ribbon of water beyond the forest. "The river Drin. We'll get horses on the other side."

"Do we swim it?" Alerio asked.

Driton and his officers laughed.

"That would mean drying out or chafing on the ride to the fort," the Admiral explained. "No, Sisera, we will not swim. There's a raft landing a short way upstream. On the far side is a military outpost with horses."

The group turned left and followed the bank to an expansive landing. At piers, they found four enormous rafts tied to anchor poles.

Alerio waited for the Admiral and his men to load. Then he joined Hektor as the youth guided the pack animal across the ramp.

"You could float a cavalry patrol or a quarter of a Century across on one of these," Alerio noted.

"It makes sense," Hektor responded while patting the mule to calm the beast. "If attacked, the Taulantii would need to move supplies and men to the fort."

"Or, move them upriver to invade Shkodër," Alerio offered.

Hektor glanced at the three empty rafts, "that is an option, Colonel. And a very real possibility."

***

The ride up to the fort required traveling on sweeping paths, ending in switchbacks that took them higher at each bend. When they finally came level with the fort, Alerio could see the walls were roughly laid rocks and not finely cut and set stones.

"The walls are impressive, are they not?" Driton bragged.

Alerio looked back to the flatland.

I could march a Century of Legionaries directly up this hill. Undercover of a ceiling of shields, we'd dismantle a section of the wall, then fight our way through the breach, before butchering everyone inside your fort.

Instead of disclosing his criticism, Alerio allowed, "They are rock walls."

With the Admiral in the lead, they rounded the fort and halted at the edge of a drill field. Soldiers sat idle on opposite sides while officers stood under an awning sipping beer.

"I've arranged a demonstration," Driton informed Alerio. "This way, you'll have firsthand knowledge of the power of an Illyrian army."

"I'm always open to learning," Alerio stated.

"Come, we'll watch from the pavilion," the Admiral instructed. Then he waved to his officers and commanded. "Prepare for the drill."

The soldiers were still setting shields on their arms and pulling on helmets when the group reached the awning. Hektor pulled up beside Alerio.

"Should I get out my medical kit?" he asked.

Legionaries were competitive. In every full contact drill, Legion infantrymen got hurt. Some injured enough to require the attention of a medic. The Illyrian soldiers picked up long spears and ambled into two opposing forces. Their lack of enthusiasm didn't forecast a violent clash.

"I don't think that will be necessary," Alerio responded. "Relax and enjoy the theater. That's what I'm going to do."

Already dismounted and holding a beverage, Admiral Driton called to Alerio from the pavilion.

"Come, Commander Sisera, the approach and transition of a terrifying, fighting force are the best parts," he exclaimed.

Alerio leaned into Hektor and whispered, "If they become a terrifying, fighting force, I'll eat my petasos."

"I believe Colonel, your hat is safe," Hektor responded.

As an enthusiastic student of the Macedonian Silver Shields, the Greek youth knew the legends and stories of a victorious phalanx. In none of the myths did uninspired officers magically raise the spirits of their infantrymen. Conversely, every losing phalanx battle could be traced back to weak leadership, a lack of discipline, rough terrain, or rarely, superior tactics of an opposing force.

Hector dismounted and took the reins of Alerio's horse. While the Greek youth took the beasts behind the tent, Alerio marched to the Admiral.

"The change to a true phalanx is awe inspiring," Driton gushed.

From either side of the practice field, the soldiers formed into files and rows. The closer they came to each other, the more compressed they became. But rather than coordinated steps that shook the earth and caused fear in the enemy, the soldiers clustered in a relaxed manner.

Just before meeting in the center, the formations closed in tighter so when they met, the men holding the forward shields were pushed from behind.

"A clash of steel," Driton shouted. "That's how it's done Commander Sisera. Belly to belly, shield to shield, man against man."

The last time Alerio witnessed a phalanx drill, the participants were Spartans. Their clash dug trenches in the earth and dislodged wagons of dirt. The Illyrian soldiers barely scraped off the top layer of soil.

"Muscle, steel, bone, and shield. I find it exhilarating," Driton asserted. "Don't you?"

"Who is in charge of your army?" Alerio questioned.

He thought maybe there was an absent General. A senior officer of the army with the knowledge to correct the sloppy maneuvering of the phalanxes.

"I am commander of both the sea and land forces," Driton answered. "The King and I decided it was the best way to keep control and prevent rebellion."

"In that case, the demonstration was a superb example of a knowledgeable Admiral," Alerio uttered. "When do we leave for Shkodër?"

"Don't you want to inspect the men and maybe offer advice?"

"Truly, Navarch Driton, I wouldn't even know where to begin," Alerio said while bowing.

"I know, it's hard to improve on perfection," Driton agreed. "Come, I'll introduce you to my Lieutenants. I trained them myself."

In the back of the pavilion, Hektor dropped his head between his knees and allowed a quiet moan to escape his lips. The strength of a phalanx started far in advance of the clash. A good unit would have their shields up to defend against arrows and flights of javelins long before reaching the enemy. And their small but ominous steps should shake the ground and trouble the hearts of the opposing force. In his opinion, neither Illyrian phalanx came close to being good at the formation.

Chapter 6 – Secrets of Fort Lezhë

They gave Alerio and Hektor a room in the lowest section of the fort. After placing their gear on the beds, the youth pointed to the doorway.

"When it rains, this room floods," he informed Alerio.

"How can you tell?"

"The streaks on the steps," the youth replied. "Someone swept them but neglected the edges of the treads."

In the weak light that came from the doorway above, Alerio examined the stone steps.

"I can see what's left from the runoff," Alerio confirmed. He ran a hand over the stone then rubbed his fingertips together feeling the grit. "But the sky is clear. I think we're safe for tonight."

"If it's all right with you, sir," Hektor said. "I'll camp out in the open."

"I can't imagine we'd drown even if there was a downpour. Is there another reason you want to sleep outside?"

"Colonel, I don't like pits or wells," Hektor stated. He shivered at the thought of being in a damp confined space. "Wet walls make me nervous."

"Seeing as the Illyrians love snakes and snakes like underground places, I can understand," Alerio allowed. "You go ahead. As for me, a roof overhead is a luxury I can't pass up."

Hektor took an oiled tarp and a wool blanket from his pack. Then he walked up the steps, leaving the low room to Colonel Sisera.

***

In the light of the setting sun, the river Drin cut a treelined path down the center of the flatland. As seen from the fort, the waterway divided farms and forest on its way south before dumping its fresh water into the sea. Beyond the farms, several villages and towns occupied land adjacent to the beach.

Hektor Nicanor admired the view for several moments before tossing the wrap and blanket over his shoulders. A pleasant night with a star-studded sky promised a good night's sleep. Before laying down, the flickering of torchlight through the trees caught his eyes.

Squinting into the gloom and over the distance, he saw that two of the large rafts had moved to the near side of the Drin River. While the pair of flatboats were edged onto the riverbank next to a third raft, the fourth raft moved northward on the river. Although it was too dark to see the content of the floating barge, Hektor had an idea. In the muted light, he made out files of soldiers snaking down the hill, heading for the raft landing.

"I'm sorry you had to see that," a voice admitted from behind the youth.

A club smacked against the side of Hektor's head. Dazed by the blow, he swung his arms in self-defense, but they tangled in the folds of his bedding. Before he could throw off the blanket and wrap, fists beat Hektor Nicanor to the rocky ground.

"You could have hit him harder," Sergeant Gezim complained.

The big infantryman lowered the club.

"But Sergeant, he treated us when we were injured," the large man responded. He touched the bandage at the sore spot on his forehead. "It didn't seem right to hit him too hard."

"Fine, it's done. Tie him up and bring him," Gezim ordered.

"Where are we taking the medic?"

"To Admiral Driton," the Sergeant replied. "He'll decide what to do with the spy."

Semiconscious and suspended between two soldiers, Hektor attempted to walk but tripped, often. Each time he faltered the right toe of his thick sandals scuffed the dirt and rocks. The youth added a moan and a head flop to assure his assailants that he was almost incapacitated.

***

Alerio lay in bed thinking while waiting for the first rays of light to reach the top of the stairs. His declaration that he preferred sleeping under a ceiling was only half true. Being out of the elements had its benefits, but the real sense of peace came from the single staircase leading to the room.

Before going to bed, he had sprinkled gravel and sand on the steps. Anyone attempting to sneak down would crunch and slip on the loose material. After a noisy trip, they would find a sharp blade waiting for them in the dark room.

Feeling safe, he released his thoughts to consider the situation. Since entering Illyrian territory, he had visited two different tribes. In one, he met an old enemy who desperately needed his help. In the other, he encountered an authoritarian figure who didn't want his interference. And for most of the trip, he traveled on a raider ship with allegiance to a queen with connections to both.

After examining the facts, Alerio decided the venture was a waste of his time. No treaty with one, two, or even three tribes could effectively protect the Maximus family trade. And it was clear, the Illyrians weren't open to exchanging trade goods. With the decision to abandon the mission firm in his mind, he threw off the blanket, got up and, strapped on his gladius. Then carefully to avoid slipping on the steps, he climbed the stairs, and went to find Hektor.

***

Rays of light came from over the mountain, illuminating the crumpled and empty blanket and oiled goatskin tarp. Alerio poked them with the toe of his hobnailed boot, then chuckled. There was no way Hektor could be under the bedding. Turning around, Alerio searched for the youth. As he rotated, he gazed over the waist high wall, down the hill and across farms to the river. The raft landings were empty, but the barges weren't his concern. He returned to the visual search of the fort for Hektor.

A couple of scuff marks in the rocks and dirt held no importance. However, the next set pointed in a direction. And a set of scuff marks beyond them begged him to follow the trail. Alerio tracked the uniformed scuff marks around the fort and out of the back gate. For several paces, he lost the marks in the grass. When the marks reappeared, they lead to the pavilion where he had watched the phalanx demonstration. Only now the sides were down, and the entrance guarded.

"You can't come in," a sentry stated. He and a second guard brought their spears to ready positions and stepped inward to block the entrance to the tent.

Alerio dropped his chin and eyed the ground. In the dirt, footprints flanked the scuff marks, one large and the other medium sized. A third set of boot prints ran right through the marks.

"Sergeant Gezim sent for me," Alerio lied while trying to find a way inside.

"Why didn't you say so?" one guard snapped. They stepped outward and away from the entrance of the tent. Both rested their spears on their shoulders and the other scolded. "You should have told us that first. And saved us the hassle."

Alerio had traveled with Hektor Nicanor through territory controlled by the Isle of Rhodes, far along caravan trading routes, and across a swatch of Punic land. Hiking, fighting, and camping with Hektor allowed Alerio to learn a few things about the Greek youth. His sleeping, snoring, and eating habits. His dislikes and favorite things. And chief among them, he learned Hektor's gait, stride, and the youth's footprints. Distinct marks for when he marched, limped, and dragged his feet when exhausted.

"Sorry, I didn't get much sleep last night," Alerio apologized while reaching out as if to reassure one of the sentries.

The fingers of Alerio's left hand slipped inside the guard's chest piece. With a hard pull, he brought the sentry stumbling forward. Alerio's left knee exploded into the man's crotch. The sudden agony of his manhood and testicles being driven up into his belly took the man's breath away. As well, his body involuntarily went rigid from shock. As silent and as stiff as a frozen rag in winter, the body of the distressed man was hoisted into the air.

At the top of the lift, Alerio slung the man at the second guard. Both guards tumbled to the ground.

Before they could untangle, Alerio stepped over them and dropped a fist on the second sentry's face. Then from on high, he added three more punches. When the Legion officer stepped back, both sentries lay hurt. One curled up and moaning. The second sentry dazed and struggling to breathe through a crushed nose and see through two swollen eyes.

"Something else you learn about a traveling companion," Alerio told the confused sentries. "You learn when a man is hurt by his footfalls. If Gezim has abused Hektor, I'll be back to gut you. Both of you."

Alerio drew his gladius, slapped aside the tent flaps, and marched into the pavilion.

***

Sergeant Gezim stood over Hektor with his fist raised for another punch. Alerio could see it was part of a series of blows from the blood running down and over the boy's lips and a bruise on his cheek. The big soldier held Hektor upright in a chair while Driton stood off to the side. The Admiral had a smug look on his face. Two officers were behind the Navarch. Farther back, the slow soldier from the beach shuffled his feet displaying anxiety.

"Hello, Hektor," Alerio greeted the boy from just inside the entrance. "Are you okay?"

"I'm sorry, sir," Hektor mumbled. "I told them who you are."

His head drooped either from exhaustion, the beating, or shame. Alerio couldn't tell which.

"Did you by chance inform them of my personal Goddess?"

Driton took a half step towards Alerio and exclaimed, "Why is your personal Goddess important, Legion Battle Commander Sisera? That's right, your valet confessed to your spying operation."

Alerio snapped the hilt of the gladius. The weapon made one rotation before he caught the hilt. Then he flipped it again.

"My deity is Nenia Dia," Alerio replied. He began walking back and forth in front of the entrance. As he prowled, he continued flipping the gladius. "She is the Goddess who comes to collect souls from dying men. For too many years now, I've been her instrument. And she, my strength. Seeing what you've done to my friend, I really want to call her into this pavilion."

The big soldier's eyes grew large at the mention of a Goddess, and he released Hektor. Free of the hands, the youth toppled to the floor. But he didn't sprawl. His hands crept under his shoulders and his knees flexed while he waited.

"You are far outnumbered," Driton gloated. Then he shouted at the closed entrance. "Guards. Guards, come in here."

The Illyrians looked at the entrance. Taking advantage of the distraction, Hektor popped off the floor. Bleeding and stumbling, he ran to Alerio's side.

"I'm sorry, Colonel," he offered.

"I demand loyalty, yes. But a verbal oath is adequate," Alerio responded. "A blood oath far exceeds my needs. Stop your bleeding while I send the souls of these barbarians to their netherworld."

"Guards!" Driton yelled.

"Admiral, please, you're embarrassing yourself," Alerio scolded. "Do you think I would leave two armed men at my back."

Gezim and his two soldiers drew their sicas as did the pair of junior officers. Only Driton left his blade it its sheath.

"You can't possibly believe you can leave here alive," the Admiral stated.

"I disabled two of your men and ran an NCO off while being careful," Alerio reminded the Navarch. He stopped flipping the gladius. "Imagine what I can do when I'm being reckless."

There was a pause before every battle, just prior to the engagement. Almost as if combat were a savage beast, requiring a beat to collect itself before coming alive in the clash of steel and the spray of blood. In that moment, one of the junior officers stepped to the Admiral and whispered in his ear.

The beast waited while Driton considered the Lieutenant's words.

***

"In my haste to believe you were here to spy on the Taulantii," the Admiral admitted, "I forgot that you were invited for a reason."

"I'm afraid your mistreatment of my medic has forced me to reconsider the offer of help," Alerio responded. He leveled the gladius and peered down the blade at the face of the Navarch. "If you think a bag of silver and empty promises of safe passage for merchant ships can buy me, you are mistaken."

Driton peered into the faces of his five men. All were Illyrian and ready to fight. However, while they vibrated with anticipation, the Latian held his blade level and steady. From the display, the Admiral realized his emotional men faced a dispassionate, professional killer.

"My sister will be disappointed if I attend the gala without Legionary Alerio Sisera," Driton confessed. "What do you need to set this unfortunate situation behind us?"

"You can all die," Alerio answered.

Alerio was angry and looking to punish the Admiral and his men for the assault on Hektor. While Colonel Sisera fumed, the youth had an opportunity to think clearly. Holding a rag against his nose to stem the flow, he bent to Alerio.

"You've come this far, sir," the youth suggested, "it would be a waste to miss meeting the architect of this mission."

Some of the fury drained away and Alerio sucked air between his teeth.

"Curse you, Hektor Nicanor," Alerio growled. "My blade was ready, my heart pumping, my mind set for battle, and my faith, all prepared to send souls to Nenia. Now, I'm thinking I'd like to meet Queen Jeta."

"She's my sister," Driton exclaimed. "It will be my pleasure to introduce you. Let's put away our blades and discuss the trip to Shkodër."

"I have two conditions," Alerio stated.

From holding the blade level, he lowered his arm and began flipping the gladius again. Every time the hilt slapped into his hand the Illyrians twitched.

"Anything to get us past this unfortunate incident," the Admiral promised.

"On the beach, I demanded blood for the insult of attacking me," he reminded the Navarch. "This time, your men drew blood."

"Yes, yes, I understand. What do you want?"

"First, I want the big soldier to be executed," Alerio replied. "Put him on his knees and chop off his head. Right here, right now."

Gezim jumped forward and raised his blade.

"Admiral, let me kill this arrogant Latian," the NCO begged. "He and his Greek are nothing."

"At another time and place, I would allow it. Even encourage it. Except Sergeant, my sister is expecting this Latian at the gala," Driton informed the NCO. "Arrest your soldier and put him on his knees."

It took both Lieutenants, Sergeant Gezim, and the third soldier to wrestle the big man to the deck. Driton drew his blade and crossed to the condemned man.

"Infantryman Pharos, I sentence you to death," the Admiral proclaimed. He raised the blade overhead. "It may not seem like it to you at this moment, but you can tell your ancestors that you died in service to your king and your tribe."

Tears rolled down Sergeant Gezim's cheeks and he patted the big man on the back. The Admiral's arm shook, then steadied, just before he swung the...

The Noricum steel of Alerio's gladius easily blocked and stopped the downward motion of Driton's sword.

"The second thing I want, Admiral, is infantryman Pharos assigned to me," Alerio stated.

"But he's under a death sentence," Driton argued.

"From his Sergeant and his commanding officers," Alerio listed. "But not from me and not from Hektor. What say, Pharos, want to live?"

The big infantryman shrugged off the restraining hands and pushed to his feet.

"I will guard your back, stand beside you in a fight, or charge into the enemy to save you," the big infantryman swore.

"I accept your oath," Alerio acknowledged. "Now, Admiral, when do we leave for the Ardiaein capital."

Sergeant Gezim reached out for the big warrior. Seeing the hand approaching, Pharos slapped it down.

"When this is over, I'm returning to my village to become a hunter," he sneered. "Not you nor any member of your Company are welcome to visit. Your names will be cursed. Consider this a blood feud."

After those words, he marched to Alerio.

"Orders, sir?" Pharos inquired.

"Take Hektor and collect your gear," Alerio told him. "Then put it with our bundles. I'll be along shortly."

"Will you be safe, Colonel?" Hektor asked.

"The question, my young friend, will Admiral Driton and his men be safe from me?"

Act 3

Chapter 7 – Enji Protect Us

"In the shadow of the next hill is the border town of Bushat," Pharos called to Alerio. The big warrior made the horse he rode appear small and the rope back to the pack mule seemed like a piece of yarn in his hand. "It's the traditional boundary between our tribes."

A rider came from a side trail, spoke to Admiral Driton, then rode back the way he came.

"That's the fourth messenger today," Hektor noted.

"At least we know where the Taulantii phalanxes went," Alerio said. "But why here? What's their purpose?"

He studied the woods between the caravan and the Drin River but couldn't see any sign of the military units.

"This puts them close to the Ardiaein border," the youth observed. "Are four phalanxes enough to conquer a territory?"

"Two hundred and fifty soldiers may not be an army," Alerio told him. "But it's enough for a precision assault."

"An assault on what?" Hektor questioned.

"We'll know more when we see Shkodër," Alerio suggested.

A rocky spine rose from flat farmland, became a massive hill, and a short while later the town of Bushat came into view. For most people, when approaching a feature on the trail, they fixated on the destination.

With everyone looking ahead, it came as a surprise when Pharos swore, "Enji, protect us."

Hearing the man's outburst, Alerio and Hektor turned in their saddles and followed his gaze. Coming along the backtrail, a woman walked beside a team of horses. Although the wagon stood taller than the average transport, it was shorter. Strong and fit, the horses seemed adequate for pulling the wagon, a couple of teamsters, and a full load of cargo. Yet, the woman paced with the horses, guiding them from the side rather than riding.

"Enji, protect us," Pharos said again.

Hearing apprehension in the big warrior's voice, Alerio questioned, "You're afraid of a woman?"

"Not a woman," Pharos protested. "Ja'Huffield is a Cleric of the Snake. May the God of Fire protect us."

While Pharos was anxious and Alerio curious, Hektor Nicanor sat transfixed.

Ja'Huffield's love charm, the vertical indentation above her sensual lips, spread to the sides as if inviting a man to caress her lower face. Below the cleft, her bowed lips could inspire a Greek sculptor. And her chin, now held level as she walked, could easily dip to display a maiden's innocence, or jut outward in anger. One a beguiling motion to beckon a man inward while the other a sharp, and painful rejection.

But the lower half of her face was all Hektor could gaze upon. From the bridge of her rosebud shaped nose and above, a snake's mask hid her features.

"Stunning," the youth sighed.

"Dangerous," Pharos corrected.

"Just another Priestess," Alerio said dismissing the Cleric.

Admiral Driton's voice broke the spell.

"Commander Sisera, please join me at the front."

Only Alerio and Pharos turned away from Ja'Huffield. They watched a cavalry patrol ride out to greet the Admiral's procession.

Alerio asked the big warrior, "Ardiaeins?"

"Yes, sir," Pharos confirmed.

Hektor ignored the approaching cavalry, and he didn't participate in the exchange. He was too busy staring at the Cleric.

***

Not counting the Cleric, in addition to Alerio, Hektor, and Pharos, Navarch Driton traveled with a personal guard of ten mounted soldiers and his aids, Lieutenants Pinnes and Fisnik. Along with four servants, teamsters drove two wagons carrying supplies and gifts for Prince Agron. Despite the size of the Taulantii delegation, the Ardiaeins sent just five mounted soldiers.

Alerio wondered at the number while searching high up on the ridge above the town.

"That's interesting," he remarked. When Hektor didn't respond, Alerio described, "They have Legion archers and drama girls on the mound."

Jolted back to reality by the oddity of the remark, Hektor's head snapped around and he inquired, "What's that, Colonel?"

"I'm beginning to think Ja'Huffield is an Enchantress, not a Cleric."

"Yes. Yes," Pharos agreed. "Witch is a better description."

Alerio ignored the big man's contention but made a note to question why he disliked this Cleric of the Snake.

"They have watchers on the heights, so they knew how many men the Admiral has with him," Alerio pointed out. "But they only sent five riders."

"What's the significance of that, sir?" the youth asked.

Alerio sat higher in the saddle and glanced at the farmland, the groves of trees along the riverbanks, and the forest farther out.

"They knew armed men were coming. Yet, we're greeted by only a handful," Alerio observed. "And from the heights, they have to have seen some sign of the Taulantii soldiers and the rafts."

"The Ardiaeins don't seemed alarmed," Hektor offered.

"Moving the phalanxes and their supplies north wasn't a snap decision," Alerio guessed. "This is a planned troop movement and must include a payoff and assurances for the Ardiaeans to ignore it. Or, the commander at Bushat is incompetent."

"Sisera, are you going to join me?" Driton insisted.

"Coming Admiral," Alerio replied. He nudged his horse forward and explained. "I was admiring the rich farmland and thick forest."

"I know," Driton teased, "excellent wood for building a merchant fleet."

***

The border town of Bushat had few amenities and less space for a large dinner meeting. To fill the gap and provide an area for the officers to talk, Admiral Driton ordered the erection of his pavilion. Behind the tent, the soldiers picketed their horses, and the teamsters parked the supply wagons.

To the rear of the livestock, Ja'Huffield unharnessed her horses and setup her camp.

"Good, the Cleric is away from decent men," Pharos observed while pulling a bundle off the mule.

He and Hektor spread their three tents on the ground in a pattern around a firepit.

"Why the attitude towards the Cleric?" Alerio inquired.

"She and her wagon of snakes arrived in Taulantii a year ago. Right off, she attached herself to my King's court," Pharos explained. "Then almost overnight, he began building more raider ships and increasing the number of men in the army."

"And you believe he did it at her request?" Alerio asked.

"I'm a hunter, an oarsman, and a warrior," Pharos responded while hammering in a tent stake. "No one has ever accused me of being smart. But, yes, I do think the buildup is because of her."

"Why?" Hektor asked.

"That's always the question," Alerio offered. He used a rag to wash off trail dust. "I'm not confident anyone knows if..."

"Sir," Hektor warned.

Ja'Huffield, in a long, flared skirt of sewn leather patches, appeared to glide as she passed the encampment. From the waist up, the garment hugged her straight form as if it was the skin of a snake. A different snake mask than the one she traveled in, enhanced the illusion of a serpent emerging from a cone of scales.

She didn't acknowledge the Latian, the Greek, or the Illyrian who had stopped to stare at the striking woman. When she was well beyond the trio, Alerio chuckled.

"If I had known the Cleric would come this way," he joked while looking down at his naked torso and the crotch wrap, the only clothing he wore, "I would have dressed for the occasion."

***

Lieutenants Pinnes and Fisnik flanked their Admiral at the head table. Alerio had a corner seat next to a local Chieftain and two of his warriors. Across the open serving space, the Captain of the Ardiaean border detachment occupied a seat separated by two empty chairs from his junior officers. Some harsh commanders refused to associate with their men to maintain discipline. Believing Captain Testimos was one of them, explained the isolation to Alerio.

In the offering were beer, wine, and spring water. Once their clay mugs had been filled, Driton stood and lifted his.

"It's always good to eat with our neighbors," Driton exclaimed. "I don't get away from Fort Lezhë near often enough. Let us drink to a secure border and peace upon the land and for the people of the region."

The attendees drank and, when Driton sat, the Chieftain stood.

"My people flourish because of the soldiers on the border," he stated, acknowledging the Ardiaean Captain. Then facing the Taulantii Admiral, he said. "And salutations to Driton. It's not often my Navarch comes upriver to pay me homage."

Driton raised his mug and bowed to the tribal leader. Local chieftains ruled regions and provided men for the raiding ships and the army. Plus, when called upon, they elected the King. The comment about the Admiral not coming upriver often was an undisguised slight to Driton.

With a final look around, the Taulantii Chieftain sat, and the diners shifted their attention to the Ardiaean commander.

Testimos curled his lips in disgust and raised his mug, splashing wine on the table.

"Greetings," he sneered. "Bring on the feast."

Servants quickly brought the food to cover for the rude behavior. Plates of roasted fish and mashed turnips with fennel, garlic, and leeks were delivered. But the relaxed atmosphere had been stifled and the junior officers sat staring at their plates. Alerio glanced around to see who would break the tension in the tent. To his surprise, it wasn't the Admiral, the Captain, or the Chieftain.

Ja'Huffield flowed into the pavilion, her feet unseen beneath the flared stiff skirt.

"What have we here?" she cooed as if soothing a fawn.

Up close her exposed skin below the mask was anything except reptilian. Smooth and clear, her face and arms might belong to a popular maiden. But the fangs, and diamond shaped eye slits of the half mask destroyed any impression of innocence.

The Cleric of the Snake glided up to Testimos and stared down at the Captain.

"You seem out of sorts," she remarked.

Slowly, as if he feared the act, he lifted his head and looked at the mask.

"I don't need help from the God Boa," Testimos told her.

"Oh, my dear Captain, of course you do," Ja'Huffield assured him. "Everyone needs to be in concert with their ancestors. Our lives reflect the heritage they left for us. Our deeds will become the heritage of future generations. Only the serpent is unchanged by the passage of time."

Ja'Huffield skimmed the palm of one hand with the back of the other. In the space of the short, sharp slap, a snake appeared on her arm.

Alerio was a skilled swordsman. Not only were his reflexes superior, but his eye for detailed movement assured his success in many a swordfight. But the Cleric's actions were so smooth and fast, he couldn't see how she generated the snake.

"This dinner, these men of destiny are gathered here," Ja'Huffield intoned while pointing a finger at the Captain. The snake curled around her forearm. Then the serpent reared up, and the head floated back and forth as if targeting Testimos with its fangs. "Yesterday would be too early and tomorrow too late for the fates. Now, today, this instant, you are here to partake of fellowship that your children will sing of when snow coats the ground and snakes sleep. Can you not feel Boa's power in this tent?"

Testimos snorted and bent towards his mug. The way his lips missed the rim, hinted at the senior officer drinking before his arrival. He took a drink and slammed the mug down.

"I feel something in this tent," he growled while pushing to his feet. "But mostly, I smell a stink."

Captain Testimos stumbled away from the table, across the floor, and out through the tent flaps.

"I fear the Captain is under the weather," Driton announced. "If Boa's Cleric has no objection, we should eat."

Ja'Huffield waved her arm as if brushing away any objection. She moved around the table, sat in Testimos' seat, but didn't touch the food. Instead, she and the snake studied the men at the tables while they consumed the meal.

***

Once the food was gone and the mugs refilled, the Cleric stood. Still puzzled by the appearance of the snake, Alerio studied her hands to see if she held another one. The tight upper garment offered no folds to conceal a snake and he didn't remember her reaching down to the patchwork leather skirt.

"Navarch Driton, there are more things in the air than another cup of wine," Ja'Huffield mentioned. In response, the Admiral for the Taulantii Navy and General of their army dropped his mug as if it was a serpent about to bite him. The Cleric bent her ear to the snake on her arm as if listening. "What's that? Someone who does not understand?"

Jolted by the Admiral's obedience to the Cleric, Alerio looked from Driton's full mug and over to Testimos' place. The Captain's mug was not on the table.

Ja'Huffield skated to the serving space between the attendees.

"When I was a little child in Germania, my family would rise before dawn and go into the fields," she explained. "There the rest of the village would gather. From sunup to sundown, we pulled weeds, turned soil, sowed seeds, then covered the rows. Backbreaking work for the weak willed."

The Cleric moved forward and around to a place in front of the Ardiaean junior officers.

"One day I heard a cry of alarm," she continued in a soothing tone. "A snake had bitten one of the men. While he was carried to the village, the rest of us continued farming.

Except we avoided the snake and gave up precious farmland to the area where the serpent lived. That night, the man's leg swelled up. As the skin stretched like a water bladder, he cried for mercy. Finally, near dawn, the skin split, yellow bile flowed from the wound and the snake delivered the man from his pain. He died."

Rotating a half circle, Ja'Huffield glided across the open space to the Taulantii chieftain.

"The next day, the sun was hot and my back hurt," the Cleric said in the same silky manner. "I hated the stones I pried up with my stick, the clumps of soil that needed breaking apart, and the endless rows. I hated the village, my family, and the man who died. So, I took my stick, marched to the snake's area, and dared him to kill me. When he didn't come out, I stabbed his hole. And I waited. When he finally poked his head out, I grabbed him and pulled his long body free. Then I carried the serpent off the farm and flung it into a stream."

She floated to Admiral Driton's area and smiled.

"I expected praise for saving valuable farmland," Ja'Huffield cooed. "But they branded me a witch and the next day my parents sold me to a Celtic trader. I cowered in fear at the back of his wagon and lived off the scraps he tossed to me in the evenings. For months, we traveled eastward, stopping at villages and towns. In each, he had me go into the fields and find snakes. He bartered for goods and sold my services while feeding me leftovers. One day, we reached a town surrounded by a stockade wall. Bright tents and people calling out prices for food and drink drew me into the crowds. It was a festival, someone said. I didn't care what they called it. I ran behind booths and took whatever I could lay my hands on. But I got caught. When called, the trader hit me, hard, and threw me to the ground.

"She's a snake girl," he bellowed.

"If that's true," a vendor challenged. "Have her bring me a snake. Or pay me for the meat pies."

"Girl, you go find a snake," the big Celt ordered. "Or I'll gut you and feed you to the prize pigs."

And so, I stumbled around the festival searching for a snake. But there were too many people. Serpents are shy and prefer peace and calm. Not finding any place a snake would be, I walked out of the gate and into a patch of woods.

When I returned, I held up two serpents for the food vendor. He screamed and backed away. The trader joined him in the retreat. An armed man slapped the snakes from my hands and used his sword to kill them.

That night, I walked from the back of the wagon to where the trader was roasting meat.

"Get back to your place if you know what's good for you girl," he shouted.

I smirked, reached into my blouse, pulled out a snake, and tossed it at him. After he backed away, I cut a big slice of meat and took it to my place on the back of the wagon.

In the night, he approached me and asked if I had any more snakes. I told him I had picked up several more after dark and asked if he would like to hold one. He refused.

"There are none in your bedroll," I assured him. "Or in your grain sack. Or the trunk where you keep your coins."

The next day, he changed directions, and we headed southeast. Rather than stopping at every farming community, he pushed the old horses to long stretches on the trail.

"Three weeks later, we rolled into the town of Raša, the Illyrian capital of the Liburni Tribe," the Cleric recalled. She turned to face Alerio and whispered. "And my life changed."

As Ja'Huffield approached him, Alerio looked beyond her right arm. Under the table on the other side, he noted the crushed remains of Captain Testimos' missing mug. Nonchalantly, he drained his cup, turned it upside down, and set it on the table next to his empty plate. Then he crossed his arms, gazed up at the Cleric, and waited for her to continue.

Chapter 8 – Deep Waters of Shkodër

"You don't belong here," Ja'Huffield bellowed at Alerio. Then, sliding back into the chant like speech, she expounded. "We are on the cusp of momentous events. As I related in my talk, to incorporate change, you must be prepared to die for your cause. But you, a scarred soldier-of-fortune, have no cause."

She stopped talking and glared at the Latian.

"I have no idea what you're talking about, Cleric," Alerio commented. "As far as dying. I'm really good at making the other guy die for his cause."

Ja'Huffield screeched and reached for the table with her left hand. At the sudden movement, the snake hissed at Alerio. Then, the Cleric raised a finger and struck the tabletop with the fingernail.

The table surged upward causing Lieutenant Fisnik, one of Driton's aids, to come out of his chair and the Chieftain and his two warriors to fall back and away. After rocking from the power of a single tap, the table settled, and the men took their seats.

The Cleric stood holding a second snake in her right hand. Weaving patterns in the air with the serpents, she stepped back and closed her eyes.

"At Raša, I became a follower of the God Boa and was instructed in his mysteries and in the ways of the snake," she chanted. "The river of time while short for humans, flows on and on for serpents. And so, my evening is done, and I bid you a good night."

Ja'Huffield glided backward and out of the tent. Once she was gone, servants rushed forward to fill mugs and clear away dishes. After a few sips, the Taulantii and Ardiaei sat talking.

Alerio was silent while thinking about what he witnessed.

The only way he knew her knee hit the table, when she tapped it with her fingernail, was a slight crease in the leather skirt. And while the diversion worked on the others, he noticed the opening in the patchwork garment when Ja'Huffield reached for the second snake.

Picking up his mug, Alerio examined it for any sign of poison. He did that because Captain Testimos had not been intoxicated when he entered the tent.

***

In the dark, Alerio returned to find his two companions lounging around a campfire.

"You had dinner with the Cleric," Hektor gushed when Alerio appeared from the dark. "Was she as beautiful up close? Did you speak with her? Did she smell nice?"

Pharos poked the fire and grunted at the youth's excitement.

"Whoa there, lad," Alerio remarked. "Give me a moment to settle in."

Dropping down to a spot at the campfire, he accepted a wineskin from Pharos, and settled back.

"She's as slick as any high Priest or barbarian negotiator," he told them. "She is pretty, but as deadly as an asp. So, don't get too close."

"That's hard to believe, sir," Hektor challenged.

"No, it's not," Pharos shot back.

"Look, you're free to believe what you want," Alerio told the teen. "Just don't let your affection blind you to what she is."

When Hektor ground his teeth and refused to ask the follow-up question, Pharos inquired, "What is she?"

"A privilege celebrant, like so many others," Alerio described, "using faith and fear to control both the poor and the powerful."

"Colonel, it sounds as if you had an unpleasant experience with her," Hektor whined. "You shouldn't judge her based on one bad meeting."

"Tell you what, Master Nicanor," Alerio suggested, "ask Captain Testimos for his feelings about the Cleric. Afterwards, we can discuss my opinion."

***

The members of the convoy woke early the next morning and packed the tents and supplies. After the Admiral spoke with the Taulantii Chieftain and one of the Ardiaean Lieutenants, the caravan moved out of Bushat.

"Well, Hektor, what did the Captain have to say about her?" Alerio asked.

"Sir, he was unavailable," the youth replied. "His aide said he was deathly ill and bedridden. So, I couldn't get an answer."

"I disagree," Alerio informed him. "You got all the information about Ja'Huffield that you need."

The caravan passed through the town, taking the road north. While the trail ran straight from Bushat, the Drin River meandered eastward and was soon lost in the trees.

***

Seven miles up the trail, the caravan and river converged. Instead of the deep waterway, the Drin's banks were far apart, and the water flowed around tree covered islands.

"This looks like a good place to cross over," Alerio remarked.

"If we ford the river here," Pharos explained, "we'll have to cross the Kini River later. It's best to get to the Drin River and ferry directly to Shkodër."

"How many rivers are there?" Hektor asked.

"Lake Shkodra flows into the Buna and the Drin doubles back on the Kini River," Pharos described. "Fort Shkodër sits on a rise where the land comes to a point between the waterways."

Hektor made a sound as if to speak.

Alerio fixed the youth with a stern look. He didn't want any public discussion about a possible target of attack by the soldiers.

"All very interesting," he said changing the subject. "Must be good fishing here."

"They say the fishermen hold up their nets and the fish jump in," Pharos said. "But I don't think that's true. Fish aren't that smart."

"Not in my experience," Hektor agreed.

The topic of an attack on the fort, even if only a guess, was lost in the light banter.

***

Several miles along the bank of the Drin, a knoll rose four hundred feet above the land. On top were the stone walls of a fort. Alerio nudged his horse in besides Hektor.

"There's a likely target for a precision assault," he whispered. He jutted his chin in the direction of the hill. "But there are water barriers."

Hektor ran his eyes up to the peak and inspected the stone walls.

"The Taulantii have four rafts," the youth reminded Alerio. Then he asked. "What are you going to do with the knowledge, sir?"

"Right now, nothing," Alerio responded.

The lead riders moved off the trail and down to a landing. They stopped at a sandbar where a single ferry raft waited.

"I'll take three guards and cross over first," the Admiral commanded. "The rest of you can..."

He stopped talking when Ja'Huffield walked her horses and wagon to the front.

"I'll accompany you," she informed the Navarch.

"Of course," Driton acknowledged. Then with less enthusiasm, he instructed. "The rest of you come over in turn."

In the rear of the procession, Pharos eased his horse and the pack mule up beside Alerio.

"I never noticed the Navarch folding to the Cleric's wishes before," the big warrior remarked. "However, I haven't seen the Admiral interacting with her much. She's usually with the King."

"A commander tightening control near the end of a plan," Alerio muttered.

"Is there a plan?" Pharos inquired.

The Admiral, the Cleric, and her horses and wagon filled the raft. Dipping and wobbling, it launched into the current. Driton's horse would cross on the next trip.

"That's not very stable," Hektor commented.

"Too stable if you ask me," Pharos added.

The ferrymen polled upstream, angling to the middle of the river. When the raft reached the center, they used the current and poles to drift to the far bank. As they traversed the river, men appeared on the walls of the fort.

"Look up there," Pharos directed. "Nobody can approach and cross the river without being seen by the Shkodër home guard."

Alerio studied the tree lined river where it weaved further north before splitting. At night, rafts and boats could row from upstream, and beach unseen by those in the fort. Eventually, the men and flatboats would be staged close enough to Shkodër for a rapid assault.

He had the battlefield, and the approach figured out. What the Legion Battle Commander lacked were the motivation and the objective of the operation. But most important of all, he didn't know who in Shkodër to inform about the suspected attack.

"Hektor. Pharos. Breakout the cooking gear and rations," he directed. "We'll be awhile. We might as well eat."

"The Commander likes his food," Pharos offered.

"A Legionary takes advantage of every opportunity to have a hot meal. He never knows when he'll have the chance again," Hektor informed the big man while untying a cooking pot. "Besides, the Colonel likes to eat when he thinks."

"I like to eat," Pharos remarked, "but it never helps me think. Mostly, eating makes me want to nap."

"Legionaries also nap when given the opportunity," Hektor agreed. "But Colonel Sisera isn't a typical infantryman or Legion officer. He's a thinker. Now, where's a good place for a cookfire."

While the two prepared the meal, Alerio walked to the top of the riverbank and watched Driton and Ja'Huffield disembark. As the raft slid back into the water, a young man and another rider came from around the knoll. They crossed a stretch of farmland and rode their horses down onto the sandbar. Alerio had no idea who the young man was until he dismounted and embraced Admiral Driton. A Celt rode with Agron and Alerio assumed he was the Prince's military trainer.

"Sir, the stew is ready," Hektor called up to him.

"Coming," Alerio replied. Then in a low tone that didn't carry, he said. "I was just getting acquainted with the Prince's weapons instructor and my opponent."

As Alerio strolled towards the campfire, he searched the far bank for the Cleric. She wasn't near her horses. Then, she appeared from the back of her wagon dressed differently.

Gone were the patchwork leather skirt and skintight top. Her traveling attire swapped for a dress and a blouse with a scarf replacing the snake mask. Without looking at the Admiral and the Prince, she climbed to the driver's seat. Urging the team forward with a snap of the reins, Ja'Huffield guided the horses off the sandbar. Once through the farmland, the rig climbed from the lowland, and vanished around the base of the hill.

"This should help you think, sir," Pharos stated while offering Alerio a bowl of stew.

Confused by the comment, Alerio took the stew but didn't question the remark. He was preoccupied with the occupants on the far sandbar.

***

You could find them in every army or Legion. Usually, they gravitated to specific jobs, such as weapon's instructor or unit disciplinarian. Those not assigned to demanding jobs, or placed in units designated for dangerous missions, typically caused dissension in the ranks.

Alerio avoided becoming a problem in the Legions by first getting drafted into a Raider Century and, later, by earning a weapons instructor's position. Yet, as he had demonstrated on numerous occasions, Colonel Sisera had no objection to ending an argument with sharp steel.

"He's a problem," Alerio stated when the raft ground onto the sandbar.

Pharos ran his eyes from the Celt's heavy sandals to the square jaw and the bushy blond mustache that jutted from under his nose before cascading down the sides of his mouth.

"He's big, but I'm bigger," the Illyrian warrior declared.

"Pharos, under no circumstances are you to cross blades with him," Alerio instructed. "That includes you as well, Hektor."

When the trio walked off the raft, details of the Celt became obvious. Small knife scars on his hands attested to blade practice and fights. And a scar from a sword tip ran across his chest before the linen of his tunic covered the old wound.

"He's seen some battles," Hector observed, "and several knife fights."

"The Celt is more than a veteran commander," Alerio deduced from the number of visible wounds. "He's a professional swordsman who enjoys his work."

"How can you know that, sir?" Pharos inquired.

Similar scars marred Alerio's flesh and, like the Celt, most of his were hidden under clothing. Plus, the Celt radiated confidence with a hint of superiority, very much like a Legion infantry officer.

"Trust me," Alerio stated. "But we're not here for a swordfight. Our job is to broaden the Prince's education."

Driton noticed Alerio and raised an arm.

"Commander Sisera come over here," the Admiral directed with a wave. "I want you to meet my nephew."

Alerio smiled at the invitation but wasn't fooled. Driton wanted him to confront the Celt as much as the Admiral wanted to introduce Agron.

"Go locate Lieutenant Pinnes and find out where he wants us quartered," Alerio ordered Hektor. "I'm going to play at being nice."

"Sir, may I remind you that we aren't here for a swordfight," Hektor cautioned.

"I know that, and you know that," Alerio acknowledged, "but does Admiral Driton and the Celt know it?"

The three separated. Pharos and Hektor went in search of the Admiral's aide, and Alerio to greet the mission principals.

***

"This is Agron, my nephew," Driton boasted. "Someday, he'll be king of the Ardiaei."

"My Prince," Alerio acknowledged with a salute. "It's a pleasure to meet you."

"I hear you are a swordsman of some note in Rome," Agron stated. "Perhaps, we'll witness a demonstration while you're visiting."

"If the opportunity presents itself," Alerio replied.

"And this is Warlord Caden Rian," Driton said, introducing the Celt to the Latian.

Alerio bristled at the unnecessary use of the title. Although the smarter choice would be to hide his skills and experience, Alerio couldn't let the Celt's title go uncontested.

"Legion Battle Commander Alerio Sisera," he stated.

'Now, shall we compare combat scars?' he almost asked. Instead, he saluted Caden Rian.

Up close, the Celt was less than half a head taller than Alerio. And while the Latian had a broad back, the Celt carried his strength in a set of wide shoulders. On his hip, Caden wore a medium length steel sword that was a little longer than Alerio's gladius.

'I'll have to get inside his guard. Or he'll cut me up and make extra work for Hektor,' Alerio pondered as he smiled into the stern face of the Celt.

The two fighters stared at each other until the pounding of hooves drew their attention away from each other.

"That's my cavalry troop and Lieutenant Enda," Agron announced. "He's Caden's man but has taken on the responsibility of training my mounted guard."

The Celtic horseman had long red hair and a thin moustache that covered his mouth. An almost three-foot long sword hung from a shoulder strap.

Where Caden Rian oozed arrogance, Enda, at least in his riding style, displayed a fiery temperament to match his hair. The observation proved correct when the cavalry troop stopped. Leaping from his horse, the Celtic Lieutenant stomped across the sandbar to Alerio.

"What's a Latian doing here?" he questioned.

Leaning forward, he put himself nose to nose with Alerio.

Admiral Driton chuckled. Prince Agron tensed but remained quiet. Caden Rian maintained a regular rate of breathing and watched.

"Warlord Rian. If this is your pet," Alerio warned, "put a leash on him."

"Or what?" Enda demanded.

Alerio dipped his chin and lowered his eyes. Seeing the downward glance, Enda followed the lead. At gut level, a curved dagger bridged the distance between the two men. The tip, aimed below Enda's belt, quivered between his lower belly and his manhood.

Admiral Driton was puzzled. Sisera's gladius was in its scabbard and the military dagger on his hip rested in its sheath. He didn't know of the assassin's dagger that resided in the small of Alerio's back. Hidden from view and theft, the weapon only came out for special cases.

"Or, Lieutenant Enda, you'll die, painfully," Alerio promised.

Chapter 9 – Pre-Gala Planning

Hektor pushed open the door to the shop and was immediately enveloped in a cloud of fragrance. His brain became overcome, causing him to stop in the doorway.

"Please, young sir, come in," a man said while taking his elbow and guiding the teen off the street.

Laughter from a pair of men snapped Hektor out of the aroma triggered spell. His right hand slipped to the hilt of his knife.

"Do you find me amusing?" he demanded.

The two men could be twins. Both carried lean muscle on slim frames. They held up identical masks that obscured their eyes, cheeks, and foreheads. Black feathers extended beyond the edges of their faces, forming soft spikes. On one mask, a long gray feather stretched to the right. On the other man's mask, the feather hung to the left.

"Good day, young fellow," one acknowledged Hektor. "We meant no insult."

The other man lowered his mask and smiled.

"When we entered the mask shop," he added, "we also had a moment of delirium."

"I believe they fill the air with heady fragrances to cloud the mind," Hektor offered.

"Possibly to make you more susceptible to their extravagant prices," the first man stated.

"How rude are we?" the second man declared. He performed a half bow. "I am Zamir."

"And I am Rezart," the first introduced himself.

He dropped his mask and Hektor could tell they weren't brothers. Their facial features were similar in shape but not close enough to be related. Yet, due to their body types, a quick glance might confuse a casual observer.

"I'm, Hektor, at your service," Hektor responded.

He dropped his hand from his knife and gave them a Legion salute.

Zamir and Rezart turned to face each other, slammed hands into their chests, and saluted each other. Then, they chuckled at their antics.

"What a peculiar custom," Zamir remarked.

"Exquisite," Rezart exclaimed. He pointed to the shop owner. "We'll take these two overpriced masks."

"Yes, Master, I'll have them put in traveling cases," the shopkeeper promised.

He collected the black masks and carried them to a backroom.

"Are you attending the Prince's birthday gala?" Zamir asked Hektor.

"No, sir, I'm...

Laughter from the pair forced Hektor to stop in mid-sentence.

"Oh, dear me," Rezart said with his mouth hidden behind his hand, "we insulted our friend Hektor, again."

"The humor comes from the title of sir," Zamir explained. "We're ne'er-do-wells with a gift for wrangling invitations from Chieftains."

"Or, in this case, a Prince," Rezart bragged. "Would you like to be our guest at the Prince's gala?"

"I don't think I'm going," Hektor answered. "I can't imagine they'll have a use for a field medic at a gala."

"A medical man," Zamir offered, "is always welcome."

The shopkeeper came from the backroom and handed them cloth bags containing their masks. After dropping several silver coins into the man's hand, they headed for the door. Then, they stopped short of the doorway.

"If you change your mind, Hektor Nicanor," Rezart advised. "Find us and we'll sneak you into the party."

They walked out chatting and laughing at some private joke.

"They seemed like nice guys," Hektor told the mask vendor. "I need two masks for the street festival and a proper one for the gala."

"Yes, young Master, come let me show you my goods," the vendor invited. "And know, if we can't find one that suits your needs, you can commission a custom mask. It's all the rage among the Chieftains and heads of families."

"Did the two who just left pick from the shelves?" Hektor asked.

"No, sir," the shopkeeper told him. "Theirs were custom masks right down to the placement of the feathers."

Hektor and the vendor began examining already made masks. It never dawned on the youth to question how Rezart and Zamir knew his last name.

***

At a small house near the beach where they landed, Pharos paced the floor.

"I should have gone with him," the Illyrian complained.

"The Admiral's assistance claims the city is safe and the mask shop's just inside the low side," Alerio reminded him. "But truthfully, I don't quite know where that is."

"Shkodër resembles a leaf shaped spearhead," Pharos described. "The fort sits on the high southern point. Downhill from the fort is the high side. Then the edges of the city flair outward. We crossed the Drin on the east side. The town faces Lake Shkodra on the other. Between us are rocky heights unsuitable for anything except birds and snakes."

"Which leaves the lower side to the north," Alerio guessed, "where the sides come together."

"Yes sir, leaf shaped, like I said."

The door rattled, then swung inward before slamming against the wall.

"Masks," Hektor announced. He held up three cloth pouches. "Two for the festival. And one so Colonel Sisera can attend the Prince's gala. I hope."

"What do you mean, hope?" Alerio inquired.

The youth handed him the sack and stepped out of arm's reach. While Hektor and Pharos watched, Alerio lifted the mask out of the bag and held it up.

"Am I supposed to wear this?" he demanded.

"It was the most unique one the vendor had in stock," the teen said defending his choice.

"It is interesting," Pharos allowed.

"Pan is the God of the woodlands, shepherds, flocks, mountain wilds, and pastoral music," Hektor explained.

"And he is known for consorting with nymphs," Alerio added. "That's hardly me."

"It's a goat mask," Pharos observed. "I do like the horns, the wild eyes, and the snout that extends over your nose."

"Just like you wanted," Hektor stated. "No one will recognize you in that."

"That's one benefit to being a goat," Alerio remarked. "What about your masks?"

Unlike the elaborate one constructed of feathers placed to resemble goat hair, the street masks used molded clay carved and painted to depict bird feathers.

"Mine's a goose," Hektor described while holding up his mask.

"If that is a goose" Pharos questioned as he examined his mask, "what's mine?"

"That's an owl mask," Hektor replied. "You can tell by the wide eyes and short beak."

"It looks like a chicken," Pharos grumbled.

"Well, it's an owl," Hektor insisted. "The man in the shop said so."

"Chicken."

"You two can discuss the masks all you want," Alerio said. He tossed a Legion cloak over his tunic. "I've got dinner with the Admiral."

"Planning strategy for the gala, sir?" Hektor inquired.

"If you're going to plan, tonight is a good time," Pharos commented. "With the festival starting tomorrow, the city is filling up with vendors and visitors. Once it starts, everyone will be too drunk to plan anything."

"I think the Admiral just wants to show me off," Alerio told them.

"Is that part of the plan, sir?" Pharos questioned.

***

"Battle Commander Sisera," Driton exclaimed when Alerio entered the hallway of a house. "I'm glad you're here. I want to show you off."

"I'll be sure to tell Pharos it was part of the plan," Alerio remarked.

"Excuse me?" Driton asked.

A servant took the red cloak and handed Alerio a glass of wine.

"It's nothing, Admiral," Alerio assured him. "Who am I meeting?"

They strolled to a crowded room where Driton steered Alerio to a group surrounding Prince Agron.

"Battle Commander Sisera, I'm glad you're here," Agron greeted him. "We were just discussing who were the best fighters in the world."

"A Spartan," a man stated.

"An Illyrian soldier," one boasted.

"A Greek Hoplite," a third proclaimed.

"I've heard the Iberians are tough," another guest stated.

"The Noricum warriors have fearsome reputations," a fifth man offered.

"Well, Sisera, which one of them is the best fighter?" the Prince asked. When Alerio hesitated, Agron prodded. "Surely a man with your experience has an opinion on the topic. Who, Battle Commander, is the best?"

Alerio took a sip and ran his eyes over the cluster of men. They were drinking and debating. No matter what he said, it would get lost in the conversation. Being lumped in with the others would defeat the mission and the reason he came to Illyria.

"The best fighter in a combat line," he finally announced, "is the shield bearer on your right. Without his shield covering your sword side, you can't win."

"Unfair," one member of the group whined. "You've avoided the question."

"He's changed the parameters," another howled. "That's not an answer."

"We weren't discussing tactics," a third stated.

But in the center of the complainers, Prince Agron remained quiet while he contemplated Alerio and the answer. Seeing the crowd deteriorate into a series of one-way comments, Driton took Alerio's elbow and extracted him from the group.

"That didn't go as well as I had hoped," the Admiral remarked.

"Who do you have there, Navarch?" a lean, but muscular man asked.

He stood with a second man, both grinning as if they shared a joke. At first glance, Alerio thought they were brothers. As the Admiral brought him closer, he could see the resemblance was superficial.

"Do I know you?" Driton inquired.

"No, sir," one replied. "We're friends of the Prince."

"Not exactly friends, but he did invite us," the other corrected. "I guess that makes us acquaintances of Agron. I'm Rezart."

"And I'm Zamir," the second introduced himself. "And this must be Decanus Sisera."

"What do you want?" Driton demanded.

"Just to say hello," Rezart replied.

"Well, you've said it. Now if you'll excuse us," Driton moved Alerio away from the two men and grumbled. "Must be the sons of some Chieftain or rich merchant. We can't waste the evening with their likes. Come, I've more important people for you to meet."

In the rush to escape the two men, Alerio didn't get a chance to ask about Zamir's use of his rank. He hadn't been a Lance Corporal for years. And the two were close enough to have heard Driton call him Battle Commander Sisera.

"Alerio, this is Chieftain Lorik, a man to know and a counselor to the King," the Admiral stated when they reached a pair of older men.

While Lorik smiled and acknowledged them with a bow, the second man stomped away.

"Please excuse Chieftain Verzo," Lorik stated. "He's uncomfortable with the Admiral."

"You're being too kind, Chieftain," Driton clarified. "Verzo doesn't like or trust the Taulantii. He's made that clear on many occasions."

"He is a man of passion," Lorik proposed. "Now, Sisera, I suppose you're in Shkodër for the gala. But why are you in the company of a rogue like Driton?"

"I'm advising the Admiral on military matters," Alerio replied.

"That is ever the problem," Lorik said. "Armies are trained and then what do you do with them? You march to war. If I could, I would disband every army and put the manpower on farms and fishing boats. Then at least, they would be too busy to destroy their neighbors."

Until the speech, Alerio had considered telling Lorik about the staged phalanxes. After it, he decided to keep the suspicion about an attack to himself.

"Lord Lorik is a man of peace," Driton explained. "But he does have ten raider ships on the water."

"I may not want war," Lorik commented. "But I don't want my family to starve for my principles."

"Well stated, Chieftain," Driton said while extracting Alerio. "I have a few others for the Battle Commander to meet."

"Please, you go and enjoy yourselves," Lorik encouraged. "I'll see you both at the gala."

"Until then," Driton promised. He and Alerio moved across the room to a deserted corner. "I was hoping Verzo would stay."

"The Chieftain doesn't seem enamored with you," Alerio observed.

"Verzo is not a friend of my tribe. But you'll need his support," Driton explained. "As for Lorik, as much as he wants peace, Chieftains Lorik and Verzo supports military spending."

"I'm confused," Alerio admitted. "Do you want Prince Agron to have a strong army when he becomes king or don't you?"

"Agron will have an army when he becomes King," the Admiral replied. "For now, we like Verzo's caution."

"And Chieftain Lorik?"

"He is the more dangerous of the King's advisors."

"But he's a man of peace."

"An idealist," Driton warned. "Break Chieftain Lorik's boundaries or betray his trust, and he will fight beyond reason."

Alerio reconsidered telling Chieftain Lorik about the attack.

***

Cities, towns, and hamlets with farms along riverbanks usually had a fresh earthy scent. Unlike pure fishing communities that reeked of rotting fish, or the stink of harbor villages with dung piles left by traveling herds. The east side of Shkodër had the clean smell until the morning.

"What's in the air?" Hektor asked.

He rolled out of bed, strolled to the window, and flung open the shutter. Baking bread and honey cakes teased his sense of smell. Below the lighter aromas, the fragrance of roasting poultry, beef, and pork flowed into the house on the morning breeze.

"In Rome," Alerio offered, "you'd smell that combination on religious holidays."

"We Illyrians don't stop work for the Gods," Pharos asserted. "But for a Chieftain's birthday, we'll drop everything and party. What you smell, Hektor, is the start of the street festival."

"Hektor. Why don't you run out and buy us breakfast?" Alerio suggested.

"I'll go with you," Pharos told the Greek teen. "Don't forget your mask."

Once they had the clay masks tied around their heads, the two left the home. Alerio hung his head between his knees and chewed on his lower lip.

"Goddess Nenia. Why am I here?" he questioned his personal deity. "I thought I could find trading partners. But all I've found is a bad Greek drama of doubts and double dealings."

In the silence of the room, Alerio Sisera listened to his breathing and felt his heartbeat. The sounds of passing vendors and their carts drifted through the window. Then, as if hands were clamped over Alerio's ears, the room grew quiet. Five heartbeats after the silence dropped, a shadow appeared on the windowsill and a gurgling croak filled the room.

"Really?" Alerio challenged. "I ask for guidance, and you send Apollo, the God of Prophecy?"

At the window, a large raven paced along the sill. From deep in the back of its throat, the symbol of Apollo croaked loudly as if stating a prediction. Then the door opened, and the raven flew away.

Hektor and Pharos came in with platters of delicious aromas.

"We have enough, sir, for you to have a good think," Pharos exclaimed.

"How prophetic of you," Alerio acknowledged as he took one of the platters.

He claimed a corner of the table. While he ate, Alerio turned over a question in his mind. What prophecy did the Gods need him to fulfill?

Act 4

Chapter 10 - Festival Day

Along the eastern side of Shkodër, people moved in bunches. Groups of young men teased and called out to women on the arms of husbands or their betrotheds and to women traveling in packs. Conversely, clusters of women laughed and flirted with men escorting their wives or fiancées and with groups of men. In masks of varying qualities, the revelers were anonymous, allowing for a lack of inhibitions.

"Oh, my," a girl squealed as a group approached Alerio and his companions. "I've always wanted a pet goat."

"Come home with me, goat-man," another one in the cluster shrieked. "I've got more than oats for you."

Alerio punched Hektor in the shoulder.

"What?" the youth questioned. "The mask of Pan is popular."

"They don't know that Pan is a God," Pharos stated. "They think the Battle Commander is disguised as a randy goat-man."

"How can that be?" Hektor inquired. "Everyone knows Pan."

The group of rowdy women had moved passed them when one turned.

"Of all my livestock," she shouted over her shoulder, "I've always been partial to my goats."

Howls of laughter erupted as the women moved farther away. Hektor shuffled away from Alerio's fist.

"Truthfully, sir," Pharos advised. "You were singled out because of the quality of your mask. Note that neither Hektor nor I were targets of their banter."

"Maybe I should take it off," Alerio pondered. "Or we can get one to replace it."

"Sorry, sir," Pharos told him. "All the shops and trading houses are closed for festival day. And no one with any sense goes about without a mask."

"Why?" Hektor inquired.

"Because, they will be pelted with rocks or garbage for insulting the Prince," the big Illyrian informed him. "So, you see Commander, you're stuck with the goat mask."

"It's a mask of Pan," Hektor protested.

They strolled northward for three quarters of a mile before turning left and entering the lower town.

***

"I could use a glass of vino," Alerio declared.

"There's a pub on the other side of the street from the mask shop," Hektor told him.

They pushed through a swarm of merrymakers and made it to the door of an inn. Before they entered, a slim girl in a linen dress with a mask resembling a white dove hooked her arm through Hektor's. She spun him back into a crowd of dancers who kept time to a drumbeat.

"Will he be all right?" Alerio questioned from the doorway.

"From what I can tell," Pharos answered, "the teen is already better off than both of us."

The girl handed Hektor a wineskin and he took a stream. His feet kept time with the chanting voices and the thumping of the drum. While the mask hid her eyes, nose, and cheeks, a very visible and welcoming smile beamed at the Greek youth. Together, they spun in the street, keeping up with the dancers and the rhythm.

"I see what you mean," Alerio admitted. "Come my Illyrian friend, allow me to buy you a beverage. There's something I need to talk to you about."

"I'd rather be dancing with a pretty girl in a dove mask," Pharos remarked. "But I'll settle for a beer and conversation."

They left Hektor and the clamor of the festival and entered a dimly lit pub. Inside, it was only slightly less noisy. At a table near the rear, they sat. Pharos so he could watch the other occupants, and Alerio so he could keep an eye on the doorway.

"A mug of wine and a large beer," Pharos called to a waitress.

When she held up two fingers to show she understood the order, the Illyrian tuned to Alero.

"You had something you wanted to discuss, Battle Commander?"

"I need you to find out where Prince Agron is being trained by Caden Rian."

"Do you want to attend as a spectator?" Pharos asked. "Or do you want to spy on them?"

"I'm not sure I like the implications of spying," Alerio said resisting the concept.

"All right then, do you want to sip wine while you watch," Pharos rephrased the questions. "Or dig sand fleas

101

out of your crotch, while keeping one eye out for snakes, as you slap flies from your neck, while you observe the training?"

The drinks arrived and Alerio paid the waitress. He took a sip before answering.

"Spying," he admitted.

"I can find out where, sir," the big soldier confirmed, "and the best place to watch unobserved."

They tapped mugs together in salute of the plan.

"I hope Hektor is all right," Alerio offered.

***

Hektor Nicanor whirled around. The girl in the dove mask clutched his fingertips and circled him. The chanting, the wine, and the press of bodies sent the youth's head spinning. Her smile provided a fixed point of focus while the world reeled around them.

"Come," she instructed. To Hektor's surprise, the girl easily stopped the movement. "Come."

Dragging the youth, she pulled him into an alleyway. Once off the street, she pushed Hektor against a wall and kissed him. The touch of their lips caused the youth's knees to weaken. After the shared passion, she eased her head back and ran her fingertips across his lips.

At the touch, the teen's legs gave way. If not for the girl's strength, he might have tumbled over.

"Who is your Latian Master?" she whispered in his ear.

"Alerio Sisera is not my Master," the youth stated. "I'm his medic."

Hektor's brain fogged, and the image of the white dove mask faded in and out of vision.

"Why is he in Shkodër?"

"We are going to help Prince Agron claim the crown," Hektor replied.

To the youth, the girl's voice sounded as if they stood in a windstorm. Her words and their meaning reached his ears in waves. Other questions were asked but Hektor couldn't remember them nor his answers.

"Which crown?" she inquired. "Are you here to overthrow the King?"

"Colonel Sisera is a weapons' instructor," Hektor slurred. "He's going to teach Agron how to fight."

Many questions or just a few later, the girl patted his cheek, kissed him again, and stepped back. Released from her grip, the Greek youth slid to the ground.

"You are very cute, Hektor Nicanor," she exclaimed before dashing to the street and vanishing into the crowd.

***

Alerio and Pharos were on their second round when Hektor stumbled through the doorway.

"My favorite medic has made an appearance," Alerio noted.

Pharos stood. Being a head taller than anyone in the room, his wave caught Hektor's attention. Staggering between tables, the youth made his way to the rear of the inn where he collapsed into a chair.

"Many lose their inhibitions, among other things, during festival days," Pharos remarked. He held up a hand for the waitress with three fingers extended. "I won't pry, but your garments are disheveled."

Absentmindedly, Hektor smoothed his tunic down, shoving the excess material under his belt. His eyes were glassy and unable to remain on one object.

"After the dancing, I remember a kiss," he explained while blinking.

"That's the best part of festival," Pharos stated. "You don't remember if she was pretty or if she was old and ugly."

"I didn't have that much to drink," Hektor pleaded. "There's no reason I can't remember."

"If you remember the kiss," Pharos encouraged, "you're better off than most. And that young Greek, is considered a win."

The waitress shoved between several men to reach them. While placing the mugs on the tabletop, she looked at Hektor's eyes.

"How long has it been?" she inquired.

"How long has what been?" Alerio asked.

"Since he was bitten by the snake. His eyes have the look, but he's up and moving, so he didn't get much venom," the waitress described. After taking the payment, she added before walking away. "The God Boa was watching out for that one."

"All I remember is a kiss," Hektor mumbled while taking a sip of beer.

"A poison kiss," Alerio guessed.

"From a girl in a white dove mask," Pharos moaned then teased. "How disagreeable?"

***

Alerio braced Hektor as the two lurched back towards the rented house. They drew no one's attention. Two more intoxicated festival goers in the crowd hardly stood out.

"Where's Pharos," Hektor asked.

The youth stumbled to a stop and peered over Alerio's shoulder.

"He's on a mission for me," Alerio replied.

"I should be on that mission."

"No, you shouldn't. You need to be in bed sleeping off the effects of the poison," Alerio informed him.

"It was only a kiss," Hektor protested.

Alerio nudged them into motion. They continued along the east side of Shkodër. Backtracking the route they took earlier in the day, the two arrived at the house. After dropping Hektor into his bed, Alerio went to his bundle.

Although the house wasn't much more than a thatched roof bungalow, it had a large courtyard in the rear. With his matched set of swords, Alerio paced from the house to the center of the yard.

He started slowly with two slashes to the side, one backhand, and two more slashes with the right sword. Mirroring the Legion recruit exercises with his left hand, Alerio Sisera continued to loosen up. Soon, he began a series of advanced drills.

***

Festival day made it hard to locate specific friends in the city. However, once Pharos found the ones he needed, getting the information from men well oiled with beer proved easy.

"Stay and drink with us," they begged.

"I would, but I've a date with a woman," he lied.

"Is she fair or wrinkled like a raisin?"

"I don't recall," Pharos admitted. "She had a mask on."

The laughter of the men followed the big Illyrian out of the pub. Once on the road, he quick walked around groups celebrating the Prince's birthday. On the other end of high side, he hooked a left and jogged to the rental house.

"Commander Sisera," he called as he came though the doorway.

But the interior was quiet and, other than Hektor sprawled on his bed, it was empty. The sounds of heavy breathing came from the backyard. When the clash of steel on steel followed, Pharos drew his long sica and charged into the rear courtyard.

Rather than intruders attempting to attack the house, he found the Battle Commander flipping through the air.

***

Alerio's right leg had kicked over his shoulder, pulling his torso back. While his body rotated head over heels, the sword in his left hand poked at the ground. As he completed the athletic maneuver, the right-handed sword tapped the left out of the way. It was this type of click that drew Pharos to the courtyard. At the end of the flip, Alerio stepped and did another. Only on the second rotation, he kicked with his left leg. Again, just before he landed, his blades clashed together.

Covered in sweat, Alerio dropped to his knees, and crossed his arms and the blades in front of him.

"If a man charged into that wicked scissor move," Pharos proclaimed, "he'd be cut in half. Thank you."

Alerio remained on his knees with his blades crossed.

"Thank you for what?" he inquired.

"For not using that on the beach at Lezhë," Pharos replied. "I have the details of Agron's practice schedule."

Kicking with his lower legs, Alerio launched himself off the ground. He went from kneeling to standing in the blink of an eye.

"When?" he asked.

"The Prince likes to start late in the afternoon," Pharos reported, "and practice until sundown."

Alerio moved out from under the branches of a tree until he had a view of the sky.

"In that case, he should be starting soon," he stated while dabbing his forehead with a cloth. "And where is this secret practice field?"

"Colonel Sisera, you need to get cleaned up and dressed," the big Illyrian informed him. "The Prince is using the drill field at the fort. Admiral Driton, and his aids, Pinnes and Fisnik, and a group of Chieftains have been invited to watch."

"So, no spying?" Alerio asked as he walked to the house. "Hold on. Will Queen Jeta be there?"

"Sir, according to rumors, no one knows when or if the queen will show up," Pharos told him. "Agron's mother keeps her own counsel."

"Something I suspected," Alerio remarked as he entered the bungalow.

***

It was only a half mile to Fort Shkodër. But for most of the trip, the path took Alerio and Pharos uphill. Stopping at the gate to the fort came as a nice break, as did relief from the late afternoon sun in the cool shadow of the defensive wall.

"Reason for your visit?" a Sergeant of the Guard demanded.

Two men-at-arms moved to flank the NCO, blocking the road.

"He is Battle Commander Sisera," Pharos answered, "the military adviser for Admiral Driton. And I'm his escort."

"The Navarch is at the drill field," the Sergeant directed. "Follow the ramp to the upper elevation."

Alerio and Pharos strolled up an incline between two short walls. At the midpoint, it turned back on itself before letting them out on a flat plain. In the distance, a group stood under the canopy of a pavilion.

"Big crowd," Alerio mentioned.

"The Chieftains have come for Agron's birthday," Pharos offered. "Today is an outing with a chance to talk before the gala tomorrow."

"Not that I'm complaining, but you seem to know a lot about what's going on."

"My cousin is a Lieutenant in the guard," Pharos told him. "The Kings and Chieftains may think the land is divided between them. But up in the mountains where my family lives, the only separation is uphill or downhill. As far as Shkodër is concerned, my cousin is an Ardiaein."

"And you're Taulantii," Alerio said.

"At least until I get home," the big soldier added. They reached the tent and Pharos began to walk towards the rear of the pavilion. "I'm more comfortable with the guards than the rich folks. Call if you need me."

"Believe me, I feel the same," Alerio stated while continuing to a gap between attendees.

"Commander Sisera, you almost missed the exhibition," Driton called to Alerio. "Come, stand with me."

While the Admiral's greeting sounded warm, his eyes burned into Alerio's chest. The Navarch wasn't please to see him attending the event.

"Have I missed anything?" Alerio asked.

Before the Admiral had a chance to answer, a striking woman pushed through the crowd. While youthful in appearance, she radiated authority. As Alerio could tell by her bold actions, the people recognized it and parted to allow her through.

"Tell me big brother," she cooed at Driton, "is this the Latian Battle Commander everyone is talking about?"

The Admiral bowed to the woman before holding out a hand in Alerio's direction.

"Queen Jeta. May I present Battle Commander Alerio Sisera," he said.

Jeta stepped up to Alerio. Her lips were set in a hard line as she studied him. Then with a twinkle in her eyes, she smiled.

"Is the best fighter in the world really just a shield carrier?"

"Bearer, ma'am," Alerio corrected. "And yes, the shield on the right is the key to winning a swordfight."

"But my husband the King, and Warlord Rian, claim the best fighter is the man with the fastest blade," Jeta countered.

"It's a barbaric assumption," Alerio replied without thinking. Then, he remembered that he was deep in Illyrian territory and inside an Ardiaei fort. And he was contradicting their Queen while surrounded by her soldiers. "I meant no…"

"I get your meaning," Jeta uttered, stopping him. "Brother. After the demonstration, send the Battle Commander to me."

She didn't wait for a reply.

"Yes, my Queen," Driton said to her retreating back. Then he raged at Alerio. "This wasn't the plan. What have you done?"

"It seems, Admiral, I met Queen Jeta."

Chapter 11 – Nest of Vipers

Prince Agron slipped off Caden's shield and whipped his blade around at waist level. It appeared to be a safe and mundane strike. Except the blade struck the Celt's shield hard, forcing Carden to brace against the assault. While his opponent paused to absorb the blow, Agron squared his shield to his blade and smashed into Caden's side.

The Warlord stumbled back. Slashing his blade back and forth over Caden's bent head, the Prince crowded forward. Only years of experience kept the Celt on his feet, preventing a humiliating defeat.

To most of the spectators, it was a masterful performance by Agron. For a few knowledgeable observers, it could have been just that, a performance. But Alerio knew the truth.

As the Prince and the Warlord fought, Alerio split his attention between the combatants and Caden's Lieutenant. Enda's face and body language revealed the truth. When Agron bullied Caden back, Enda vibrated with the desire to dash to the aid of his Warlord.

"I fear Agron isn't as good as he and King Pleuratus believe," Driton whispered to Alerio. "If he tried striking the center of a soldier's shield in a real fight, he'd get hurt."

The Prince's advanced moves to an untrained observer appeared too simple to be successful. But Agron's mastery of his sword and shield were on full display during the demonstration. Realizing this, Alerio knew two things. He had little to add to the Prince's education and the Admiral was lying.

"Individual combat has a lot to do with the student's natural ability," Alerio remarked.

The assertion didn't confirm the Admiral's falsehood or contradict the statement. Navarch Driton knew Prince Agron required no extra training but insisted on the need for Alerio.

"So, can you help him?" the Admiral inquired.

"Yes," Alerio lied.

There would be no peace treaty or trade agreement because there would be no training of the Prince by Alerio. In the back of his mind, he began to plan an escape from Illyria for him and Hektor.

"Did you see that?" asked a voice with delight.

"Fluid, I tell you," a second declared. "Prince Agron moves like water."

Alerio looked to the other side of the pavilion. Standing with arms extended, two men mimicked sword fighting. Their black masks with the single long gray feathers jutting to the sides identified them.

"As devastating as a broken dam," Rezart exclaimed.

"As forceful as a three and a quarter foot tidal wave from a fall storm," Zamir added.

They stopped the mock combat, clinked their mugs together, and drank.

"Excellent analogies," Zamir stated.

"We are ingenious," Rezart confirmed.

They lifted their mugs and drank again.

"Agron has made poor choices of friends," Driton complained.

"I believe Admiral, they are just acquaintances," Alerio reminded him.

On the drill field, cavalrymen rode to the pavilion. Agron mounted a horse held by Lieutenant Enda. As the troop galloped to a position opposite a practice foe, a voice spoke behind Alerio

"What did you think, Battle Commander?"

Alerio pivoted to face Caden Rian. Rather than engage the Warlord, Alerio took the Celt's arm and guided him to an empty area outside the pavilion.

"My compliments," Alerio said when they were away from the other guests. "You've armed the next king of the Ardiaei with deadly skills."

"I'm surprised to hear you say that," Caden remarked. "Most swords-for-hire would try to remove me and take the commission for themselves."

"I could save them some coins," Alerio suggested.

"Oh, really. How's that?"

Alerio pointed to the cavalry engagement taking place on the drill field.

"Illyria is mostly mountains, valleys, islands, and shoreline," Alerio listed. "Where do you plan to hold the gallant cavalry charge?"

Caden Rian chuckled.

"I needed them to pay my Lieutenant," he admitted. "Besides being a ferocious warrior, Enda is an expert horseman."

"I'm not going to challenge your position," Alerio told him. "After the gala, I'm taking my medic and leaving."

"Enda and I are going to stay," Caden ventured. "I'm beginning to like Shkodër."

On the hike up to the fort, Alerio had peered down at the high section, and out over the east and west sides of the town. From the trail, he had an unobstructed view of the unfriendly rocky heights separating the sides. While large in scope, the city was an oversized working village. Fish racks and fishing boats lined the shorelines. Warehouses with open fronts were rickety and seemed as if they would tumble down in the next storm. And rather than merchant vessels, raider ships lined the beaches. All the commerce had to do with food for the crews and stolen goods. Other than the fort, nothing in Shkodër, including the bungalows, were well built. To Alerio, he might as well be in Massina with the equally uncivilized Sons of Mars. Nothing about Shkodër made it a desirable place to visit, let alone a place to settle down.

"Well, I plan on leaving," Alerio advised, "unless…"

The city and the odd occurrences he's seen since arriving in Illyria had Alerio's brain questing for answers. The 'Unless' was a fishing expedition.

"Unless what?" Rian asked.

"Unless something is going on that I'm not aware of," Alerio responded.

"I have no idea what you're talking about," the Celt asserted, but too strongly.

"How about your agreement with the Taulantii."

Caden Rian stepped back, and eyed Alerio.

"How did you find out?"

"Two things. Admiral Driton had no interest in us when we left the pavilion. Before, he was so excited for us to meet, I figured he wanted to see you kill me. But now, he's dismissed us," Alerio replied. "Plus, you just admitted you have a deal with the Taulantii."

"I'm a simple northerner who came to teach a Prince how to fight," Caden told Alerio. "And I found myself in a nest of vipers."

"Then why stay?"

"Among my people, I am a warlord," Caden explained. "But our land is poor and while my warriors are fierce, they are few. Here, I can command an army and get rich."

"If the Taulantii win," Alerio noted. He rested his hand on the hilt of his gladius before warning. "You should know, there are a few things I could teach the Prince."

"There's no reason for us to fight," the Celt said. He lifted his hands away from his blades. "As long as Prince Agron wins, everything will go as planned."

"How can you be sure you understand the plan?" Alerio cautioned. "You said it yourself. Illyria is a nest of vipers."

***

Late that afternoon, a pair of guards walked Alerio through a portal and down a corridor of rough stone. At a double doorway of iron bound oak, his escorts nodded at a heavily armored man standing sentry.

"Whose quarters are those?" Alerio asked.

"It's not," one guard answered.

"That's the Ardiaei treasury," the second added.

The three continued to a door at the end of the hallway. One guard knocked.

"Send him in," Jeta called from inside.

Before he entered, Alerio glanced back at the door to the treasury. Between the soldiers in the fort and the one at the doorway, the tribe's coins were secure from a random robbery. Then, he walked through the doorway.

Torches lit a sitting room with a variety of furniture. The tables were from Greece, the sofas from Republic craftsmen, and the chairs displayed Egyptian design. The accommodations served to remind Alerio that he was dealing with pirates.

"Queen Jeta," he greeted Agron's mother with a bow.

"Pour us glasses of wine, Battle Commander. It's from Syracuse, I believe," she directed. "And join me."

She patted the chair across from her.

"Agron is an excellent swordsman," Alerio informed her.

He handed one glass to Jeta before taking the other seat.

"I've been informed Caden is going easy on him."

"I'm not sure I want to know who," Alerio said, avoiding the subject. "Agron is very good with the blade and shield. You don't need me."

"It seems I do," Jeta remarked. She took a sip, rested her head against the chairback, looked down her nose, and studied Alerio. "You told me the truth. Keep it up and tell me about my brother."

"Admiral Driton has two hundred and fifty soldiers staged on the border," Alerio replied. He thought about what to say and decided if anyone needed to know it was the Queen. "He placed them there for a reason."

"Do you find him ambitious?"

115

Alerio thought back over the time he spent with the Admiral.

"He's very proud of being Navarch over both the Taulantii army and Navy," Alerio described. "I've a feeling he likes the authority. But I didn't detect a desire for absolute power."

"Then who is the driving force behind the placement of his troops?" Jeta questioned.

"Ma'am, I don't know," Alerio admitted. "But one of my traveling companions suspects the Cleric Ja'Huffield has control over the King of the Taulantii."

"As a Queen, I have fifteen raider ships with sixteen hundred loyal men," Jeta submitted. "While my husband has twenty-five ships and as many Ardiaei Chieftains with their own ships and men. My husband allows me to keep mine because I analyze information and advise him."

"I'm sure King Pleuratus appreciates your efforts, ma'am."

"My husband appreciates results," Jeta countered. "He was a Chieftain of a fishing fleet and I his new Taulantii bride when the old king died. I advised my husband to take the name Pleuratus and challenge for the Kingship. The first Pleuratus was a warrior king from my tribe. Ninety-two years ago, Pleuratus fought the forces of Phillip of Macedonia. Yes, that Phillip, the father of King Alexander. Even though Taulantii lost territory, the warrior king wounded Phillip and killed a vast number of his elite soldiers. Taking the name Pleuratus, along with having a Taulantii wife, assured my husband of peace in the south. He fought, was elected, and took the name Pleuratus. During the changeover of leadership, neighboring tribes invaded

Ardiaei lands. With his southern border secure, my husband was able to marshal his forces and win back the stolen territory."

"Ma'am, what's changed?" Alerio inquired.

"My son is only a couple of years from being able to challenge for the Kingship if his father dies," Jeta responded. "With a Taulantii mother and an Ardiaei father, Agron is fit to become King of either tribe."

"Or King of both tribes," Alerio suggested.

"That would mean war," Jeta warned. "Few Chieftains want a regional King."

"If I might offer a couple of scenarios, Queen Jeta. The soldiers on the border are there to murder Prince Agron to prevent him from becoming King. Or to assassinate King Pleuratus so a regent, with your support, can take control until Agron can fend off challengers. Someone like the King of the Taulantii."

"That would mean kidnapping my son," Jeta exclaimed. She tossed the glass. It shattered against the stone wall, and she jumped to her feet. "Over my dead body."

"Ma'am, that is another worry," Alerio commented. "But none of these concern me. With your permission, my medic and I will take a ship back to the Republic."

Jeta stomped around the room, burning off the rage. In her motions, Alerio could see where Agron got the fierceness he displayed on the drill field. Finally, the Queen stopped at the wine table.

"More?" she asked.

"None for me, thank you."

Jeta filled a fresh glass and strolled back to her chair.

"Tell me about shield bearers, Battle Commander," she prompted.

Alerio assumed the audience was over. Now, he wished he had taken the second glass of vino.

"The front line of a phalanx presents interlocking shields to an enemy, but the formation is not flexible," he described. "When an individual fights, the shield only covers his left side. If his sword or spear gets out of place, his entire right side is open for an attack. Yet, unlike the phalanx, he is mobile and can retreat. But put a second shield with his or more in an assault line and they form a moving barrier. The soldier is protected while he recovers without him having to give ground."

"If my son is able to win his fight," Jeta projected, "King Agron will face challenges from neighboring tribes. Without, I suspect, the comfort of having his southern border secure."

"I can't disagree, ma'am," Alerio responded. "But those are tactics and Cleric Cetea said he wanted me for personal instructions."

"Phillip, when he fought King Pleuratus the First, used his elite shield-bearers at the front of his formation," Jeta reported. "The ground was too rough for the phalanx and too steep for his cavalry. My son will face the same situation in his land battles. I want him to have shield-bearers, so he never has to give ground and retreat to recover."

"You're looking to train bodyguards for King Agron," Alerio summed up.

"An elite force that will protect my son and spearhead his army," Jeta corrected. "A force trained by the man who claims the best fighter is the shield bearer on a warrior's right. How much for that service, Battle Commander Sisera?"

Like Warlord Caden Rian, Alerio could get rich and become a commander. But he was already rich and a Colonel of the Legion. What he needed was a different form of payment.

"I want a trading pact with the Ardiaei and passage for Senator Maximus' transports," he demanded. "Armor for sixty men, and a private place to train them. Oh, and payment for my companions."

"How much time do you need before the shield-bearers can be tested?" Jeta asked.

"Four weeks," Alerio replied without hesitation.

"The price is acceptable. You'll have everything you need," she declared. "Until the gala tomorrow, I bid you a good evening."

Alerio marched to the door, opened it, and stared down the hallway.

"Queen Jeta, there is one situation that we didn't discuss," he informed her.

"What's that, Battle Commander Sisera?"

Alerio faced the Queen and inquired, "What happens to a tribe if their treasury is stolen?"

"The King would be unable to pay his army and his vendors," Jeta replied. Her eyes opened wide, and she continued. "He'd lose the respect of the Chieftains. And that would make it hard to raise funds."

"Almost as crippling to a tribe," Alerio questioned, "as say, murdering the King?"

"Yes, Battle Commander," Jeta confirmed.

"In that case, ma'am, bring extra warriors into the fort. Keep them here until Admiral Driton departs. And for a few days after he leaves."

Alerio had entered the Queen's chamber ready to leave Illyria. Now he left the room with a mission, a chance for an agreement, and a quandary.

As retired Centurion Tomas Kellerian often warned, *'Don't train the enemies of the Republic on how to kill us. Keep Legion tactics for our Legionaries.'*

Alerio would have to work within those constraints. But somehow, he would build an effective fighting force of shield-bearers for Queen Jeta. And afterwards, he'd get a trade agreement and safe passage for his adopted father's merchant ships.

Chapter 11 – Poison Gifts

When Alerio and Pharos returned to the bungalow, the house was empty. After a quick inspection, they found Hektor sitting in the courtyard.

"Flames and embers make you contemplative," the youth uttered when Alerio came through the backdoor.

Light from the firepit cast shadows against the back wall of the house and the tree branches overhead.

"Are you reflecting on your mortality?" the Illyrian inquired. "Snake poison has that effect on survivors."

"No, Pharos. I'm thinking about the kiss from the girl in the dove mask," Hektor admitted.

"Sounds as if you've fully recovered," the big soldier teased.

Alerio and Pharos sat on benches near the pit. All three were quiet for a spell, listening to the crackling of the fire.

"How was the demonstration?" Hektor asked, breaking the silence. He held up the piece of leather with Alerio's note. "I really wanted to see the fort. But I guess I'll see a lot of it when you start training the Prince."

"There's been a change of plan," Alerio told him.

"We're leaving Shkodër and going back to Rome?"

"We're leaving the city," Alerio confirmed. "But we're not leaving Illyria."

"The Battle Commander is going to be an Ardiaean General," Pharos announced.

In the firelight, Hektor's eyes appeared huge as he expressed surprise.

"Is that correct, sir?" he questioned.

"I'm going to train a detachment, and that's the designation they gave me," Alerio answered. "However, before we leave Shkodër, there are things we'll need."

"Like what, sir?" Hektor asked.

"You'll need extra herbs, thread, needles, and bandages and a couple of medics to train," Alerio listed. "As far as practice, I'm going to train them hard. Your students will have plenty of injuries to treat."

"What about me, General?" Pharos asked.

"Find us a leatherworker, carpenter, and a metalworker," he directed. "We need to arm fifty shield-bearers with shields and spears. And I want them to have armor and capes of the same color. I don't care what color as long as they match and stand out."

121

"You're creating a branded unit?" Hektor guessed. "Like King Alexander's Silver-Shields, and his elite Shield-Bearers?"

"Pride in one's unit will hold a man on a combat line longer than skill, training, or fear," Alerio explained. "I need Jeta's soldiers to have an identity to brag about."

"It took King Alexander a year of campaigning before the Silver Shields solidified into a branded unit," Hektor advised. "How long do we have, sir?"

Alerio picked up a stick and flung it into the fire. Burning cinders exploded from the pit, sending flickering embers into the air. After a pause, while the hot ash settled, he replied, "We have four weeks."

***

The main streets of upper town were crowded for the second day of the festival. Just as the first day, roaming groups of men and women flowed around each other. They called out suggestions that elicited squeals of excitement or groans of disappointment for inept or clumsy remarks. The half masks allowed everyone to be as loose or as judgmental as they dared.

"Goats are sturdy creatures with endurance," a woman shouted. "If you know what I mean."

Alerio jabbed an elbow into Hektor's ribs.

"I thought everyone would know it's a mask honoring the God Pan," the youth protested.

"Next celebration, I'm going to save up and buy a goat-man mask," Pharos announced. "So much attention, it'll be glorious."

"You can have this one after the gala," Alerio scoffed.

"Really, General? It'll be a big hit," Pharos gushed. Then he bellowed while patting his chest. "Lookout ladies, the goat-man cometh."

Several women stopped to look at the big man. But their eyes quickly dropped to Alerio and the mask. They watched in anticipation of Alerio putting on a show.

"It's bad enough I have to wear this on my face," Alerio whined, "now you're calling attention to me."

"Hey, goat-man," a woman sang, "hey goat-man, I've a plot of land but no man. Hey goat-man, I've a two-acre span, but no man. Hey goat-man, hey goat-man, I've a house with a large floorplan, but no man. Hey goat-man, I've got a loose blouse, but no man."

"See, see," Pharos exclaimed, "it's the mask."

Alerio shoved the big Illyrian to get him moving. They walked away from the woman as a group joined her in the song.

"Hey goat-man, hey goat man…"

"It's a mask of the God Pan," Hektor mumbled. Then louder while searching faces in the crowd, he asked. "Has anyone seen the girl in the dove mask?"

"Yesterday, she almost killed you," Alerio reminded the youth.

"It's a festival," Pharos asserted. "During a festival, all things are forgiven."

"Not everything," Alerio stated while tapping the goat mask.

***

Where Hektor and Pharos continued along the main street, Alerio took a side road. Here, rather than exuberant revelers, the road was lined with soldiers. Not braced and ready for inspection, this was a festival, they were more-or-less sober and kind of on duty.

"Sir, may I help you," an Ardiaei officer inquired.

"I'm Battle Commander Sisera," Alerio replied. "A guest of Navarch Driton, and, I assume, Queen Jeta."

"General Sisera, yes sir," the Captain saluted him. "At the end of the road, take the stairs up to the pavilions."

Alerio thanked the officer and proceeded to a set of steps cut into the stone. As he climbed, Alerio noted the rough rocks that sat in the center of Shkodër. As if a huge bird had buried a giant egg in a nest, the land rose on both sides. Only, rather than a smooth exterior, the heights had jagged peaks and ankle breaking basins. At the top, he saw the reason for the steps.

For a large area, the rocks had been cut flat and the valleys filled in with dirt. Off the western edge, a twelve-foot cliff overlooked a section of the main street. Chieftains, their guests, and their entourages stood waving and calling to the people below. From the street, voices shouted up to the flat expanse.

Away from the edge, three large tents had been erected and wooden flooring installed. From one of the pavilions, a musician plucked a lyre, a flute complimented it with higher notes, and a pair of tympanons, one beaten with a stick, and the other drummed by hand, kept rhythm.

"General Sisera," a navy officer stated.

The man marched from the third pavilion and stopped in front of Alerio.

"And you are?" Alerio inquired after a few heartbeats.

"Captain Mergim."

Then the Ardiaean officer stood mute.

"Are you always like this?" Alerio asked.

"Like what?"

Alerio pursed his lips and blew out in frustration. Then he cocked his head to the side and waited. When the Captain didn't volunteer anymore information, Alerio strutted around the man and headed towards the last pavilion. He wasn't in the mood to play power games with Mergim. Plus, the third tent had tables filled with food and he was hungry.

"Sisera," the Captain called after him. "If we're going to work together, there are a few things we need to get straight."

"If," Alerio replied without turning his head.

Mergim stopped at the edge of the tent. As Alerio sidestepped around the tables filling a platter, the Naval officer glared at him. Once the platter was piled high with food, Alerio left the tent by a side exit.

Although he pretended not to notice, Alerio saw Mergim dash to the music tent and take up a position where the Captain could watch him.

"Battle Commander Sisera, are you finding everything to your satisfaction?" a woman asked as she crossed the floor.

Her dress was light green, and the linen chiton, hanging over one shoulder, was a pale salmon color. A burst of red, yellow, and black feathers hid her eyes and hair. Yet, even with the elaborate mask obscuring her features, the way she carried herself left no doubt who was behind the mask.

"Queen Jeta," Alerio greeted her. "The food is excellent and the music pleasing to my finely trained ear."

"Are you a musician?" she inquired while looking around at the players. "I could have one sit out and you can play."

"No, ma'am," Alerio informed her. "I am blessed of the Goddess Canens with a beautiful singing voice. Would you like a serenade?"

"Maybe later, Battle Commander," she said, turning down the offer. "I want to talk about Captain Mergim. Where is he?"

Alerio caught a glimpse of a figure arriving at his side.

"Mergim? A Captain you say?" Alerio questioned. "I haven't made his acquaintance."

The officer stepped forward and bowed to the queen.

"We were just getting to know each other," Mergim assured her.

Alerio stripped meat off a bone with his teeth and stood chewing.

"If you were introducing yourself, but the Battle Commander doesn't know you," Jeta suggested, "then you may be an outstanding Captain of the King's Phalanx, but you aren't the officer I thought you were."

"Ma'am, it was a simple misunderstanding," Mergim pleaded.

"Sisera?"

"I don't know him, Queen Jeta," Alerio remarked. "Men looking for their self-worth in minor confrontations are a waste of the days you've allotted me. Ma'am, I need fighting men who can follow orders."

"I can..." Captain Mergim started to protest.

Jeta snapped her fingers and pointed at the exit to the tent.

"I'll find you another Captain," she commented. "When you've finished eating, join me in the King's Pavilion. It's time you met Agron's father, King Pleuratus."

Alerio plucked a baked radish from the platter and munched on it while the queen moved through the crowd. He approved of the fluid moves of her hands as she extracted herself from knots of admirers. What Battle Commander Sisera didn't notice was the seething Captain Mergim, staring daggers from the back of the pavilion.

Queen Jeta finally broke through the entanglements, reached the exit, and gracefully made her escape. Alerio picked up a baked turnip. After raising it in salute to the queen, he popped it into his mouth. Shkodër didn't offer much, but the food was good.

***

The musicians took a break just as Alerio finished the plate of food.

"Chieftains and guests, we will return shortly with more music," the flute player announced.

As his voice faded, the sounds of a pair of hands clapping carried from the far side of the pavilion. Then, as if trying to outdo the clapping, snapping fingers alternated from one hand to the other of a second person. Curious about the enthusiastic pair of music lovers, Alerio began to turn but then he recognized a voice.

"Excellent renditions," Rezart declared while he continued to clap.

"A fine set of songs for a gala," Zamir added his words between the snapping of his fingers.

Alerio grinned at the acquaintances in the black masks with the single gray feathers resting at jaunty angles. The pair seemed to be at every event. And as usual, the 'twins' stood apart, not mingling with any groups or individuals. But Alerio had seen similar relationships in the Legions. Men from different regions who meet, immediately formed a bond, and spent all their time together.

Their affection had nothing to do with the blessing of Philotes, the Goddess of Sex. When men fused to the exclusion of other companions, they shared the bonds of Zagreus and Dionysus. As the storytellers related.

Born to Zeus and Persephone, the infant Zagreus was sent to Mount Ida for protection. But Hera, Zeus' wife, and queen of the Olympians, had the Titans butcher and eat the baby. During the feast, Athena managed to save the child's heart.

When Zeus and Semele had a child, Zeus used Zagreus' heart for the infant. Therefore, Zagreus, the God of Butchering Small Animals, and Dionysus, the God of the Vine and Wine, shared the most precious of gifts.

Much like Rezart and Zamir, Alerio assumed, they shared one heart in brotherhood. With a grin at his cleverness for figuring out the look-a-likes, Alerio left the music tent and made his way to the King's Pavilion.

***

Inside the tent, a servant handed him a glass of wine. Alerio studied the clear container with the gold wire wrap.

"Piracy does pay," he admitted while looking around the tent.

Everyone in the King's Pavilion was adorned in jewelry, draped with gold and silver chains, wrapped in fine fabrics, and held glasses of various types. All the merchandise was the work of craftsmen from other regions.

A quick scan located Queen Jeta on the far side of the pavilion and the King in the center. Thinking to wait until she moved closer to Pleuratus, Alerio sipped his wine and continued looking at the occupants of the tent.

He spotted Admiral Driton. Although three men stood near the Navarch, their backs were to him. Alerio started in the Admiral's direction to keep him company.

But Queen Jeta shifted. Not just moved, but suddenly appeared in another part of the pavilion. Alerio couldn't figure how she reached the new location. Then, the three men near the Admiral spun around.

Alerio stopped in mid stride.

Expected were Driton's aids, Lieutenants Pinnes and Fisnik in matching molded ceramic masks. However, with the Taulantii officers was a man in a plain clay mask with a bandage on his arm, Sergeant Gezim. Seeing the Admiral's knifeman, Alerio momentarily forgot about the queen. Gezim wasn't the type of soldier one brought to a social event.

Alerio looked for the Queen and blinked. She had doubled. Two women wearing masks of radiating red, yellow, and black feathers and dressed in light green dresses with pale salmon linen wraps greeted crowds of admirers.

"Good day, Colonel," two voices addressed him.

Rezart walked by Alerio on one side and Zamir strolled passed on the other. Their footfalls so soft, Alerio hadn't heard them approaching.

Between the two men sneaking up on him, the suspicious appearance of Sergeant Gezim in the King's Pavilion, and the two versions of Queen Jeta, Alerio's combat instincts kicked in. To what effect, he didn't know as no threat presented itself.

***

The Queens moved through the throng heading for King Pleuratus. But as Alerio witnessed before, people crowded both the Jetas delaying their progress.

"Which one is the real Queen?" Zamir demanded.

His partner snapped his head from side to side, looking from one Jeta to the other.

"I can't tell," Rezart admitted.

They had stopped several feet in front of Alerio and he heard the question. It clarified his thinking, and he studied each Queen. Both used their arms to signify their path so people could politely move aside while speaking to her. Both displayed fluid moments when flowing between groups. But one Jeta touched admirers with her fingertips. It was an intimate gesture that brought smiles to the faces of those receiving her touch. The other Queen used the back of her hands.

"The imposter is on the left," Alerio blurted out.

His voice low, the announcement used more to get himself in motion. Alerio didn't think, he started forward.

While racing ahead, he pushed between the look-a-likes, and took one more step. Something tangled his legs and Alerio went down. As he splattered against the floor, he noticed Rezart's foot extracting from between his ankles. Then the man raced after his partner.

Zamir stutter stepped, to allow Rezart to catch up. Alerio recognized the precision in the maneuver that brought the two online. They came abreast for three strides, before separating. Ruthlessly shoving attendees out of their way, the twins angled for the fake Queen.

In response to the commotion of them charging, the bogus Jeta extended her fingers as if they were claws. She bent forward and raced at King Pleuratus.

While dashing froward, Alerio watched in horror as Jeta elbowed aside a Chieftain, extended her arms, and raked the air, almost touching the King. He leaned out of reach, but she stepped closer and again clawed with the fingernails.

The shocked attendees circling the King, gawked at seeing their Queen attempting to scratch the King. Most assumed it was a domestic dispute and didn't want to get involved. Crossing either had consequences.

Reaching the final barrier of people, Zamir and Rezart flung bodies aside and emerged in the circle. From opposite edges, they plucked the gray feathers from their masks, jumped at the fake Queen, and stabbed the back of her hands. From a tense attacking animal, the phony Jeta crumbled to the floor.

Blades came out at the sight of their Queen being stabbed and men surged forward, threatening the 'twins'. Before anyone else got stabbed, the real Queen shoved her way into the circle.

"What's the meaning of this?" Jeta demanded. "Who is that woman?"

Chapter 12 – Stacking Failures

The ring of attendees glanced from the red, yellow, and black feathered mask on the ground to the one on the woman speaking. Their blades hovering, the men still couldn't sort out one Queen from the other.

Zamir bent, hooked a finger behind the fake Queen's mask, and flicked it off the unconscious woman's face.

As peaceful as a sleeping infant and appearing as innocent as a newborn lamb, the woman lay in repose on the wooden planks. Alerio recognized the rosebud shaped nose and the lips that could sneer or smile. A smile that was identifiable under a dove mask on lips that could entice a youth into dancing on the street. And have him wanting to go back for another poisoned kiss.

"She's known as Ja'Huffield," Rezart explained.

"And who are you?" King Pleuratus inquired.

He as well held a blade in his hand.

"I'm Rezart, and my partner is Zamir."

"We're agents of the Cleric of the Snake, sir," Zamir informed Pleuratus. "Sent to watch over you and Prince Agron."

Rezart pulled two small bags of heavy cloth from under his tunic. With twine, he tied a bag around each of Ja'Huffield's hands.

"Her nails are dipped in poison, sir," Rezart reported. "One touch and the birthday gala would turn into a tribunal to elect a new King."

Pleuratus sheathed his knife. Seeing their king's action, the men in the crowd put away their blades.

"So, agents of Cleric Cetea," Jeta asked, "what now?"

"My Queen, you are free to enjoy the evening," Zamir replied.

"We'll be transporting Ja'Huffield to Risan in the morning," Rezart described. "There, she'll answer to the God Boa for her oath breaking."

A sigh of relief escaped from the crowd.

As Driton had brought the rogue Cleric to Shkodër, Alerio wondered what the Admiral's reaction would be to her apprehension. A quick glance failed to locate the Navarch and his guests.

"Where is Prince Agron?" Alerio inquired.

"In one of the other tents, maybe?" someone proposed.

Alerio sprinted to the music tent. After a moment of searching, he raced to the food pavilion. Agron was nowhere to be found. The Legion Battle Commander didn't return to the King's Pavilion. Instead, Alerio ran for the steps and the side road.

***

At the bottom of the steps, he questioned the officer in charge.

"Have you seen Prince Agron?"

"The Prince was ill," the Captain replied. "His uncle, two officers, and a guard escorted him home."

"That's what I was afraid of," Alerio said before running down the road.

At the main street, he looked left and right, attempting to see though the groups of people enjoying the festival. The undulating masses blocked his view in both directions. With no visual clue, he turned eastward towards the road leading up to fort and, beyond, the trail heading down to the riverbank.

***

Pushing through the crowd, Alerio neared the road leading to Fort Shkodër. High above, the reinforced walls loomed over the street. Because the hill dominated the skyline, few people looked up or bothered checking the path heading to the fort. Alerio did and caught glimpses of movement on the twisting road. For a heartbeat, he assumed the men staggering down were friends assisting drunken companions. But through the crowd, Alerio noted the bloody bandages, the leather armor, and naked blades.

On the crown of the hill, Ardiaeins stood with shields and spears daring the Taulantii assault units to come up one more time.

"I guess the Ardiaei treasury is safe," Alerio whispered, "even if their Prince isn't."

Weaving in and out of revelers, he followed the retreating Taulantii soldiers. In the distance, he observed where the festival hooked a left. While the celebration continued along the main street of the east side, straight ahead, soldiers blocked the trail leading down to the Drin River.

"Goat-man, come drink with us," a woman offered.

Around her were five friends with swaying hips and smiles on their lips.

"An invitation I cannot resist," Alerio declared. He held out his arms and stepped into the midst of the group. "Let us explore the best of the festival."

With three women under each arm Alerio guided them towards the intersection.

"The goat-man has lofty standards," he warned. "You must have a pulse, and a name, to play the goat-man's game."

"What game?" the women shouted with glee.

"First, close your eyes," he directed. "Keep them shut and tell me your names."

Laughing and saying their names, the women didn't notice when they failed to turn at the intersection. In several steps, the group ran into the shields. Opening their eyes, they found themselves standing in front of a line of soldiers.

"Ooh, men," a few exclaimed.

Confronted by a pleasant line of fetching women in masks, the soldiers relaxed and engaged the group in conversation.

"Where's the goat-man?" one woman inquired.

The goat-man had vanished. But two of the women noticed the goat mask laying on the side of the street.

***

When the women approached the picket line of shields, Alerio dropped his arms from their necks, discarded the mask, and stepped into the flow of wounded soldiers.

"You look bad," he said to one.

"I caught a spear tip in my thigh," the soldier reported. "But I can…"

Alerio's fist buried itself up to the wrist in the man's solar plexus. With the air driven from his lungs, the injured man collapsed.

"Here, let me help," Alerio suggested.

He slipped his arm under the staggering man's shoulder and reached for his shield and helmet. Lifting them off, Alerio settled the iron head gear on his own head and the shield on his arm. Then they shuffled forward leaving the picket line of distracted soldiers and happy women behind.

At the bottom of the trail, a Taulantii NCO demanded, "How bad is he?"

"A cut on his thigh, but I bandaged it," Alerio lied. "I'm more worried about broken ribs and his breathing."

The wounded man erratically sucked in air as if to confirm the diagnosis.

"Put him on the first raft," the Sergeant ordered. "And stay out of the Admiral's way."

Supporting the weight of the injured man, Alerio crossed the farmland, shuffled through the sandbar, and walked onto the first raft.

Driton stood near the front with his back to the river, observing developments along the shoreline. His two Lieutenants knelt over a sleeping Prince Agron. And while Sergeant Gezim was nowhere in sight, Alerio knew the knifeman couldn't be far away.

At an empty spot, Alerio lowered the injured soldier to the deck. With his body and the shield screening the man from view, Alerio punched him in the temple. After that, Alerio proceeded to fuss over the leg wound of the semi-conscious man to be sure no one ordered him off the raft.

***

The last of the Taulantii soldiers ran down the slope. In a wave they sprinted over the farmland, scurried across the sandbar, and leaped onto the other rafts. As the flatboats launched, the six women stood at the top of the slope. Smiling, they waved until a company of Ardiaei spearmen pushed them aside and sprinted towards the riverbank. Spears flew, but the rafts were already in midstream. Polemen fast walked the side boards pushing the crafts faster than the current.

During the extraction, Prince Agron sat up, leaned over the side, and vomited into the water. Unfortunately, the drug they used to subdue him didn't sit well with him. As one of Driton's aids handed the Prince a waterskin, Alerio eased the soldier's helmet off his head.

He placed the headgear on the deck, but kept the shield attached to his arm. At first, he appeared to be a soldier stretching his legs. But in a few steps, Alerio picked up his stride. When he plowed into Driton and his Lieutenants, it became obvious the soldier wasn't simply out for a stroll. Hands reached for Alerio, but they were too late.

Alerio Sisera hooked an arm around the Prince's waist, snatched him from the deck, and together they nosedived into the river. Iron spearheads and shafts plunged into the river around the shield left floating on the surface,

"Stop. Stop you fools," Driton screamed. He continued yelling as his aides pulled the Admiral off the deck. "Stop. Stop this before you injure the Prince."

The last three rafts poled by the drifting shield while men scanned for the Prince and his assailant. But the surface of the river displayed no sign of the two missing men.

On the shore, a few soldiers tossed spears which fell short of the retreating rafts. Then, two heads broke the surface of the Drin River and the spearmen ceased throwing.

Ardiaei waded out to meet a man towing the body of the Prince. A few took Agron, and other spearmen formed a semicircle around the swimmer.

"You're under arrest for the kidnapping and murder of Prince Agron," an officer barked. "Those are both capital offences. Give me one reason why I shouldn't carry out the sentencing right here, right now."

Knee high in the river, Alerio wiped excess water from his face and head.

"Captain, I have a reason for being here," he assured the officer. "But let me say, I am under contract with Queen Jeta to protect the Prince. I suggest, you let her decide when to execute me."

They pulled Alerio to the sandbar, bound his wrists behind his back, and pushed him towards town.

As the escorts marched the Battle Commander away, farther down the riverbank, a figure swam to a grassy area where he crawled onto the shore. Although the river water soaking the bandage on his arm stung, Sergeant Gezim ignored the pain. He had a mission to accomplish.

***

Troops guarding Alerio parted and pushed back the gala attendees, allowing his captives to move rapidly. At the start of the fort road, Alerio spied Hektor in the crowd.

"The Prince was drugged," he shouted. "He was breathing but ill when I pulled him under the river. See what…"

A soldier hit Alerio in the back with the staff of his spear.

Alerio stumbled forward, loosing sight of the Greek.

"Keep moving, Latian," the soldier ordered.

When Alerio stabilized, he searched the crowd for the medic. But the mob of partiers had swallowed Hektor. The escorts left the street festival and started up to the fort.

***

While they climbed, Hektor ran down the slope, and sprinted across the farmland to the beach.

"Where do you think you're going, Greek?" an officer asked.

"I'm a medic and your Prince had been poisoned," Hektor replied.

"How can I trust you?"

"If he's dead, what harm can I do?" the youth suggested. "If I revive him, then you'll get credit for locating a medic."

The Captain waved a hand signaling the youth to proceed. Hektor ran across the sandbar and slid to a halt next to the body of the Prince. Stretched out on a shield and ready for transport, Agron appeared lifeless.

"He's not coming back, lad," an NCO said.

Hektor dropped to his knees, leaned over the Prince's face, and sniffed. Then he thumbed Agron's chest.

"I need a cup, a piece of bone, and some salt," he instructed while continuing to beat a steady rhythm on the Prince's breast. "And water."

"What's going on?" a Lieutenant demanded.

"The bad news is your Prince is drowned."

"Everyone can see that."

"The good news is he was poisoned," Hektor stated while pounding on the chest.

"What's good about that?" the officer questioned.

"The poison slowed down his heart," Hektor described. "If I can give him something to counteract the poison, he may recover."

"What do you need, lad?"

"A dry bone, salt, a cup, and water," Hektor listed, "and someone to act as the Prince's heart. Oh, and a piece of charcoal."

Moments later, Hektor scraped down the edge of a dry bone. The upper part was still wet. The soldier who donated the bone, chewed off the meat before handing it over. Once a large pile of bone dust collected under the knife, Hektor scooped up the meal and dropped it into the cup. Once he added salt, the medic stirred in water until he had a liquid mixture. Finally, he dumped in a dose of ground charcoal.

"Stop the pounding and sit him upright," Hektor directed.

With Agron supported in a sitting position, the youth opened the Prince's mouth and splashed in a portion of the brew.

"Pat his back, hard but slowly," Hektor instructed. At the second slap, Agron coughed, and opened his eyes. "Prince, you've been poisoned and drowned. Drink this."

Between coughs and bouts of spitting out river water, Hektor coaxed the drink down his throat. When his breathing evened, Agron was placed on the shields.

"Take him home and post guards," the medic instructed.

"Why guards?" the Lieutenant asked.

"Anyone who is poisoned is likely to be targeted again," Hektor advised.

He had no idea what happened on the beach. But Master Sisera had been arrested and the likely heir to the Ardiaei tribe had been poisoned and drowned. Giving an order of protection seemed appropriate.

"You will accompany him," the officer insisted.

"I've done all I can," Hektor pleaded. "Besides, I don't have my medical kit."

"You'll be escorted to your quarters to get your kit," the Lieutenant directed, "then to the Prince's bedside, just in case."

"In case of what?" Hektor asked.

"In case Agron dies. Then you'll be killed for failing to save him."

"Again," Hektor grumbled.

"What did you say?"

"I said, for saving him again."

***

Alerio fell into the cellar and dropped to his knees.

"How about something to drink," he asked

A kick from a guard sent him face down onto the dirt floor.

"There's your meal," the guard sneered.

The door closed and Alerio heard the locking bar drop to secure it.

"I didn't ask about food," he complained with his cheek still pressed to the hard packed earth. "I asked about something to drink."

But he was the only occupant of the storage room. In the dark, Alerio scooted to the stone wall and sat with his knees drawn up to his chest.

"Hektor and I should have left when I first thought about it," he said to the darkness. Then he laughed, changed his tone, and addressed the Goddess of Death. "Nenia, if we must meet tomorrow, I would ask that you take my soul quickly."

His personal deity didn't reply. She never did. Although, occasionally before a battle, she made presence known. In the dark of the cellar, the Goddess offered no response. But the cool and dark environment lulled the Battle Commander to sleep.

***

A wisp of bright smoke appeared in the air above Alerio's head.

"Finish your business here," a female voice urged, "and get home. You will be needed in Rome before the end of the year. As will I."

The screech of the locking bar being lifted woke Alerio and with consciousness, the smoke and voice vanished.

"A waterskin and a blanket," the Captain from the beach stated. He dropped the folded fabric and the water container next to Alerio. "The Prince lives, thanks to your medic. For that, you'll not go thirsty."

The officer marched out and the door closed. Alerio picked up the skin and took a stream of water.

"I don't know how you did it, Hektor," Alerio said to the dark room. He drew the banket over his shoulders. "But I appreciate your work."

***

In a house in the hills on the west side of Shkodër, Hektor Nicanor dipped a rag into a bowl of water. After ringing out the excess, he dabbed at Agron's forehead.

"Prince, we need you to live," he explained to the feverish man, "both Battle Commander Sisera and I are depending on you."

A guard standing in the doorway nodded at the declaration. From the other side of the house, a door slammed, and the sounds of feet running proceeded a procession of people. One was Agron's mother.

"How is my son?" Queen Jeta asked.

She moved to the bedside, reached down, and rested a hand on Agron's head.

"He's breathing well," Hektor told her, "resting comfortably and the aroma of almonds has gone."

"Almonds?" Jeta questioned.

"Yes, Queen, the poison made from the pit of the plum fruit," he described, "releases an aroma resembling almonds."

"And the smell being gone is good?"

"Ma'am, it's certainly better than not being gone," Alerio offered.

Act 5

Chapter 13 – Murder of Opportunity

The squealing of the locking beam being lifted woke Alerio. He threw off the blanket, jumped to his feet, and crouched in a fighting stance. Maybe if he hit the guards hard, he could make it out of the fort, get to the river, and steal a boat. Except, this deep in the fort, there was no light to give him an idea of the phase of the day. Without the cover of darkness, any escape plan was doomed.

Torch light pushed back the dark and Alerio shielded his eyes.

"Good morning, General Sisera," a man greeted him.

"Who are you?"

Alerio blinked until he could see a large body and a youthful face.

"Altin Breuci. Oh, sorry, sir. Captain Breuci reporting," the Ardiaean officer replied. "Sir, we need to get moving. The Queen is waiting for you."

"Judgement day," Alerio mumbled.

"No, sir," Altin corrected. "It's breakfast, General."

"I'm not exactly dressed or clean enough for polite company," Alerio noted.

"No problem, Lieutenant Pharos is meeting us with a change of clothing," Altin explained. "And Captain Nicanor will join us at the Queen's residence."

"Captain Nicanor?"

"A title bestowed by the King himself for saving the life of Prince Agron."

Alerio looked up at the arched ceiling. Torchlight flickered across the rough stone.

"It appears that we'll be staying a little longer," Alerio stated.

"Excuse me, sir," Altin inquired.

"I wasn't talking to you, Captain," Alerio responded.

They walked out of the cellar, through a stone tunnel, and out into the morning sun. Pharos stood next to a trough filled with clean water.

"Good morning, sir," the big warrior greeted him. He held out a clean tunic and Alerio's red Legion cape. "I see you've met the Captain of the Queen's shields."

"Altin, are you my shield Captain?" Alerio asked.

"I am General," the big officer replied.

"How much experience do you have?"

"The Queen said you wanted a fighting man who could follow orders," Altin responded by pounding a fist into his chest. "On my last three voyages, I took my raider ship up against Athenian warships."

"How did that work out for you?" Alerio asked as he washed his face and arms in the water.

"We had to retreat from two when their oarsmen joined in the fighting," the young officer described. "But they were good fights while they lasted."

"What about the third one?"

"Well sir, as we rowed away, the Greek got her oars in the water and her ram into our side."

"How is the ship?"

"Under repair," Altin admitted, "and under command of another Captain."

"Let me guess, the Queen is not happy with you."

"Sir, she said I was inexperienced and bold beyond my years."

"You're just the officer I need," Alerio stated while pulling off his dirty tunic. "Welcome to the shields."

Once dressed, Alerio and his two officers marched from the fort. The trip down the twisting path to Shkodër and over to the Queen's residence wasn't what Alerio envisioned. It was better than going to an execution, much better. But odd in that he was following Nenia's advice and staying in Illyria until the job was done. Whatever the job was.

***

Alerio, Lieutenant Pharos, and Captain Altin Breuci walked into a room with a view of the Buna River. Opposite of the balcony, Hektor Nicanor stood with a glass of beer wearing a blue cape over a white tunic.

"Are you well Battle Commander?" the youth inquired.

"I've had rougher nights in more uncomfortable places," Alerio assured him. "Tell me what happened with the Prince at the beach?"

The three moved to the beverage station and poured drinks.

"He was dead, Colonel."

"Drowned. I know because it was me who pulled him in," Alerio confessed, "and me who held him under the water."

"That's not what I meant, sir," Hektor corrected Alerio. "Prince Agron had been poisoned. He wouldn't have made it much longer."

"But they kidnapped him for his birthright. He's qualified to be a leader of both the Taulantii and Ardiaei tribes."

"I don't know anything about politics, sir. But I know medicine, and he wouldn't have made it very far down river."

A side door opened and Jeta strolled into the room. She dipped her head in Hektor's direction as a sign she heard the last part of his statement.

"My son is resting under guard safely in his own bed," Jeta stated. She walked to Hektor and took his glass. After taking a gulp, she handed the beer back to the youth. "Thanks to Captain Nicanor's medical treatment and to you Battle Commander Sisera. If you hadn't pulled him off the raft, the Ardiaei would have lost their next King."

"But I thought he was respected in both tribes."

"By some, yes," Jeta explained. "But also, some fear him because of his legacy. It's now obvious to me there are ruthless people who want to harm my son. As a mother and a Queen, it feels too soon, but now that they have acted against Agron because of his potential, he needs to display his authority."

"The elite shields?" Alerio ventured.

"Yes, Battle Commander," Jeta replied. She pointed to Altin. "Is my former raider Captain agreeable?"

"It's yet to be seen if he is my kind of commander."

"And what kind is that?" she questioned. "A man looking for a fight?"

"If it'll protect the Prince, my Queen," Captain Breuci swore, "I am ready to fight."

"If I might add something," Hektor offered. "Colonel Sisera never looks for combat. But when called upon, he brings all his skills to the battle. And a large part of his success comes from discipline."

"That's not what I think of when I ponder the talents of a warrior," Jeta commented. She pointed to another room and began walking in that direction. "Discipline sounds so removed from the clashing of blades."

"It's discipline that marches men into a fight," Alerio described. "It's discipline that allows a line to shift and take advantage of an enemy's weakness. And it is discipline that holds an assault line together when men, on either side of a Legionary, fall."

Queen Jeta stopped in the doorway. Beyond her, the aroma of hot food wafted back to the room with the view.

"Tell me Captain Breuci, do you have that kind of discipline?" She asked.

"Truthfully, I don't know, ma'am," Altin admitted. "But I'll put everything I have into learning it."

"And that, my Queen," Alerio revealed, "is my kind of commander."

***

At mid-day, Alerio, Hektor, and Pharos sorted their gear and placed the items in stacks for easy packing. After they had piles beside their bags, Alerio waved them into the rear courtyard.

"We're going out with fifty or sixty warriors," Alerio said while Pharos started a fire. "I'll be imposing a new fighting system on them."

"That's what the Queen's excited about," Pharos remarked.

He blew on the kindling until a flame grew and began consuming the twigs and wood shavings.

"She may want it. But men accustomed to tribal warfare or even the phalanx will balk at the change," Alerio warned. "And to make it worse, we only have a few weeks. That means extra training. I want you both to be aware that disgruntled men may try to get back at me by attacking you."

"Let them try," the big Illyrian responded.

To highlight his strength, he used two fingers and his thumb to pick up a large log and place it in the firepit.

"I should be going with you," Hektor whined. "You'll need a medic."

"The Queen wants you in Shkodër until Agron recovers," Pharos reminded the youth. "You know, to make him another of those disgusting drinks."

"If I shove anymore charcoal down his throat," Hektor stated while patting the pouch on his side, "he'll start coughing it up. Really, all he needs now is rest."

"There are worse jobs than being the medical adviser to a Prince," Alerio suggested.

The three sat and watched the fire for a portion of the afternoon. Then, Hektor stood, stretched, and saluted Alerio.

"I'm going to finish packing and head to Agron's house," the youth announced. "Unless you need anything."

"I don't need anything," Alerio replied. "But I owe you a debt of thanks."

Hektor strolled to the bungalow and walked through the doorway. Halfway to his bed and stacks of things, he stopped. His extra tunics and sandals and rags, herbs, and other items from his medical kit lay scattered on the floor.

Thinking a burglar had broken in, the youth smiled. In his days as a thief, he would have taken a steel weapon and run. He glanced at Sisera's stack. Puzzled that the Battle Commander's dual sword rig was...

The blade sliced the edge of the tunic and would have cleaved into Hektor's flesh above his hip. But the pouch of charcoal, although a soft and crumbly substance, absorbed the slash. Pieces of charcoal spilled out as the Greek youth threw himself down and away from the blade.

"Attack, attack, attack," he bellowed.

After crashing to the floor, Hektor flopped to his belly and crawled towards the backdoor. All the while, he called out the warning to Battle Commander Sisera.

Feet straddled the youth, and a man laughed. With the blade held high for maximum penetration, Sergeant Gezim adjusted his grip then stabbed downward.

***

At the first 'Attack', Alerio rolled off the bench. Not bothering to come fully erect, he used his hands and feet to propel himself to the bungalow. Most normal people would stop and survey the situation. Colonel Sisera was not a normal person. He bolted through the doorway and caught sight of the plunging knife.

Powering off his bent legs, Alerio leaped across the room. Stretched out as if flying, he reached even farther with his hands. And while his body fell short, his arms slammed into the NCO's knife hand, throwing it offline.

Hektor Nicanor crawled under Alerio before the Battle Commander dropped onto the floorboards. But Alerio didn't remain down. Popping to his feet, he drew his Legion dagger, and crouched in a fighting stance.

"Good afternoon, Sergeant," he growled. "Fancy meeting you here."

"You surprised me, Sisera," Gezim informed Alerio. "I figured I had a moment or two to finish off the interfering Greek before I got a chance to kill you."

The two men shuffled around until the Taulantii NCO, and the Colonel had exchanged positions.

"Well, here I am," Alerio challenged, "step up and take your chance."

"No tricks like you did on the beach," Gezim cautioned. "This time..."

Hoping to catch Alerio off guard, the Sergeant jumped forward in midsentence.

After parrying the advancing knife with his blade, Alerio took half a stride forward to set up a counterstrike. The move proved unnecessary.

Sergeant Gezim's eyes closed, and he wilted to the floor. Following him down was a large piece of firewood held by Pharos.

"Sorry I was late, sir," the big Illyrian apologized. "It took a beat to find the right sized piece of wood."

***

The Taulantii NCO lifted his head and a moan escaped from his lips.

"What happened?" Gezim groaned.

"Allow me to sum up the events," Alerio said. "You tried to murder Hektor and failed."

"The Greek was not my primary assignment," the Sergeant admitted. "He came in while I was preparing for you. You might say he was a target of opportunity."

After testing the ropes tying him to the chair, Gezim settled down. Hektor moved around the NCO, examining the gash on top of his head.

"The blow didn't do much damage," the Greek declared.

"What now?" Gezim inquired.

"Who poisoned the Prince?" Alerio asked.

"He was drugged to appear ill," Gezim replied. "Ja'Huffield said he might be sick to his stomach, but it would pass."

"That answers a couple of questions," Alerio offered.

"What are you talking about?" the Sergeant asked.

"We didn't know if Driton wanted his nephew dead," Alerio remarked. "Or if he wanted Agron as a hostage and if someone else poisoned the Prince."

"He's dead?" Gezim exclaimed. "No, no, he's a Prince of both tribes. The Admiral wanted to get him away during the distraction caused by the two Queens. Well, he also wanted the treasury, but somehow, the Ardiaei had extra warriors in the fort."

"Are the Taulantii always like this?" Alerio questioned.

"Like what?" Gezim demanded.

"Gullible and easily led astray?"

***

The morning sunlight caught on the jagged stone center of Shkodër, casting shadows over the Buna River and the boats along the riverbank.

"I don't envy Gezim," Pharos remarked. He tossed his and Alerio's gear into a raider vessel. "The Queen is still angry."

"That's his problem," Alerio said brushing off the comment. "Our problem is on those other boats."

Warriors stepped into four raider ships. Fifteen men and their gear overcrowded the vessels already full of their normal compliment. But they weren't going to sea. The flotilla of boats would row a mile upriver to Lake Shkodra.

"It'll take our supplies, the leather man, carpenter, and the metalworker a couple of days to reach Ivanaj," Pharos informed Alerio. "Wagons don't travel as fast as raider ships. That means we won't have quarters until they arrive. Maybe you should wait another day, sir."

"I'm good with camping on the ground," Alerio replied. "Besides, it'll help with the training."

"How can sleeping on the ground help with training?" the Illyrian inquired.

"You'd be surprised," Alerio answered.

Altin Breuci appeared on the upper bank. He hiked down a path to the water's edge.

"General Sisera, I hope all is to your satisfaction," the youthful officer greeted Alerio.

Before Alerio could respond, the Captain of the nearest boat spit over the side.

"Is this waste of my crew your idea, Breuci?" he demanded.

"I'm in charge of it," Altin answered in a small voice.

"You'll probably sink this expedition too," the other Captain accused Breuci.

Alerio expected the brash young man to defend himself. But Altin hung his head and didn't challenge the insult.

"Pride is not awarded," Alerio mumbled, "it's a brand on your soul that you earn."

"Excuse me, sir," Pharos inquired, "did you say something?"

"I said sleeping in the mud builds character," Alerio replied. "Captain, get us launched and moving upriver."

For a moment, Altin Breuci looked as if he would respond. But it was the raider skipper who acknowledged Alerio's instruction.

***

Accustomed to rowing and sailing at sea, the smooth waters of the lake proved easy for the rowers. In fact, the five crews competed, racing, and exchanging the lead several times. While those destined for the shields and the soldiers on the raiders cheered, Alerio studied Altin Breuci.

The officer's eyes hungered for the command of a ship and a crew. Alerio could tell by the way his attention snapped from vessel to vessel. He was analyzing stroke rate, the fitness of each oarsman, and the wakes that would disturb the way a ship cut through the water. But the young officer never voiced his enthusiasm or talked with the raider's skipper. While his excitement wanted to burst out, the shame laid on Altin by the Captain held him in check.

"Not to worry," Alerio said so low no one could hear him, "The fleet may not have given you pride. But soon, you will eat enough dirt, Altin Breuci, that the infantry will brand your soul."

Chapter 14 – Camp Ivanaj

The rain started twelve miles into the journey. It didn't slow the ships, but the weather dampened the enthusiasm. Instead of joyously racing, the oarsmen hunched over and settled into a rhythm.

"Captain, how far to our location?" Alerio called to the commander of the raider ship.

After a glance at the land to get his bearings, the skipper replied, "We're over halfway there, Latian."

"General," Alerio corrected.

"What?" the Captain asked.

"Per your Queen, I am an Ardiaei General," Alerio told him. "And you will address me as such, or I'll take command and you can swim back to Shkodër."

"You take command of my raider?" the Captain exclaimed. "How do you expect to do that?"

"I'll gut you, then the next man to step up," Alerio described. He stood and tossed back his red cape revealing the gladius and legion dagger. Water dripped down his face and caused the fabric of his tunic to stick to his muscular chest. "Then I'll cut the next man to step up. Then the next, and so on. Until I find men who honor their Queen."

Grumbling came from the oarsmen and warriors on the ship, as they protested the challenge of their loyalty to Jeta. Their declarations weren't lost on their skipper.

"About eight miles, General," he reported. "I want to beach the ships until the rain stops. This is a good spot."

"It's perfect," Alerio confirmed. "Signal the boats to beach and have them set up for a day's stay."

"We're more than ten miles from Ivanaj," Altin protested. "Without our gear, we'll be cold and hungry when we arrive."

"Captain Breuci, will you also be telling me it's raining?"

"No, General Sisera, that's obvious," the young officer said. Seeing Alerio nod at the comment, Altin's eyes grew large with understanding. "As apparent as the ten-mile hike."

"I suggest you jump ashore and organize a march by columns of five."

"Five abreast," Altin repeated. "I thought most Companies march by twos?"

"Not just five across, but five ranks deep," Alerio clarified. "That'll give us two units plus half of another. And you'll be in the lead making sure they all arrive at the same instant."

When the ship's prow tapped the muddy shore, Alerio and Altin jumped off. Pharos followed with General Sisera's baggage.

"Put the bundles back on the ship," Alerio ordered.

"But sir, I can easily carry them."

"Back on the boat," Alerio insisted. "Come to think of it, you stay with the raiders, as well."

In moments, the boats were all out of the water, the oarsmen spreading oiled tarps to reduce the collection of rainwater in the hulls. As the crew set up lean-to tents, the Queen's new shield bearers stood in the downpour.

***

The Navy escaped the fat drops, but not so the volunteers for the Shield Company. Drenched, they stood in clusters, none of them gathered near the officers.

"Five across," Altin ordered. He lifted his arms and designated a starting line.

The warriors didn't move. As if the young officer hadn't given them directions, they continued to complain to one another.

Altin Breuci might have been capable of supplying and navigating a raider vessel and leading attacks on warships. But he was incapable of organizing unmotivated men. For long moments, Alerio let him stumble around in the rain asking for obedience.

To the sixty men idling in the downpour, Alerio shouted, "Who is your best swordsman?"

Several glanced at the Latian before returning to their groups.

"Do I have to start a tournament," he bellowed, "to find one man with courage?"

All the warriors pivoted to stare at Alerio. Although they lacked discipline, none were short on courage. One stocky individual opened his mouth, then sneered, and remained silent.

"You, step over here," Alerio ordered him.

Not overly tall, the warrior had broad shoulders and thick limbs.

"What do you want, General?" the man inquired.

"I'm going to make you the Company Sergeant," Alerio replied.

"What if I don't want the job?"

"What would you say to Queen Jeta?" Alerio asked.

The warrior strode to Alerio, looked him in the eyes, and remarked, "My name is Edon. I'll take the job, General. But don't turn your back on me."

Alerio leaned forward and whispered in Edon's ear, "Threats work both ways, Sergeant. Now get these men in lines."

While Edon bullied and shoved men into the first five columns, Alerio waved Altin over.

"Lesson two. Do not let disobedience fester," he warned. "Find a way to get your men moving. It doesn't matter the action. As long as they're in motion you can direct them."

"What's lesson one?"

"You witnessed it on the boat," Alerio told him. "Figure it out."

The sixty men were in three formations. Several had been trained in the phalanx and instructed the tribal fighters on how to square up with the men around them.

"Lead your Company to Ivanaj, Captain Breuci," Alerio ordered. "Sergeant Edon, keep the lines straight."

"Over rough ground, General?"

"Especially over rough ground," Alerio replied. "Get them moving."

As the warriors shuffled off, trying not to step on the heels of the man in front, Alerio fell in behind the last row.

On the shoreline with the lake as a backdrop, the crews of the five raider ships sat under rain proof covers while fires radiated warmth. The difference between the Navy and the men assigned to the infantry was not lost on the volunteers.

***

Three miles into the march, the forward men stumbled into a wide, muddy lowland area with a creek in the center.

"When you reach the stream, pick up your feet but slow down," Alerio shouted. "And maintain your spacing and the alignment with your neighbors."

Edon heard the instructions and soon both the General and the Sergeant were patrolling the formations issuing the same orders.

"Watch your distance," Edon bellowed. "You think I like this job? I don't. But it's obvious someone has to keep the livestock in line."

The front ranks stepped down and struggled across the soggy ground, through the channel, back across more swampland before they stepped up on solid ground. In a typical cross-country march, the ranks to the rear would bunch up at the drop. Then stretch out as the forward elements made it through the obstacles and increased their rate on the far side.

"Slow it down, Captain Breuci," Alerio shouted as he ran to the front. "Everyone in line, at all times."

After delivering the message, Alerio jogged back along the lines.

"After you cross the stream, step high but slow down," Alerio shouted. "And maintain your spacing and the alignment with your neighbors."

He passed Edon and the NCO glared but continued to repeat the directions.

***

Four miles along the march, rolling hills rose in front of the formation. Before Captain Breuci could order a change in course to circumvent the obstacles, Alerio appeared.

"Straight over the hills," he said. "And Captain..."

"I know sir, keep our alignment and spacing."

"I couldn't have said it better myself," Alerio stated before turning and jogging to the rear.

For Alerio, running around or through a formation was the job of an infantry leader. He dismissed the activity as being part of the job. While he didn't notice, the warriors did. After passing Edon marching beside the center rows, Alerio continued to the rear and didn't hear the Sergeant's comment.

"General Sisera is crazy," Edon offered. Several men heard him.

"This is the worst march I've ever been on," one volunteer stated. "Through the deepest part of the swamp, directly over the hills. What else can the madman want?"

"I trust you'll get him out of our lives soon?" another suggested.

"After his antics on the trail, he'll be asleep before any of us," Edon boasted. "I'll send him back to Shkodër for treatment after he collapses."

Alerio heard none of the conversation. But even at the rear, he noticed the laughter in the center formation.

***

They stumbled down the far side of the hills and hit a long stretch of level ground. While the landscape remained flat it wasn't empty or smooth. They marched through thickets, over bushes, and anything in their way.

The job of the infantry was to defeat an enemy. Not to simply push them around, but to wreck their foes. A side effect of the training caused infantrymen to enjoy crushing things. Although the new shields bearers hadn't officially started training, they began stomping bushes. Mostly out of the frustration from being shoulder to shoulder with another man during an overland march, while having to match steps with the man in front. So, with glee, they kicked, stomped, and wrecked everything in their path.

None saw the smile on Alerio's face as he glanced at the even path of destruction left by the volunteer shields.

Seven miles into the march, the forward rows stopped at the steep bank of a small river.

"What's the hold up?" Alerio shouted.

"The drop off is over six feet, General," Altin Breuci responded. "And the water is deep. We should find a place to ford the river."

"I've climbed mounds of dead stacked higher than that," Alerio scolded. "And survived a storm at sea on a vino cask. Jump. And move fast before the next row lands on your heads."

In response, Altin shouted, "Follow me."

And then, the Captain jumped into the water. With a nod of approval, Alerio stood aside as row after row of warriors reached the embankment and jumped.

"You're going to get people hurt," Edon warned when he approached, "or get someone killed."

"You keep them together and moving," Alerio responded. "I'll worry about the burial details."

Edon bristled as if he would challenge Alerio. But the sixth row moved forward, and the Sergeant jumped with them. At the rear, Alerio followed the twelfth row into the water.

***

The village of Ivanaj straddled a main trading route. On several occasions, the formation crossed the winding path. Each time, the volunteers eyed the flat surface as it faded away and they traipsed through more undergrowth. With the village dead ahead, two columns had the advantage of the hard packed road while the other three marched on the soft soil.

"Keep your line straight and your columns together," Alerio bellowed.

To maintain formations, the two columns on the road stepped high to slow their progress.

"Sergeant, where is the lake?" Alerio asked.

"To the west, General, just south of the hills. It's about two miles and a quarter," Edon told him. "Where are we camping?"

"Find us a defensible location," Alerio responded.

Ahead and to the left of Ivanaj, a hill covered by thinly spaced oak and fir trees rose twenty feet into the air.

"That hill, sir?" Edon inquired.

"That helps," Alerio responded.

"Helps?" Edon asked.

"Trees for the stockade," Alerio answered.

"A stockade, of course," Edon stated, "why not."

***

The sixty men moved away from the road. As they angled towards the hill, a group of four old men strolled from Ivanaj. Altin Breuci stepped away from the formations and went to meet them.

"Who are you?" one demanded.

"We are the Shields of Queen Jeta," Altin bragged.

Alerio jogged up but stopped away from the group.

"That Taulantii girl?" one old man asked. "Why does she need shields?"

"Because she is the Queen," Altin explained. "She has to defend Ardiaei."

"Shouldn't we be protected by Ardiaean Shields?" another questioned.

"One of you is the Chieftain of the village," Altin pointed out. "May I have your name?"

"I am Gazmend of the Ivanaj region," the Chieftain identified himself as the head of the entire area. "Are you going to kill me now or later?"

"Sir, why would we kill you?"

"When over sixty men show up, muddy and obviously destitute," Gazmend replied. He expanded his chest to make a target. "I expect you to plunge a knife into my breast before you rob my people."

"Sir, I am Captain Breuci, and we have no intention of violating your people or murdering you," Altin assured him. "We're here to train. And while we appear impoverished, our supplies are coming on ships and in wagons."

"Our well on this side of the trading road has the sweetest water in all of Ardiaei," Gazmend stated. "You are welcome to take all the water you need."

"Thank you, Chieftain," Altin responded with a salute.

Gazmend ignored the salute, turned, and guided his three advisors back to Ivanaj.

After the ten-mile hike, most men had gone through their personal water supply. Alerio sent groups to the village well to fill their waterskins. He also sent Sergeant Edon to be sure no one took advantage of the residents.

***

Without tools, bedding, or personal items, the sixty men crowded around campfires. Dirty, exhausted, chilled, and hungry, they huddled near the warmth of the flames as daylight faded.

"I left a good wool blanket on the boat," one man complained.

He shivered and placed his hands over the fire.

"My cook pot is there, along with a supply of vegetables and dried beef," a second volunteer whined. "What about it, Edon?"

A silence fell over the assembly as the men stared into the flames.

"I told you I would handle him," Edon promised. "In a while, I'll…"

"General Sisera," the man on the far side of the campfire uttered.

Edon froze and ran back in his mind what he said aloud. Then a hand wrapped around the back of his neck and a chill ran down the NCO's spine. Sisera wasn't approaching, he stood right behind the Sergeant.

"How are you men doing?" Alerio inquired.

He stepped into the circle and sat beside Edon. Something in the General's hand caught the firelight and gleamed for a moment. Fearing a knife attack, Edon pulled an arm back and rested his hand on the handle of his knife. Unfortunately, everyone around the fire saw the movement and fixated on the hand and the hilt.

"Tomorrow, we'll begin shield training," Alerio mentioned without commenting on the fingers wrapped around the knife.

"But sir, we don't have shields," a man protested.

"That's true," Alerio allowed. His hand jerked up and Edon half drew his knife. Seeing a section of steel, the General inquired. "Is something wrong, Sergeant?"

Edon's knife remained half drawn until Sisera waved a stick in the air. With the bark peeled away, the length of white wood glowed. And as it did before, when Alerio tossed the stick into the fire, light reflected off the pale segment of the stick as if it were metal.

Then Alerio stood and offered advice to the men around the campfire, "Get some rest. Tomorrow will be a busy day."

When Sisera vanished into the dark, conversation returned to the circle. All the men speculated on how they would run shield drills without shields, all except Edon. Although the Sergeant knew it was his imagination, he could still feel General Sisera's fingers on the back of his neck.

***

Before dawn, before the first trace of sunlight, and during the waning light of a setting moon, Edon rolled over and his arm fell away from his body. It hit the toe of a hobnailed boot. The NCO jerked upright.

"Good morning, Sergeant," Alerio whispered. The scraping of a rock sliding down a steel blade accompanied his voice. "I left my filing gear on the ship. I had to find a piece of granite to hone my blade."

"That can work, sir," Edon uttered. "Can I help you, General?"

"No, just making the rounds to be sure everyone is all right," Alerio replied. "That does remind me, we need to set an overnight watch."

The granite squealed along a steel blade from the hilt to the tip. Lasting much longer than the length of the General's dagger, Edon realized, Sisera had an extra knife. The General's message was clear. Turning your back on an enemy, worked both ways.

"Sorry to have woken you, Sergeant," Alerio offered before slipping silently away.

Edon shuddered. Partially at the stealthy retreat of General Sisera, and at how easily the man had snuck up on him, twice.

Chapter 15 – Drills and Ducking Duty

Griping and complaining about the lack of food, the volunteers formed a semicircle around General Sisera.

"Make fists and cross your arms at the wrists," Alerio demonstrated. "Left arm to the front."

Only a few of the sixty followed directions.

"Why?" one warrior demanded.

"An excellent question. Step up here and let's find out."

He was taller than Alerio but leaner. That didn't mean he was skinny. The man just had no excess fat on his body.

"Cross your wrists, like this," Alerio instructed. Sliding his right leg back, he angled the foot to the side, dug it into the dirt, and bent his knees. "Now, move me."

"What if I hurt you?" the slender warrior asked.

"You're not man enough," Alerio mocked.

"My name is…" the man started to say.

"I haven't all day to jaw with you," Alerio snorted. "You can tell me about your pathetic childhood some other time. Now, push me out of your way."

The tendons in the warrior's neck threatened to burst from his skin. And the sinew along his arms flexed in response to the insults. In a sudden, but not unexpected reaction, he charged.

The Illyrian came at Alerio with his hands extended away from his body, his legs straight, and his back rigid.

Alerio allowed the man to grab his crossed arms. His rear leg stopped the man's forward movement. As the warrior attempted to wrestle, Alerio shifted but didn't used any unarmed combat techniques. What the Legion weapon's instructor did was hold the man stationary for a few beats. Then, Alerio dipped his left leg and shoulder, forcing the man off balance. With a twist and shove, he flung the warrior to the ground and stepped over him.

"We don't have shields," Alerio explained while straddling the prone warrior. "But the movements are the same."

"It's not the same," Edon disagreed.

Alerio dropped. His left forearm smashed into the chest of the lean warrior. Grunting as the air exploded from his lungs, the man coughed and doubled over in pain.

"You're right," Alerio admitted as he stood. "If I had a shield, I could have struck him in the head and the chest at the same time."

The lean warrior rolled over and worked his way to his hands and knees. A final cough cleared his lungs and he inhaled deeply.

Alerio squatted beside him, rested a hand on his back, and asked, "What's your name?"

"Arvin," he replied.

"Arvin, you are the second squad leader," Alerio declared. "I hope you're fast."

"I am, sir," Arvin confirmed. "And I had a happy childhood."

"I'd like to hear about your family and village," Alerio told him. He hooked a hand under Arvin's arm and helped him to his feet. "But right now, we have to do shield drills."

"Shield drills," the squad leader for Second Squad stated. To reinforce the statement, Arvin crossed his wrists and lifted his arms for the Company to see. "Even though we don't have shields."

Alerio demonstrated the stance for bracing and described the weaponless shield drills. Then the Company divided into four groups. Alerio took one, Altin Breuci another, Arvin a third one, and Edon, on the far side of the practice field, took command of the last group.

The Sergeant didn't like the repetition of men colliding with each other and driving with their legs. To him, it amounted to uselessly digging up dirt. But he ran the drills.

"You two are almost hugging," Edon accused two of his men. While strutting to them, he glanced at the other side of the field to see General Sisera with his hands on the shoulders of a pair of volunteers. The NCO was happy that his group wasn't the only one having trouble getting men to commit. "You're not here to lean on each other. You're supposed to drive each other out of the way."

"This is dumb," one of the warriors stated. "I've held a shield and a spear since I was a little boy."

The other slacker added, "We both know how to fight."

"I don't know what Sisera has in mind," Edon told them. "But Queen Jeta thinks he knows something. If not for him, let's give the Queen the benefit of the doubt. Try it again."

They nodded in agreement and faced off. Edon spun to retrace his step to a place where he could watch his men push and dig ruts in the ground. In mid turn, he jumped back. General Sisera's face was a hand's width away from the NCO's nose.

"That's three times," Edon alleged.

Sisera rested a hand on his gladius when the Sergeant backed away.

"Three times, what?" Alerio inquired. "Do you have a problem? I was going to wait, but we can start with a sword demonstration if you don't mind bleeding a little to help the exhibition."

"Are you that confident, General?"

Alerio's gladius came out of its sheath but didn't stop at the tip. In a smooth motion, he hurled it overhead with his right hand. Whirling, the blade snapped around and around as it peaked before falling back to earth. It never touched the ground.

"I'm that confident," Alerio admitted after catching the rotating sword in his left hand. "Your turn. Draw."

Edon's group and Arvin's had stopped their drills to watch the exchange between the Sergeant and the General. Farther away, more volunteers halted their activity to watch the bloodletting.

At first most assumed Edon would draw and cut Sisera. Yet, after the flashy sword handling, the most dwindled to a couple of long odd's gamblers.

"Three times you snuck up on me," Edon clarified. "Three times you could have slipped a blade between my ribs. I have to say, sir, it's wearing on my nerves. Can we call a truce?"

"Sergeant Edon, I never realized we were at war," Alerio responded by putting away his gladius. "If I had thought we were at war, I'd have cut off your left arm."

169

"My left arm, General?"

"An NCO doesn't necessarily need to hold a shield," Alerio informed him. "It's a luxury for a Sergeant."

Edon swallowed and reached across his body to touch his left arm.

"I don't understand this drill," the NCO shot back.

Alerio understood Edon's remark was to change the subject and help him salvage his dignity. He had no issue with helping his Company Sergeant keep his pride.

"If this one confuses you," Alerio replied, "the next drill may help you see my reasoning or not."

A voice called from the direction of the lake.

"The boats have landed," Pharos shouted. "General Sisera, the men can claim their gear."

"Sergeant Edon, in an orderly fashion, march the men to the lake in columns of seven," Alerio ordered.

"Yes, sir," Edon replied while saluting. Then in a booming voice, the NCO instructed. "Shield Company fall in on Captain Breuci's position."

Alerio remained in place as the Sergeant, the Second Squad leader, and the men jogged to their Company commander.

Pharos hiked up, stopped, and set the bundles on the ground.

"Did I miss anything, sir?" he inquired.

"Just an inkling of cohesion and organization," Alerio replied while watching the volunteers march towards the lake. "And you missed a damp, sleepless night."

***

By midday, tents had gone up and the air filled with the aromas of cooking food. After eating a hot meal, Alerio allowed Pharos to keep watch while he napped.

"I need to speak to the General," Altin demanded.

"Captain, he is sleeping," the big Illyrian protested.

Alerio heard the commotion and rolled out of his blanket.

"Captain, what seems to be the problem?"

"Edon has sent men around the back of the hill to cut trees," Altin complained. "I thought we were going to continue the drills."

"Why can't we do both?" Alerio asked. "Half working on the stockade while the rest train."

"When I trained my oarsmen, we had the entire team working together," Altin explained. "It seems to me we need the same togetherness with the shields."

"You aren't wrong," Alerio said as he draped the red Legion cape over his shoulders. "But for this phase, splitting the Company might be a good idea."

Altin followed Alerio to the formation.

"Sergeant, are you cutting out a logging team?"

"I am, General," Edon replied.

"Before you do, have them line up by height," Alerio instructed.

Height presented a problem. Not because short men don't know they were below average or tall men were oblivious to standing over the others. The challenge with dividing the volunteers by height had to do with separating friends. Breaking close bonds could prove detrimental for unity in the future. Despite the issue, Edon walked the line moving and adjusting men until their heads resembled a gently rising slope.

"Arvin," Alerio beckoned the squad leader from near the tall end. "I want you to stand behind the fifteenth and sixteenth slots."

Once Arvin looked over the designated men, Alerio announced, "If anyone from the middle to my right has a relative or a short friend on my left, move behind that man."

Taller men shifted until they stood behind their shorter associates.

"Sergeant Edon, place the rest of the tall side behind the short side," Alerio directed. "The second line are your tree cutters. I'll be working with the front rank."

As the second rank marched to collect axes, wedges, saws, and hammers, Alerio walked the line of men remaining on the practice field.

"There are three distinct maneuvers you will learn," he told them. "The center must know split, and the wings need to understand envelope. And everyone must master the straight line."

The volunteers laughed because they knew the definition of a straight line.

"Who is a fast runner?" Alerio inquired.

A man stepped forward.

"Name?" Alerio asked.

"Monunis," a man of average height answered.

"You're the First Squad's leader," Alerio told him. "Move to the center of the combat line."

"This is a combat line?" someone called out.

The thirty volunteers had on different types of clothing, mismatched capes or wraps, and weapons of all sorts. They were all different, except, they were close to the same height.

"Here's the next drill," Alerio described. "You will fast walk to the tree line and back. However, you must remain in a straight line. Go."

The group stepped off and within a few feet presented a bowed line with snake like ends.

"They don't look straight," Altin observed.

"They better learn, Captain," Alerio warned, "because on the next circuit, Monunis is going to be the pace setter."

"How many cycles up and back, General?"

"Until they put their shoulders together and arrive at the same time."

***

The next morning, half the Company was happy. Felling oaks and pines, splitting boards from tree trunks, or cutting young trees and making spear poles had the men singing and moving at a smooth and steady pace. They all started as oarsmen, at one time or the other, and the regulated rhythm of building a stockade sat comfortably with men who understood rowing.

Quite the opposite, the other half of the Shields sweated and cursed as they attempted to stay abreast while jogging across the practice field.

"General Sisera, the slower men are holding up the rest," Captain Breuci noted. "Just like yesterday except the fast ones have longer legs."

"Lesson number three, Altin," Alerio responded, "your unit's strength is in arriving at the battle as a single wall of shields and spears."

"So, we're limited," Altin Breuci summed up. "We can only move as fast as the slowest man."

On the practice field, a vee that would do migrating birds proud passed the senior commanders. Unfortunately for the potential Shields, it was far from a single straight line.

After Alerio jerked a thumb towards the far side of the field, Arvin shouted, "Let's run it again. This time keep your line straight."

The thirty huffing and puffing men fell into a sloppy line. When they jogged forward, the Captain addressed General Sisera.

"Separating the Company into two rows, having the men move in shoulder-to-shoulder formations, running until they keep pace with each other," Altin Breuci listed. "In the past days, you've only had them face off and fight once. Why?"

"Every battle starts with intimidating your enemy," Alerio lectured. "The Celts scream and jump around before attacking in a chaotic horde. Once they break your line, it's a melee one-on-one fight until one side loses enough men. The Spartans on the other hand comb their hair, do calisthenics, and act nonchalant about the coming fight. But they have decades of reputation. That affects their enemies, even before the Spartans form their attack lines."

"Illyrians don't have any reputation besides being fierce fighters," Altin pointed out. "Usually that's enough."

"What happens when Illyrians fight Illyrians?" Alerio questioned.

"The side with the most men," the Captain suggested, "is victorious, usually."

"If the Taulantii came across the border, your sixty warriors, as they are now, will be murdered trying to protect

Queen Jeta or Prince Agron. You need an edge, Altin. And that is a stable wall of moving shields," Alerio said while indicating an almost straight line coming back up the practice field. "Give them a rest and a talk about the benefits of being an assault line. I'm going to check on the stockade."

***

Three completed sides of the stockade separated the crown of the hill from the lower slopes. A fresh scent from the boards of green lumber permeated the air and everywhere men chopped, secured boards to posts with rope, or shaved and trimmed wood with axes.

"Any trouble, Sergeant Edon?" Alerio asked as he climbed the final grade.

The NCO stood on a platform constructed on the crest of the hill. From the elevated height, he had a view over the walls.

"We've skinned and smoothed over one hundred spear shafts," Edon reported. "And you can see the progress on the walls. As far as trouble, it's like you have the God Boa sneaking around listening to me."

The idea of trouble and issues was a universal worry for military commanders. Healthy men trained in combat tended to be adventurous. From ducking duty to go fishing or hunting, to fighting each other, to theft from civilian settlements, there was no end to the list of possibilities.

"I've got a confession," Alerio admitted, "I only asked because things are going so well. What is it?"

"Vegetables, sir. We've got men pulling nighttime raids on neighboring farms," Edon reported. "I wasn't going to mention it to you, hoping our supply wagons would arrive soon. But three of our men were caught by a farmer and his sons last night."

"Are they being held?"

"Two managed to get back to camp, but both are hurt," Edon offered. "And so were the farmer's sons. I expect you'll be getting a visit from Chieftain Gazmend about Skender, the third Shield involved in the fight."

"Things were going too well," Alerio cursed. He leaped up to the platform and gazed around at the countryside. Then he addressed the NCO. "You've done an excellent job, Sergeant. But you need help, and the assault lines need a left side commander. Get with Arvin and Monunis. You and the squad leaders select a trustworthy man who can read, write, and do numbers."

"At first General, I wasn't sure if you knew what you were doing," Edon admitted. "Or if you were simply a sadistic war pig who enjoys us wallowing in the mud."

"And now?"

"In three days, you've created a command structure, built a fort, and have taught sixty men to move in straight lines over rough ground," Edon replied. "I'd say you know what you're doing."

"Not true," Alerio remarked. "Right now, I'm going to see the Chieftain of Ivanaj. And, I haven't any idea of what I'm going to say to him."

Alerio hopped off the platform and began the hike off the hill.

"You'll think of something, General Sisera," Edon called after him.

While the expression of confidence by the Sergeant felt good, Alerio didn't reply. He was preoccupied with how he

176

would appease the most powerful man in the region and get his Shield back.

Act 6

Chapter 16 – A Horror of a Promise

The trading route out of the mountains split the village of Ivanaj. Alerio crossed the hard packed road, asked directions, and proceeded to the chieftain's residence. As expected, it turned out to be one of the largest homes in the village. It had to be as the house served as the regional seat of government.

Alerio assumed there would be a few farmers, fishermen, shepherds, and craftsmen waiting to petition the Chieftain. Unexpectedly, he found a mob gathered in the front courtyard.

"There's another one of them," a man cried out while pointing at Alerio.

"Get him," a second man screamed.

In Rome during emergencies, the Central Legion supplemented the Capital guardsmen. As a result, training in crowd control became one of the lessons for arriving officers. Having spent several weeks in garrison with the Legion, Alerio picked up a few pointers about dealing with unruly masses.

Paramount in the training, an angry mob didn't possess a brain, a heart, or logic. No one person led it, therefore no one person could curtail its actions. Like a blind bull long past his prime, a mob could only snort, rip, and tear. Compassion required focused thought, something lacking in a mob.

Sadly, a swarm of furious citizens recognized only two emotions - anger and fear.

The men around the door to the Chieftain's house had reached a hysterical pitch. They had the angry covered. Alerio tossed back his red cape, drew his gladius and his Legion dagger, and introduced the second emotion.

"I can gut two men at a time," he bellowed. "Who are my first victims? Come on, don't be shy, let's spill some blood. It's what you want, isn't it?"

Faced with two lengths of sharp steel, and a ferocious Legion officer, the mob leaned back as if hot flames from a fire threatened to burn them. In an instant, fear won over anger and the mob settled into a less emotional crowd.

"Make a path," Gazmend instructed from the doorway. "Let Jeta's General through."

Here was an opportunity for a dignified approach. And a chance to get hit in the back of the head by a farm implement. Alerio chose a brutish approach.

"These are Noric steel," he warned while slashing the air with his blades. "They are sharp, and because of a curse, they have a habit of slashing out on their own. I suggest you stand back and let my blades pass."

With those words hanging in the air, Alerio marched forward holding the weapons at hip level, the blades facing outward towards the men lining the walkway. Respectfully, the citizens of Ivanaj moved back, giving Sisera's cursed blades plenty of room.

"Come in, General," Chieftain Gazmend invited from the doorway.

***

Obviously, a setting for business, the room had an abundance of chairs, a small table, and a large one for conferences. What wasn't part of the normal furnishings lay bloody and curled up in a corner.

"Is that my man?" Alerio inquired. "Or one of the farmer's sons?"

"Skender is one of yours," Chieftain Gazmend acknowledged. "But, one of the farmer's boys was stabbed and died last night. Therefore, the mob and justice demand a fitting punishment."

"You're going to execute him for a fight? Surely you suspect it was an accident," Alerio said, trying to find reasons to get the young man pardoned. "Plus, he's a soldier of Ardiaei."

"It's for that exact reason I'm going to have him drowned," the Chieftain admitted. "I'm praying that he dies of his wounds. But if Skender lives or I allow him to live, the farmer will send his other sons to avenge their brother's death. And then soldiers from your phalanx will come to revenge their brother-in-arms. I've seen these blood feuds and they can go on for years. But not this time and not in my region. The best solution is a quick execution and an end to the affair."

Alerio crossed to the badly beaten volunteer. Kneeling, he felt Skender's forehead and checked for broken bones.

"You're not going to die of your wounds," Alerio reported. "Which is good news for a day or two."

"General, I don't want to be drowned," the young soldier pleaded. "Nor crucified, or impaled, or put on a board for the crows, or..."

180

"I get the idea," Alerio told him. "Let me talk to the Chieftain some more."

"Please, sir," tears rolled down Skender's cheeks. When mixed with the dried blood on his face, they sent a slurry of red over his chin. And he sobbed, "Please, save me."

Alerio pushed to his feet, suddenly feeling every bit of his thirty-one years. The old arrow wound in his thigh throbbed, and the crescent shaped scar on the crown of his head itched. It would be so easy to walk out and let justice be done. Then he remembered being young and in trouble. And how a Centurion and an Optio had conspired to spirit him out of town before the Spilled Blood gang could have him executed.

Conscience being a tough task master, Alerio raised a hand and pointed to the head man of the region.

"Chieftain Gazmend, let me propose a few things to you."

***

Later in the day, Alerio and the condemned man left the Chieftain's residence. With his arm under Skender's shoulder, Alerio supported him as they limped across the road. Slowly, they left the village behind and entered the woods. Three quarters of a mile later, they emerged from the forest and spotted the stockade. And at the base of the hill, a caravan of wagons with their supplies.

Hektor appeared from behind a transport, spied Alerio hauling Skender, and ran to fetch his medical bag.

"Are you injured, Colonel?" the young medic asked as he dashed up. "Where is Pharos?"

"I'm fine. The blood is his," Alerio answered. Together they stretched Skender out on a bed of pine needles. "And I don't need a bodyguard."

"In a Legion camp with mostly Latians you need guards to watch your back," Hektor offered as he probed bruises and swollen spots and checked for broken bones. "Yet here, deep in Illyria, you're safe walking around alone?"

"It was dicey for a day or so," Alerio told him. "How's Skender?"

"Beaten badly, but not to death," Hektor diagnosed. "All he needs is rest."

"I need you to set up a medical clinic in the Chieftain's residence," Alerio informed Hektor. "And to claim that you are a doctor."

"Colonel, you know I don't have the training," the youth protested.

"Hektor Nicanor, your hands have been inside more wounded men's bodies than ten surgeons," Alerio countered. "And you've treated more Legionaries than a dozen doctors. I think you can handle it. If you get stuck, just prescribe a dose of vinegar. It's what most physicians do when they're mystified."

"Then I'm afraid, Colonel, Ivanaj will soon have a major shortage of vinegar."

***

By late afternoon, a command tent with wooden flooring occupied a space next to the gate. In the rear, near the stockade wall, a metalsmith, a carpenter, and a leather worker had set up their tents and worktables.

"We have a candidate for your consideration, sir," Edon submitted to Alerio. "Arvin and Monunis agree that Sabaia is your other NCO. He's respected by the men and meets your educational requirements."

They strolled through the compound inspecting the supply tents and the stored gear.

"Speaking of Arvin and Monunis," Alerio advised. "Have them take sixteen men and a wagon of wood to the farmer. They have two days to do whatever he asks. Build something, plow a field, dig a well, chop firewood, whatever he needs, for two days. Then they're to come back here."

"The word is spreading that you saved Skender, and the men appreciate it," the Sergeant told Alerio. "What did you promise the Chieftain, sir?"

"Mostly things that I can measure and control. A medical clinic while we're in the region, and to appease the farmer, workers, and supplies at his property," Alerio listed.

"Sir, you said mostly," Edon said picking up on the hint of something not in the General's control.

Alerio stopped at an area where men were leveling the ground for their tents. After a few words with them, the General and the NCO strolled away.

"What I promised, Sergeant, was a personal guarantee that we would stop the thefts," Alerio answered. "Plus, if the Chieftain needed anything, we would respond without hesitation."

"You swore an oath to a regional Chieftain?"

"I did."

"May the God Boria have mercy on us," the NCO prayed.

"What's the problem?" Alerio questioned. "A moment ago, you were delighted with my deal to save Skender. Now you're invoking the God of the Mountains."

Edon lifted an arm and indicated the mountain ranges that dominated the horizon. Swinging from the peaks to the north, the spikey heights to the east, and towards the serrated tops to the south, he pointed out the landscape.

"Chieftain Gazmend commands warriors to defend a large area," Edon explained. "Blood feuds hold him and the neighboring Chieftains in check and prevent raids. What you did was hand him sixty armed outsiders to use against his adversaries."

"We will not murder farmers or destroy villagers," Alerio vowed.

"That's not my worry, General. He couldn't hold any new territory we claim for him," Edon disclosed. "For the Chieftain, it's enough for us to weaken his rivals along the border."

"And it doesn't matter what happens to us, while we strengthen his position," Alerio suggested.

"That's the core of it, sir," Edon confirmed.

"May the God Boria have mercy on us," Alerio prayed.

***

The next morning, while the men ate a full meal, Alerio went to the leather worker's shop.

"What I want are two pieces of leather over their shoulders," Alerio described to the craftsman.

"Like belts, General?" the craftsman questioned.

Grabbing a teamster from where he sat watching, Alerio squared off with him. Then he drew his gladius and raised his arm in the air. The driver flinched when the blade dipped as if it was bridging over the top of a shield.

"Their shoulders need protection from overhead slashes," Alerio explained.

The craftsman selected two strips of leather that were a hands' width wide and draped them over the man's shoulders. Then he pulled the ends together at chest level.

"I can stitch them in place by inserting a torso piece. Is that what you had in mind, General?"

Alerio studied the wide epaulets. Then he raised his gladius before dropping the edge onto the man's shoulders. The blade hit the leather, and other than a minor cut in the material, it didn't cut the man.

"How did that feel?"

"Sir, I couldn't feel anything," the teamster reported.

"We'll need sixty-three sets of shoulder and chest armor."

"What color, sir?" the craftsman asked.

Alerio Sisera had years of experience training for war and in fighting. What he didn't have was an eye for color. Or even the knowledge that he could select a color for the leather.

"I'll need some help," Alerio admitted. "What are my choices?"

"I have blue dyes made from berries, it's very popular," the craftsman offered. "Or you can have Kermes red. We make that by crushing the bodies of insects that live on the sap of oak trees."

"I don't want a popular color that can be seen everywhere. I need the Shields to stand out," Alerio mused. "And red, well that's too close to Legion colors. What else do you have?"

"Yellow from onion skins, or brown from the mighty oak's acorns," the craftsman described. "There's a sickly green but it's closer to puke than leaves."

"Yellow, brown, green, it'd be like looking at a forest in the fall," Alerio complained. "Is there nothing else?"

"I'm in short supply of the raw material, but I can make a bright, pale salmon color."

"How can something be bright and pale at the same time?"

The leather worker vanished into his tent and came back a moment later with a piece of brightly dyed cloth. He held it up to the light.

"That's a pale representation of the meat of a salmon," Alerio acknowledged. "And it's dazzling. I like it. What raw material do you need to dye the armor, the shield covers, and sixty-three capes?"

"General, I'll need a wagon load of chestnuts," the tradesman said. "It's a lot of work and I'm afraid…"

"Chestnuts?" Alerio inquired. "What else?"

"Urine, sir. I'll boil the leather with the husks of chestnuts and stir in urine to set the color."

Alerio spun on his heels and marched to the command tent. The day's training had been replaced.

"Captain Breuci, the Company, at least those not working on the farm, will hunt for locations with sandy, clay soil and good drainage," Alerio instructed.

"Sandy soil, sir?" Altin inquired.

"It's the preferred environment of chestnut trees," Alerio responded. "Lesson number four, Captain. Create pride within your unit by any means necessary."

"With chestnuts?" Altin questioned.

"With the color of brilliant, pale salmon."

***

Four days later, the men faced off with shields. In a great pushing match, they grunted, turned up soil, and attempted to shove the other line backwards.

"We've been playing the part of draft horses for a long time, General," Sabaia told Alerio. "Shouldn't we do something else?"

"An excellent idea Corporal. Break them into four groups and let's practice pivoting."

Sabaia saluted and marched to Edon.

"I thought some spear or sword practice would break the monotony of pushing," he whined. "But the General said to pivot them around the practice field. If we are fighting men, shouldn't we be fighting. I wonder if he even knows anything about spears or swords?"

The Company's Sergeant smiled at the new Corporal.

"The General has some strange ideas," Edon remarked. "I'm sure we'll get around to fighting, eventually. Now get control of your section and dance them around."

While lines of fifteen men pirouetted around a pivot man, creating concentric patterns at the commands of Alerio, Altin, Edon and Sabaia, a wagon rolled off the hill. At the practice field, the teamster and a helper drove the team to the edge of the tree line.

"Corporal Sabaia. Take your group and clear the branches from sixty hardy trees," Alerio ordered.

The NCO marched his men to the edge of the woods. Setting to work, they quickly chopped and hauled away the branches.

"What's in the wagon?" the Corporal asked.

"Poles," the teamster replied.

Alerio strutted to the wagon, reached into the bed, and lifted out an eight-foot pole.

"We have plenty. Come get one," he exclaimed while holding the shaft over his head. "I expect to have none left by sundown."

The sixty men picked up a wooden pole each and fell into their two-line formation.

"Our enemy is there," Captain Breuci directed.

"Sir, that's the forest," a voice noted.

"Not today," Altin corrected. "The bare tree trunks are enemy warriors. Move forward and stop three feet from the tree and attack it with your spears."

"Are we just going to beat on trees all day?" another voice inquired.

"No," Alerio assured him. "Part of the time, we'll be pushing the trees down with our shields. Now, attack."

Groans escaped for several men, including Corporal Sabaia.

As they poked the tree trunks, the NCOs and officers worked with the ranks.

"Stab low with an underhanded grip," Alerio instructed the forward line. "Rear rank, use an overhanded grip and stab down over your shield. Keep the enemy warriors off your front rank."

Someone laughed and said, "It's not like the trees are going to move."

"An excellent observation," Alerio shouted. "If the trunks aren't coming to us, we will go to the trees. Attack in lines and push the trees down."

None of the trees so much as swayed. But with encouragement, the volunteers grunted, dug in their feet, and attempted to move the unmovable.

"Is this more to your liking, Corporal?" Alerio asked.

"Sir, I didn't mean to question."

"Of course, you did," Alerio assured him.

Hektor jogged across the practice field, his medical kit bouncing on his shoulders. His two helpers following with kits of their own.

"Are we too late, sir?" the medic inquired.

"No, we haven't started yet."

Hektor and his team laid out bandages, tubs of ointment, and sharp knives. Once the medical supplies for treating blisters were on display, Alerio pointed to Sabaia.

"Corporal, back them off and have them attack the trunks," Alerio ordered. "It's hard to splinter a pole by stabbing a tree. But after a team cracks their poles, they get to rest and get treatment. When every team has broken their shafts, we'll rearm and attack again."

"How long does this drill last, sir?" the new NCO inquired.

"Until we run out of shafts, or it gets dark," Alerio replied. "Luckily, we have plenty, so we'll continue tomorrow. Captain Breuci, Sergeant Edon, rattle some trees."

Sounding as if a swarm of woodpeckers had dropped from the sky to pound on the bark, the forest rang with impact after impact. Soon another sound joined the cacophony. That of men howling in pain as the skin on their hands ripped while they hammered the ends of poles into the trunks. Everyone wanted to be the first to shatter their shafts and take a rest.

"I'm exhausted from watching you boys tap, tap, tap on the trees," Alerio bellowed. "Take a break. Shields up. Charge. Push a tree down."

Chapter 17 – Border at Ducaj

Two weeks later, their hands had toughened, as had their leg and arm muscles. Swift in changes of angle, and as tight in the turns as they were in a straight-ahead formation, or a sweep, the Company had all the movements of an elite unit. Plus, due to their fierce thrusts, they shattered wooden poles almost at will.

"General Sisera, I'm impressed with their responsiveness," Altin noted. "No one, including me, thought you could train us this fast."

On the practice field, Arvin and Monunis pulled their squads back. As the First and Second faked being overrun, the flanking squads moved inward while stabbing with their spears and hammering with their shields. In a few steps, they closed the gap, reestablishing the assault line.

"There're still missing two things, Captain Breuci," Alerio explained. "They haven't been tested in battle and they are, as yet, unbloodied."

"But most have been in fights, some at sea, others in border skirmishes, and a few in phalanxes," Altin protested. "Doesn't that count?"

"There's only one way for a two-rank fighting system to be successful. The lines must hold in tough situations," Alerio replied. "As they stand now, some will be tempted to break ranks and fight solo or runaway. They need confidence in each other to hold the line."

Across the field, Sergeant Edon and Corporal Sabaia called a halt to the drill. The NCOs looked towards the officers.

"Put them in formation, Altin," Alerio said. He turned his back to the practice field and signaled to the hill. "We'll do a quick inspection. Then we'll add to their pride."

Alerio and Altin marched to the gathering of men as two wagons rolled from the stockade. The officers reached the formation long before the wagons arrived.

"You've come a long way," Captain Breuci addressed the Company. "You should be proud. But there are a few things missing. Most of you are almost as naked as a Celtic warrior."

Restrained chuckles ran through the ranks. Not because the image of a bare skinned savage wasn't humorous. It was to the Illyrians. The reason the Company didn't laugh was the jest hinted at the truth. In the weeks of practice and drills, their clothing had ripped, been stitched, and patched until they stood in rags of different material.

"First, we need armor," Altin continued. "And not simply helmets. Our armor needs to identify us and strike fear in our enemies."

"How can the sight of armor strike fear in anyone?" Corporal Sabaia questioned. "A sword, a spear, or a knife, we understand. But armor is, well, just protection."

The horses pulled the transports in behind Alerio and Altin. After stopping, the teamsters pulled tarps off the wagon beds. An odd hue glowed from stacks of leather. To a few, the shade reminded them a maiden's lips. Others thought of bright flowers and others thought of the meat of a salmon or trout, only paler.

"Let's test your premise, Corporal," Alerio stated while climbing on a wagon. "First line, your armor is in the first wagon. Second line, your armor is in the second."

"You heard the General," Sergeant Edon instructed. "Put down your poles and shields and go get your armor."

It took a while for the shorter men to find which armor rested comfortably on their shoulders. For the taller men, they had to locate leather rigs where the center piece sat high enough to guard their chests. At the bottom of the leather armor, they found iron helmets.

Even though they tested the gear, the closest fitting items wobbled on their heads or threatened to cut into the flesh of their shoulders.

"Back in the stockade, you'll find sheepskin to pad the armor and line the helmets," Alerio informed them. "For now, first rank put on your armor and helmets, pick up your shields and poles, and move off twenty feet. Second rank, get dressed and face the first rank."

They still wore rags for undergarments. But the rows of matching leather over their shoulders and across their chests presented a view of what an enemy would see. A uniformed row of soldiers as if the perfect fighter had been duplicated and then placed shoulder to shoulder to form a wall of armor.

"Corporal Sabaia, do you have an opinion now?" Alerio called to the NCO.

"General Sisera, I take back my previous statement," the Corporal admitted. He glanced from one combat line to the other, stood a little straighter, and declared. "Sir, the Queen's Shields are frightening."

"That they are," Alerio acknowledged. "Sergeant Edon, dismiss the formation. I'm sure everyone wants to get padding in place before the gear rubs them raw."

"Men of the Queen's Shields," Edon shouted, "fall out."

Some men removed the armor and carried their leather rigs. Others kept the armor on. All of them fussed over the wide strips of their shoulder covers and the chest guard as if welcoming a new friend. In a way, they were.

***

For two days, the mood inside the stockade and on the practice field reflected pride. Being a member of an elite force carried through to every action performed by the Company, including the viciousness of their drills.

"Another bloody scrap," Altin grumbled. "I'm afraid, if we ever put blades on the spears, they'll happily slash each other to pieces."

The Captain had called for a break to get the injured treated and everyone a chance to get a drink and to catch their breath. Around the practice field, men sat kneading bruised right arms, or holding their hands over bloody noses. But thanks to the leather armor, no one suffered a broken collar bone or a dislocated shoulder.

Alerio stood off to the side with Pharos scanning the Company.

"I've fought Greek Hoplites, Iberian and Noricum infantry," Alerio opined. "Between the shields and the armor, the Queen's Shields aren't as heavily armored, but they certainly qualify as heavy infantry."

"My people like stationary targets," Pharos scoffed. "The Shields look pretty, but put them in the center of a battle, and my tribe would chew them up and leave them for the crows."

Alerio looked at the big Illyrian to see if he was grinning or serious.

"What's the problem with the Shields?" Alerio inquired.

"They're standing in one place, beating on each other," Pharos replied. "No offense to your double line, sir. But the Shields are fixed in place. Sure, they move to get into position but once the fighting starts, they become no more than tree trunks. Hard and stationary, and waiting to get chopped down."

Caught in the quandary between revealing the secrets of the Legion's rotating lines and the unified 'advances' with gladii and spears, Alerio had focused on what not to teach the Illyrians. He still wouldn't teach a potential enemy how to beat a Legion, but he could give them movement for tribal warfare.

***

"I think we're ready to take on any tribe," Edon advocated.

"Or phalanx," Sabaia added.

"We still have a week before we report to the Queen," Altin reminded them. "Let's make sure we used them wisely."

"Yes, sir," the NCOs replied.

Before they could get the Shields up and into formation, Alerio walked to the command staff.

"This afternoon, I want to try something new," Alerio offered. "We'll separate the Company into four sections. Have them move sideways back and forth across the practice field, two facing two."

"So, they'll battle one section while passing, then fight another section," Edon said describing the drill. "What's the purpose, sir."

"If I had a hundred warriors to use as an enemy force for the drill," Alerio answered, "you'd see us reacting to their attempt to get around us. As it is, try to imagine a horde of warriors angling to get behind our lines."

"Get up, tighten your shields, rest time is over," Edon and Sabaia bellowed.

"I'm relieved by the change in tactics," Altin disclosed. "By moving, they won't do as much damage as they do when standing and pounding on each other."

"There is that," Alerio confirmed.

***

Clouds moved over the sun as it dipped below the horizon. With the early loss of light, the evening darkness came quickly. As they had been coached, at the end of each day, Captain Breuci, Sergeant Edon, and Corporal Sabaia roamed the camp talking with the men. When they first arrived, Alerio did as well. But as the Shields solidified into a garrison command, General Sisera curtailed his visits.

"Not going to grace the campsites with your presence, sir," Pharos asked.

His back was suddenly outlined by flames as he puffed and blew a campfire to life.

"It's more important that the Captain and his NCOs are seen," Alerio replied.

Not far from the command tent, two guards paced in front of the gate. Their shadows grew long as they approached one of the torches beside the portal and shortened when they marched away from the lights.

Alerio leaned his head back and studied the black sky.

"You'll be heading home I imagine," Alerio remarked to the Illyrian, "when Hektor and I return to Rome."

"I've talked to Captain Breuci, and he asked me to stay on as his supply man," Pharos stated. He lifted a pot of stew and hung it on a hook between the iron tri-legs of a stand. "I'm thinking it might be a good career move."

"What happened to returning to your village and becoming a hunter?" Alerio asked.

"General Sisera, what you've built here will sustain the Queen and the Prince," he replied. "And when Agron becomes king, the Shields will help him crush his enemies."

"I thought you were unimpressed by stationary targets," Alerio teased.

"In a boat crew, we row one way in good weather, another when the waves are peaking, and stroke differently in a storm," Pharos described. "The best crews can adjust quickly. You've trained these men to adapt on the run. I'm thinking about hanging around to see what they can accomplish."

Alerio lifted a wineskin and toasted himself.

"I guess I did do good..."

From the gate, a sentry shouted a warning.

"Alert," he called out. "Men approaching."

The two guards leveled spears and soon a squad assigned to the watch joined them.

"Stand down," Hektor called from the dark beyond the gates. "It's the medic with Chieftain Gazmend and company."

The last comment brought Alerio off the chair. With his gladius in hands, he sprinted to the gate.

"Explain your company, Hektor," Alerio demanded.

"A single warrior from the border," the Greek replied.

"Split your squad and line the road, just in case," Alerio told the squad leader. When the Shields were in position, Alerio said. "Hektor, bring the Chieftain in."

For once, Hektor Nicanor didn't have his medical kit. Alerio knew of only two times the youth failed to carry the bulky package. Once when a nobleman tricked him out of it, sold the medical equipment, and used the coins to sail home while leaving Hektor stranded. And the other time when Hector needed to travel fast.

Behind the youth, the old Chieftain walked through the gates and behind him, a dirty, hard looking warrior marched into the fort.

"Close the gates," Alerio ordered. Then to the guest, he invited. "Chieftain Gazmend, come to the fire where there's warmth, light, and nourishment."

"I'm glad you're in an amicable mood, General Sisera," the old Lord commented. "Because I'm about to call in your favor and ruin your evening."

***

Gazmend sat staring at the fire and sipping from a mug of wine. War injuries from long ago prevented him from raising his face and drinking from a wineskin. But he seemed to be at peace and lost in memories. Watching the ancient Chieftain, Alerio wondered if one day he would end up stiff from his war wounds. Hopefully, he would also find solace in a campfire.

When Altin, Edon, and Sabaia returned to the command tent, they were surprised to see the Chieftain seated at the fire and a warrior stationed behind the old man.

Respectfully, they greeted the regional Lord and didn't take offense when he failed to reply. They took glasses of beer and sat quietly around the campfire. Finally, Gazmend pried his eyes from the flames and his mind from the past.

"Ballaios is my warden at Ducaj," he said, introducing the warrior. "He's fresh off the mountain. If you can call his present state fresh. He has a tale."

Ballaios stepped closer to the old man and with affection, briefly touched the Chieftain's shoulder. Then he stepped close to the fire and the flames reflected off his tall, straight frame.

"I patrol from Ducaj, over the mountain to Rahovic on the other side, and back," the warden stated. "It usually takes me a week to hike the trails. Three days ago, I left Ducaj. It was early and the sky clear. The first day out is the toughest. I must climb from the valley. But once on the mountain, it gets easier as I follow the animal trails."

Pharos handed the warden a mug of beer. After a long pull, Ballaios continued with his story.

"I hunt small animals along the way to supplement my grain," he described. "On that day, I walked up on an injured deer. Her leg broken, she waited in pain for the boars or wolves. I put her down, but it left me with a problem. It was too much meat to haul over the mountain and too much to waste. I gutted the animal and tossed the entrails off a cliff to keep the predators away from my route. Then I headed back towards Ducaj."

Ballaios glanced down which for most people was a sign of shame. But the strong warrior hadn't admitted to anything disgraceful.

"Go on," Gazmend urged, "General Sisera is unusually talented at untangling knots."

Ballaios lifted his chin and nodded.

"As I neared the edge of the slope to the valley, I caught the aroma of smoke. A good distance north, a haze lay over the gorge," he said. "Fearing a forest fire, I dropped the deer and worked my way along the heights. About halfway to Boge, I saw a military encampment."

"Boge is a Labeatae village three miles up the valley from Ducaj," Gazmend informed the group. "Our tribes have clashed in the past but not recently. There's no reason for an armed camp to be there to darken the sky and blacken my disposition."

Alerio stood and smiled at Ballaios.

"How many men in the war band?" he asked.

The warden seemed to shrink in statue.

"I don't have numbers in my head," he divulged.

And there was the challenge. Ballaios couldn't count and therefore had no way to express the number of soldiers. Alerio accepted the fact and suggested the warden finish his story.

"Thinking to find Ionios, the Boge warden, and ask who the soldiers were, I crept along the ridge. But then I spotted Ionios in their camp. And a thought came to me."

"What thought?" Alerio inquired.

"Ionios and I patrol at the same time in the same direction," Ballaios answered. "We will cross paths at certain spots. There's an agreement that if one of us gets hurt and can make it to the meeting spot, the other will help."

"Three days ago, Ionios should have been heading over the mountain," Alerio summed up. "Do you think he waited for you to leave before bringing the soldiers from Boge?"

"I do, General."

"If they have a big enough raiding party to gather on the border," Altin ventured. "Why stop halfway between the towns? There can't be that many of them."

Alerio pulled a stick out of the fire, blew out the flame, and handed it to the warden.

"Draw what you saw of their camp."

Edon and Sabaia leaned around the fire to watch Ballaios smear lines on the boards. As small boxes appeared, Alerio inhaled deeply and exhaled hard.

"Two men per tent or ten men?" he inquired when the warden finished.

Alerio held up two fingers than flashed all ten digits.

"I saw a handful of soldiers at a few tents," Ballaios replied. "They were eating, and each had a bundle of spears next to him."

Alerio paced from the corner of the command tent to the fire and back several times. Then he stopped and fixed the NCOs in his gaze.

"In your opinion," he inquired, "how good are the Shields?"

"They need seasoning," Sabaia answered. "But General, they are the best I've seen since I tangled with a phalanx of Greek mercenaries."

"I agree," Edon confirmed.

Turning to the Lord, Alerio dropped to a knee, so the old man didn't have to look up at him. "Chieftain Gazmend, call in your favor."

"General Sisera, I have enemies on my border at Ducaj," Gazmend stated. He raised his arm and rested a shaky hand on Alerio's shoulder. "I ask you to remove the threat."

"The Queen's Shield-Bearers hear your request, and we will respond."

Chapter 18 – Not a Pretty Knot

The clouds hung low, threatening rain, and blocking the sun. Under the gray sky, fifty-seven Shields, their commander, and their NCOs marched from the stockade.

"Why aren't you with Captain Breuci?" Pharos asked.

"I've done all I can to make them a functioning Company," Alerio replied. "From now on, they'll win or die by their own deeds."

"Yes, sir, but can I point out that you're accompanying them into the mountains," the Illyrian noted.

"Just because a mother bird kicks the wee ones out of the nest, doesn't mean she ignores her young."

Behind Alerio and the Illyrian, four draft horses pulled a single transport. It was more pulling power than normal, but Alerio wanted to be sure, the Company's supplies kept pace with the marching troops.

They were a mile from the stockade and approaching the trade road when Hektor and Ballaios caught up to the procession.

"The Chieftain is home safely," the warden reported.

"Gazmend argued all the way to the village," Hektor informed them. "He wanted to come on the expedition."

"In his younger days, my Chieftain was a great warrior. He said he would have given you competition, General

Sisera," Ballaios remarked. Then the warden added. "Please understand, that's a compliment from the old man."

"And that's exactly as I took it," Alerio assured him.

It started to rain and, ahead of Alerio's group, the Shields pulled out oiled skins and covered their armor and helmets. Suspended on poles held over their shoulders, the men made sure the colored leather and iron head gear were covered. Even though, it left the Shields wet and unprotected from the downpour.

***

A half mile south of the village, the cavalcade left the trade road and took a southeast heading. Somewhere during the three miles to the river with the swampy banks, the rain stopped. However, the deluge in the mountains collected, flowed down, and swelled the watercourse.

While the men struggled to ford the rapidly flowing water, the double team of horses easily splashed through the current.

"The rain stopped," Hektor declared while peering at the sky. "It'll make the climb more comfortable."

"And let the Labeatae forces move faster if they've finished," Alerio said.

"Finished what, sir," Pharos questioned.

"The number of tents showed a war party of forty," he answered. "If they're raiders, they shouldn't have stopped on the border. There's something else going on. Camping between Ducaj and Boge feels like an incomplete maneuver. And it makes me nervous."

"You think they haven't finished gathering and aren't ready for what they have planned," Ballaios remarked.

Pharos laughed and mumbled, "So much for mommy birds."

While Ballaios and Hektor stared at the big Illyrian in confusion, the Company turned north and entered a mile wide valley. Ahead, the mountains dominated the landscape.

***

The grade underfoot climbed subtly, but steadily, as they hiked up the valley. Where it ended, the base of two mountains rose sharply on either side of the trail. As the Company climbed out of the valley, the elevation steepened.

"Ballaios, scout ahead," Alerio instructed. "If you spot trouble, get the word back to Captain Breuci as fast as you can. Don't wait for details. You've already proven your worth."

"As the Chieftain said," the warden commented, "you are very good at untangling knots."

Ballaios easily jogged up the footpath, soon passing Breuci and his command group, then the forward columns, and finally the advanced squad. In moments, he was lost to sight in the greenery along the mountain trail.

"I've heard the phrase, but don't understand," Hektor pondered. "Just what does good at untangling knots mean?"

"On an ocean voyage, crewmen get into arguments and sometimes fights," Pharos explained. "Being trapped with an adversary can lead to more fighting which disrupts the rest of the crew. A Captain, or first mate, who is good at figuring out why the men are arguing and finding a solution to restore peace is said to be good at untangling knots."

"Then I agree, Colonel Sisera is good at untangling knots," Hektor granted.

The Company continued to hike into the higher reaches of the mountains, and deeper into Chieftain Gazmend's northern region.

***

At midday, they reached the village of Bzhetë, and Captain Breuci called for a rest period. As the troops settled to the ground, he hiked back to the supply wagon.

"General Sisera, any suggestions?" he asked.

"Ballaios said Bzhetë sits halfway to Ducaj," Alerio replied. "From here up is the most dangerous segment of the trip. You're susceptible to an accidental engagement or even a planned ambush."

"I guess it's time to gear up and arm up," Altin decided.

"You're the Captain."

For the rest of the period, Shields came back to the wagon and exchanged their poles for spears with steel broadheads. Pointed at the tip, the blades swelled outward before arching inward and clamping around the top of the shaft. The wounds inflicted by the leaf design were both deep from the point and wide from the flare.

"Be careful you don't hurt yourself," Edon teased.

"I'm sick of breaking poles," Skender said while stabbing with the underhanded grip of a First Line Shield. "I've been waiting to get my hands on a real spear. So where is the enemy?"

"You'll get your chance later. Move along," the NCO instructed. "Next man, step up. Put your pole in the wagon and take a spear."

On the way up the trail, brightly colored leather rigs and iron helmets swung from poles held over the shoulders of average men. When the same men stepped off after the break, much had changed.

Fifty-seven spears jutted above a formation of uniformed warriors. While the shiny spearheads above reflected the midday sun, down in the formation, men strutted. Each looked around at the superb gear and the attitude of his neighbor and he beamed with pride.

It might have been half the distance. But riding the emotional high of being the Queen's Shield-Bearers, they came within sight of Ducaj before anyone of them realized they had traveled that far. They would have marched straight into the village except the warden signaled a halt.

Captain Breuci and Corporal Sabaia jogged forward, leaving Sergeant Edon in the center of the formation. If something were to happen to the officer and the other NCO, the Shields would still have leadership. It was another of General Sisera's rules - Someone must always be in command.

***

Sitting on a stone shelf and looking miserable, Ballaios offered only a wave of his hand to greet Breuci and Sabaia.

"We're too late," the warden complained. "The Labeatae force has grown."

"How many more?" Breuci asked.

"Just as many more spears as they had before," Ballaios replied. Then he held up ten fingers and added. "Plus, a double handful of slingers. We need to retreat back down the mountain and warn the Chieftain."

"Figure eighty spears and twenty slingers," Breuci said after totaling the count. "What do you say, Corporal. Do we retreat or advance?"

Ballaios glanced from the NCO to the Officer. He'd never witnessed the chief of a war party ask any of the warriors for their opinion. Of course, the warden had no way of knowing it was Sisera's sixth rule. Ask your NCO's advice before making any decision.

"Is there a spot in the valley where our men can block the pass?" Sabaia inquired.

"The valley is wide on both sides of the Prroni I Thate," Ballaios answered. "It allows us to have farms on both sides of the river all the way to Boge."

The Corporal glanced at the mountain river and imagined the difficulty of crossing it.

"Captain, I can't see us setting up a blockade," the NCO advised. "If we're going to fight, we'll need to entice them to focus their attack."

Ballaios recoiled and reminded the officers, "they have more warriors."

"Are you going to tell me it rained this morning?" Breuci asked.

The Captain spun away and marched downhill, leaving Ballaios confused.

"Everyone knows it rained this morning," the warden commented.

"He knows the odds," Sabaia informed him. "We also know, thanks to you, that they have bundles of spears."

"Yes, that's right, they have bundles of the weapons," Ballaios gushed. "We need to retreat. This is not a pretty knot."

"Spearmen throw spears before they charge while slingers stand off and toss rocks or pellets," Corporal Sabaia clarified. "We are the Queen's Shield-Bearers. With an emphasis on shields. And, you should know, we have spears of our own. Let's get back. I want to hear what General Sisera has to say about this knot."

***

The warden guided thirty-nine Shields up a winding ridge, through a small gap, and onto a high meadow. Where they had tree cover on the slopes as they climbed, at the upper elevation the vegetation consisted of scrub pines, fields of wild grasses, and weeds sprouting from rocky mounds. But they traveled far above the valley and out of sight from the spearmen.

With Ballaios' knowledge of the mountains, they marched four miles until he called a halt. Between the Shields and the crest were pines. Beyond the foliage lay the empty air over the valley with the opposite mountain in the distance.

"From here," Ballaios announced, "you can reach the spearmen. Although, it's a little steep."

"How steep?" Edon asked.

In reply, the warden dropped to his belly and crept forward to a spot under the pine boughs. Captain Breuci and Sergeant Edon followed in a low crawl until the three were looking out over the valley. Below them was a steep slope and, on the valley floor, the backside of the Labeatae camp.

"Yup, there they are," the Sergeant remarked with little enthusiasm.

From his perspective, they might as well have been on a raft, a mile from shore, without a paddle. He could see their objective but no easy way to reach it.

"Is there a better way down than falling?" Altin Breuci questioned.

"Interconnecting ravines from runoff," Ballaios answered. "One of the ditches starts a short way from here."

"How connected?" Edon demanded. "Most mountain gullies are a series of waterfalls. It'll take us days to scale down multiple cliffs."

Breuci looked at the sky, noting the location of the sun.

"If we're going to be ready for General Sisera," the Captain reminded them, "we better get moving."

***

Miles to the south and down in the valley, Alerio and Corporal Sabaia marched the First and Second Squads into Ducaj. Before the supply wagon reached the mountain village, farm families came out of their cottages to gawk at the Shields.

"Are you here to defend us from the spearmen camped in the upper valley?" the village elder inquired. "Or are you just unlucky?"

"A little of both," Alerio admitted. "Have they bothered you?"

"Not so much as a patrol onto our lands," the elder replied. "But no one brings that many spears to a border with good intentions."

"I can't argue that," Alerio agreed. "We'll be spending the night."

"I figured," the old farmer said. "You'll be wanting food."

Men who farmed the high country were a tough breed. They survived where the weather and flooding caused as much trouble as drought and wild animals did in the lowlands.

"We have our own provisions," Alerio informed him.

"What, our food's not to your liking?"

Another thing about high country farmers, they were hard to read.

"There are twenty-three of us," Alerio warned.

"Better to feed your men than send it to Shkodër as tax levies," the old man stated. "Have the teamster put the horses in the barn. We get wolves early in the morning."

"Corporal Sabaia, we're not going to have to unpack as much as I thought."

"That will help us in the morning, General," the NCO responded. "I'll set a guard rotation for the night."

"General? We don't get many Generals up here," the headman said. "Come General, let me introduce you to the families. Then we can go sit by the fire and chat."

One trait was shared by all farmers. Once they trusted you, they liked to talk.

***

Darkness came quickly in the mountains. Unfortunately for Sergeant Edon, he still had men traversing the rocks of the ravines. Wearing armor with shields strapped to their backs and holding a spear in one hand, they didn't move as fast as the lightly equipped warden.

At the bottom of the system of gullies, Captain Breuci collected the men as they backed down the final chute. From there, he passed them off to a squad leader who guided them to a grove of trees. Ballaios waited there to warn them to be silent.

While Alerio and Sabaia's detachment walked sentry or sat around fires eating hot food and talking, Breuci and Edon's squads experienced the evening differently. They drank cold water, chewed on tough dried meat, remained quiet, and silently cursed the evening. Because cruelly, the aroma of cooking stew and the sound of pleasant banter drifted to them from the Labeatae war camp. And as much as the smell tortured the Shields in the upper valley, the glow of warm fires just a quarter of a mile away, tormented them the most during the chilly night.

***

At dawn, two columns of men marched up the valley. Behind the sixteen soldiers, a wagon pulled by four horses paced to their rear. Guards in the war camp shouted warnings and in moments clusters of spearmen and slingers raced downhill to meet the threat.

"I believe, sir, we've gotten their attention," Sabaia offered.

"Monunis, Arvin, keep your columns steady," Alerio called out before acknowledging the Corporal's remark. "I count fifty."

"It's difficult with all the jumping around, but I see closer to sixty spearmen," the NCO reported. "And ten slingers."

The committed slingers lined a rise and allowed the warriors to rush ahead.

"Maintain your pace," Alerio encouraged. "We need to give the Captain's element a chance to get into position."

If the spearmen had run directly towards the Shields, they would have arrived quickly. But they stopped to hop around and bellow challenges.

"Come on and fight me."

"If you want some of this, I'm here."

"I'll take your life and that pretty armor."

All were words to bolster their morale and the spirit of the warriors around them. A necessary precursor to battle as no one wanted to charge in alone. The delays also gave the slingers an opportunity to throw slugs.

"Shields," Sabaia ordered when he saw leather slings whizzing over the heads of the slingers.

Drilled and prepared, the Queen's Bearers snapped the shields from their backs and caught the first volley. With projectiles in the air, the spearmen stopped their antics and waited for the slingers to do damage.

"Watch the horses," Alerio reminded the six men assigned to providing barriers to protect the draft animals.

Many a traveling caravan, and King Pyrrhus' army, had been routed by wounding animals and sending them into a frenzy.

"Teamster, get ready," Alerio issued the warning.

The sixteen soldiers, Hektor, and Pharos continued to march the gentle incline. Down the riverbank, water ran over rocks babbling and splashing. Other than the buzzing of slings, and the occasional bellow from a spearman, the valley was almost peaceful. Then, getting their blood hot and their lungs expanded, the spearmen renewed their screaming of war cries and dashed towards the columns.

"Teamster, get the wagon out of here," Alerio barked.

While the horses hauled the transport around, Corporal Sabaia instructed, "Form your assault lines and offset by three."

Arvin stepped out of a column and backed up three steps. Second Squad rotated as if on an axle until they stood beside their squad leader.

Monunis stepped out and First Squad wheeled a half turn, forming a line with their squad leader. Both squads side stepped until the center had a double row of five men, creating wings with three single shields on each end.

Sabaia jogged to the right side, leaving the squad leaders to backup the center. The entire maneuver took only a few heartbeats. Pride in the snappy response swelled Alerio's chest as he jogged to back up the left flank.

***

Pellets rattled the shields, but the Queen's Bearers appreciated the sound. Not because they didn't fear the damage a slinger's projectile could do if unblocked. They treasured the rattling because when it stopped, spearmen would attack. And they far outnumbered the Shields in the lower valley.

The rattling of the slugs stopped.

"Brace!"

Act 7

Chapter 19 – Birth of the Shield-Bearers

A spearhead dipped over the shield wall, glanced off the iron helmet, and bounced from the shoulder armor. Before the spearman reset, Alerio stabbed over the Shield-Bearer. Crying out in pain, the spearman fell away from the barrier.

"Hold your line," Alerio encouraged while hopping to the next Bearer.

Forty, fifty, or sixty enemy warriors might have been against them, but it didn't matter. Only so many spearmen could swarm the eleven-shield line. Stacked up, the Labeatae should have moved the formation. But the Queen's Shield-Bearers had pushed trees and each other while grinding trenches with their feet. Thanks to the drills, they held against the waves of attackers.

Two enterprising spearmen scrambled up the hill on the left. Hunched over, Alerio churned up the incline, slashing as he rounded the last Shield. One blade severed a spearman's hand. As the appendage flopped to the ground, the warrior gripped his wrist. Tumbling down, he fell into the legs of his comrades at the face of the shield wall.

In the confusion of tangled legs and spewing blood, the last Shield-Bearer on the line had a moment without pressure to his front. As he had been trained, he angled his spear to the right and helped the adjacent Shield with his opponents.

Alerio ducked below the thrust of the second warrior. Before the man could pull his spear back, the Legion officer ran his other blade between the spearmen's ribs. Pulling back, Alerio drew the dying man towards him. Before Alerio could twist and free his blade, they both tumbled back, fell down the slope, and ended up behind the shield wall.

"Need help, sir?" a Shield-Bearer asked.

"Watch your front," Alerio sneered while pulling his blade free.

On the far right, Sabaia had the opposite problem.

"Hold your line," he screamed while dashing to the top of the riverbank.

Three warriors had dropped into the river and were splashing forward to get around the end of the defensive line. Chasing the spearmen, pulled Sabaia away from the shield wall. Without backup, the three Shields on the end gave a half a step. Then another, and the defensive line curled.

"Arvin. Stop that deterioration," Alerio called out.

But the squad leader for Second Squad held the weak spot between the last pair of Shields in the doubled center and the first single man on the right.

In situ means in its original place, and a steady, unmoved combat line had an advantage. But once the men shifted their feet to adjust, the integrity of interlocking shields crumbled. With the movement on the right flank, the Shields of First and Second Squads were moments from folding.

Alerio slashed over the shoulders of one man. Raced to another and stabbed to dislocate a climber. No sooner than that one fell into the arms of his comrades, then another spearman attempted to scale a shield. Trapped by his duties, Alerio had no option. If he stopped fighting on the left to help on the right, the left side would falter.

Bellowing reached his ears, and Alerio snapped his head around to look right. Pharos with a shield on each arm bulled his way in behind the weakening line. Bolstered by the reassuring pressure on their backs, the Shield-Bearers got rock solid and increased the stab rate with their spears.

"We can't hold much longer, Colonel," Hektor warned. The youth stepped forward with an armload of new spears. "The Shields are representing themselves with honor. But some are fighting with cracked shafts and several with broken shields. It's time for a change, sir."

Alerio peered over the fighting and scanned up the valley to the war camp. Warriors, a Chief, and slingers stood calmly watching the battle. Seeing no sign of the Captain or the other Shield-Bearers, Alerio indicated an area in the center of the formation.

"We're folding the line," he informed the youth. Then in his command voice. "Collapse the line. Flanks fall back and circle up."

Withdrawing while in contact with an enemy was the maneuver that gave commanders nightmares. If he had Legionaries, Alerio would call for an advance. A healthy dose of hardwood shields hammered into faces would slow down the pursuit and separate the fighters. As it was, he had to depend on each Shield-Bearer to fight his way back and into the defensive circle.

While Hektor carried the replacement spears to the center, Alerio ran to the end of the withdrawing line.

"Back slowly, control the man in front of you," he directed the three Shield-Bearers on the flank.

"General, I've got three against my shield," one of them complained.

Alerio didn't reply. He had five warriors trying to get by him.

***

From up the valley, Astius fumed as he studied the fighting. His spearmen flooded the shield wall and pressed forward. Yet none managed to breach the defensive screen.

"We have them three to one and still they resist," the Labeatae War Chief spit out.

"They seem to be well trained," a warrior noted.

"Too well. I may have to send the reserves across the river to circle behind," Astius mentioned. "I want this over with so we can proceed to Ivanaj."

"It's a long hike, Chief," his Lieutenant of slingers pointed out. "You'll need men with fresh legs when we get there."

"I'm the one who planned this march," Astius reminded the officer. "And it didn't include a protracted battle in this valley. The less time we spend in Ardiaei territory the better."

He wanted to pace or grab a spear and charge into the fight. He did neither. Other than to show his displeasure before punishing an infraction, his status as the chief for a war band required him to be indifferent and above emotional outbursts.

Astius settled for folding his arms across his chest. Then, the shields collapsed, and he felt relief. It lasted until a circle ten feet across formed and his warriors returned to beating uselessly on the shields.

"Send the reserves forward, now."

Before his instructions could be passed to the waiting spearmen, a terrified voice from behind Astius screamed, "Fire. Fire."

With a fatalistic shrug of his shoulders, the War Chief turned around.

***

A double line of shields drove the Labeatae reserves back as if herding a gaggle of geese. Some spearmen resisted and died on the moving wall of spearheads and hardwood. Others stumbled away as their tents, supplies, and provisions went up in flames.

"Sound the retreat," Astius directed. "Everyone across the river."

"We can regroup in Boge," another Lieutenant offered. "Then we'll attack again."

"With what?" the War Chief shot back.

Men in armor the color of a maiden's lips advanced behind a solid wall of shields and in front of a curtain of smoke from the burning camp.

***

Alerio and Sabaia stood back-to-back. While they pressed together, Hektor remained low as he bandaged an injured Shield-Barrier. Over his head, the butt ends of spears poked back into the circle before thrusting ahead. To stand or move from the center of the circle would disrupt the fighting men and get the offender punched by pairs of retracting spears.

With his head turned so Alerio could hear him over the war cries and grunts of men fending off spearmen, Sabaia ask, "What do you suppose happened to Captain Breuci?"

"I have faith he and the Shields are out there and moving towards us," Alerio replied.

Pharos stood behind a short Shield man from First Squad. The disparity in height gave a false impression to the warriors attacking the circle. They assumed the shorter man would be easy while the big Illyrian in the rear rank was the dangerous one. The result of the misunderstanding was a semicircle outside the defensive ring filled with men suffering from wounds to their lower extremities.

"Smoke, General," Pharos shouted.

Alerio didn't need to raise up on the balls of his feet to see the gray smog billowing into the sky.

"I think that's the work of our missing Shields," Alerio suggested.

***

The battles at the upper valley and the lower valley ended abruptly. Warriors flaked off in layers from around the defensive circle and dashed for the riverbank. Already across and hiking northward was War Chief Astius, his command staff, and the surviving spearmen from the reserve force. Soon a long string of freshly dipped warriors and slingers stretched from the lower valley to the village of Boge.

"Do we give chase, sir?" Sabaia inquired.

"I'd say no," Alerio responded. "But that's up to the Captain of the Shield-Bearers. You should ask him."

The rows of shields parted and Altin Breuci strutted through the gap. Standing tall, the young officer had soot and blood on his face, a sword in his hand, and his eyes shown with a fierce pride.

"Sorry it took so long to get here, General," he stated. "They had a mob stashed on the backside of the camp."

"Captain, a smart commander sends in his less competent fighters to soften up the opposition," Alerio mentioned. "The reserves are usually his best warriors."

"Compared to the Queen's Shield-Bearers," Altin shouted, "they were a herd of sheep."

His comment elicited a roar of approval from the men.

"He's become pretty arrogant," Pharos whispered.

"I wouldn't say that too loud about their Captain," Alerio warned. "You're surrounded by his Company of elite soldiers."

***

After Hektor finished treating the injured spearmen, Captain Breuci sent the wagon to Boge with the wounded and the dead. Along with the return of the warriors, there was a note for the Labeatae commander.

War Chief Astius,

We are here. Come fight us and die. Or clear out. In either case, you will be gone from this valley by tomorrow.

Signed,

Altin Breuci, Captain of the Queen's Shield-Bearers

The return note on the back of the parchment was less straight forward but clear in its intent.

Captain Altin Breuci,

Its not out of fear that I leave. My mission has concluded although not to anyone's satisfaction. The valley is yours.

Astius, War Chief of the Labeatae

***

The next day, Ballaios spied on Boge as the war band marched from the village. By midday, the last of the wounded limped away, and peace returned to the border valley. He slipped down the slopes, shimmied over short cliffs, and jogged to Ducaj.

"They're gone," the warden declared.

Alerio fingered the parchment while rereading Astius' message.

"What mission?" he asked. "And who is not satisfied, other than the spearmen and slingers of the war band?"

"Good questions, General Sisera," Breuci acknowledged. "Should we gear up, go after Astius, and find out?"

Alerio chuckled then caught the look on the Captain's face. It would take very little to convince the Shields' officer to go marching after the Labeatae commander.

"No, let them go," Alerio replied. "We've almost reached the deadline. The Queen invested coins in us and it's time she sees the result of her investment."

"Sergeant Edon, in the morning, we march for Ivanaj," Altin directed.

"And Shkodër after that, sir?" the NCO asked.

"As soon as transportation can be arranged," Breuci confirmed.

***

Due to aching muscles, painfully deep bruises, and stitches that pulled on fresh wounds, the parade down the mountain moved slowly.

"The healthy men want to bolt ahead," Sabaia reported to Edon.

"What did you tell them?" the Sergeant inquired.

"That the strength of the Shields' comes from arriving as a solid wall," the Corporal answered.

"Someone should make that a rule," Edon teased.

A man walking behind offered, "It's rule number three, Sergeant."

"It is," Edon verified.

***

After spending the night on the trail, the Company reached the trading road the next morning. Although trees blocked their view, they recognized the location, and the men increased their pace as they neared their camp.

"When we built the stockade, I hated the idea of it," a Shield confessed.

"You hated the idea of coming to Ivanaj in the first place," another man reminded him.

"That's true, but I disliked having to build the fort more," the Shield added. Men marching around him laughed, and he protested. "No, really, I don't like woodworking. I'm a soldier, not a carpenter."

"You like cookfires, don't you," someone joked. "Cutting firewood is woodworking."

Chuckles ran through the ranks.

"Can anyone else smell that?" a Shield in the third row questioned. "It smells like there was a forest fire."

In the center of the formation, Captain Breuci also noticed the aroma of burnt lumber.

"Sergeant Edon, take a squad to Ivanaj and see if they've had a fire in the village," he directed. "Report to me if Chieftain Gazmend needs anything. I'd go myself, but I want to get the men settled in."

The NCO jogged to the front and pulled Third Squad out of formation. In moments, the Sergeant and the squad vanished around a bend. Shortly after, the main body of the Shields turned off the road. As they marched through the trees, the stink of burned wood grew stronger.

**

The flames had died long ago, the smoke cleared, and the ash cooled. What was left of the stockade were a few stubs of beams with charred tips.

"Sabaia, take some men and check to see if the craftsmen made it out," Breuci ordered. "We'll start the search for bodies and personal goods at the gate. Or what's left of it."

They didn't have to shift through much rubble before uncovering bodies. The three Shields left to tend the fort were buried under scorched boards just inside the old gateway.

"They were dead before the fire or smoke got to them," Hecker informed Alerio and Altin. "The sword cuts and spear punctures are deep. And sirs, they have no wounds on their backs. These men died fighting the enemy."

"What enemy?" Alerio asked. "We stopped the Labeatae. Who else carries hate for us?"

"General Sisera, my father had a saying," Pharos described, "if you lose sheep every night and there's no blood trail, stop hunting for predators, and look to your neighbors."

Sabaia picked his way through the wreckage of the camp. As he got closer to the gates, Altin could see an object in his hand.

"What have you got, Corporal?"

Sabaia balanced a piece of bright, but pale salmon colored leather in his hand.

"The leather craftsmen, carpenter, and metalworker died at their wagons," he related. "From their wounds, I'd say they didn't even put up a fight."

"Neighbors," Pharos mumbled. Then aloud, he repeated. "Look to your neighbors."

***

A long while later, Edon and Third Squad escorted Chieftain Gazmend to the burned-out fort.

"When the smoke was reported, I brought men to investigate," the old Lord explained. "But the raiders had already rowed away by then."

"How do you know they used Lake Shkodra?" Altin inquired.

"When it got light, I followed their footprints," Gazmend answered. "Once, Captain, I was the best tracker in the region. A band of sixty men came from the lake, did the foul deed, and retreated back to the lake."

"Are there outlaws around the lake?" Alerio asked.

Altin ground his teeth and answered, "Not with boats or sixty armed men."

"Then who has sixty men and boats?" Alerio asked.

"A King's phalanx," Captain Breuci replied.

"Neighbors," Pharos whispered.

Chapter 20 – Audition by Combat

One of Gazmend's trusted fishing boat captains took two days to row to Shkodër, sell his fish, and locate Captain Epulon. When he returned as a solo boat, he explained.

"Epulon said it would take him a few days to find the right raider ships," the fisherman informed them. "I was surprised as the beach at the city was crowded with raiders."

"Just not the right ones," Captain Breuci guessed. "You did well, and I thank you."

"My brother has a farm at Ducaj. I should be thanking you."

"You just did," Altin assured him.

After the fisherman left the campsite, Alerio questioned Breuci, "Why is a Queen's Captain being selective about which ships come for us?"

"I'm sure Epulon has a good reason," Altin replied.

**

Three nights after the report from the fisherman, a sentry woke Altin Breuci and Alerio Sisera.

"There's a man at the perimeter, sirs," the Shield whispered. "He claims to be a Captain Epulon."

Altin and Alerio tossed off their blankets and jumped to their feet.

"In the middle of the night?" Alerio questioned.

"I have no idea," Altin admitted. "Let's go collect Epulon and find out."

In moments, they returned to the campsite with the raider skipper.

"Having trouble sleeping?" Alerio joshed.

"Yes. But it's more than this midnight run," Epulon replied.

Alerio placed a piece of wood on the fire and blew on the embers until flames crept up the sides of the log.

"Shkodër has become an armed camp," Epulon said. "King's men are checking everyone coming in or out. It started after the attempt on the Prince. But then the Dardani moved warriors to our northeast border and the Labeatae attacked you."

"So, what are you doing out in the dark?" Altin asked.

"Hold on," Alerio interrupted. "How do you know about the Labeatae attack?"

"Captain Mergim returned and reported the destruction of your stockade," Epulon replied. Breuci jumped to his feet and stormed away from the fire. "What's wrong with Altin?"

"Finish your thoughts," Alerio urged.

"Mergim told us the Labeatae attacked your camp. And although he searched, his men couldn't locate you, Altin, or any of the volunteers," the raider Captain continued. "He said based on the fire, not to expect survivors. But then the fisherman arrived and said you needed about five ships."

"We have fifty-seven in the Company, and they are very much alive," Altin said from the dark. He stepped into the light and Alerio could see the anger on the young Captain's face, "plus equipment. We need six but five will do."

"I have four more raiders loyal to the Queen, coming in over the next two days," Epulon told them. "We can take you out a few at a time and you can sneak into the city."

His plan sounded reasonable, and, for a few moments, the three commanders were silent. The fire crackled and the flames cast a flickering light that pushed back the darkness. Then Captain Breuci sat, picked a branch from the fire, and smashed it against the burning log. Sparks burst into the air.

As the embers rode the hot flames towards the sky, Altin announced, "No, that doesn't work for me or the Shields. We will not sneak into the city like driftwood washing ashore."

The command campsite rested in the middle of the Company bivouac. Men awake heard their Captain and a buzzing of agreement came from out of the darkness.

"The phalanxes won't like you bringing an armed unit into the city," Epulon advised.

"Rule number four," Altin responded.

"What's that?"

Alerio tapped the raider Captain on the shoulder, held up four fingers and said, "Rule number four, create pride in your unit by any means necessary."

"What does that have to do with anything?"

Altin stood, filled his lungs and across the dark encampment, he shouted, "Shields. March in or stealth?"

Voices exploded from the dark.

"March in, Captain."

"It's modified, but that's rule six," Alerio mentioned. "Ask for advice before making any decision."

"I don't understand," Epulon whined. "You need to get approval from your spearmen before acting."

"We aren't simple spearmen," Altin boasted.

***

Three days later, five raider ships rowed across the lake heading for the beach at Shkodër. First to land was Epulon's ship making Captain Breuci, General Sisera, and a squad the first men ashore.

"Altin," the raider skipper who ferried Breuci out to Ivanaj sneered. "Heard your venture as a ground commander failed. Messed that up as badly as your turn at commanding a ship, did you?"

Altin tried to ignore the skipper. But when he turned to look at the lake to be sure his other men made it to the beach, the crews of neighboring ships laughed. Spinning around, Altin marched to the skipper.

"What are you going to…?" the raider began while pulling a knife.

Altin Breuci kicked him in his right thigh. The leg flew back forcing the skipper to lean forward to keep his balance. It placed his face in the path of Altin's uppercut. Flying backward the raider skipper, who moments before was full of derision, landed hard. Straddling him, Altin kicked the knife away and poked the raider in the chest.

"Never again insult my Company or me," Altin exclaimed before heading back to the landing area.

Alerio bent over the skipper and hissed, "Captain Breuci figured out rule number one."

The ships began reaching the shore and Shields jumped to the beach. Pharos leaped from the last ship and ran up the embankment. Moments later, he returned with two porters and a two wheeled cart. They began transferring items from the vessel to the cart.

In short order, fifty-seven men in pale salmon colored armor, holding battled scarred shields, and long poles formed up on the beach.

"Where to sir?" Edon inquired. "The fort?"

Altin lifted his face and stared at the fort on the hill. A beat later, he shook his head as he decided on a destination.

"Sergeant, march us to the Queen's residence," he directed. "She should know that we have returned."

"Yes, sir," Edon acknowledged. "Corporal Sabaia, take a squad out front and clear the street."

A moment later, the Shields marched off the beach, up the bank, and into Shkodër. Close behind the last rank, Pharos and the porters pushed the cart up the incline, trying to stay close to the formation.

***

Due to the threat against the Prince and pressure along the borders, five spearmen were assigned to guard the house overlooking the Buna River. Two sat in the rear, their spears resting against the home's exterior wall, and two stood in the courtyard under the room with a view. The final sentry blocked the front door as the last line of defense.

None were ready when men in bright armor raced to encircle the house and disarmed four of the guards.

"No one may pass," the last one standing declared.

Corporal Sabaia stood at the bottom of a short flight of steps.

"Please have the Queen come out," the NCO directed.

"No one may pass," the sentry stated again.

"You aren't very smart, are you?" Sabaia suggested. He glanced at the Shields standing on either side of him. "Bring him down to me."

The guard lowered his center of gravity by dropping into a fighting stance. His blade extended, he waited to defend the door, to the death.

Two poles, thrown with power and accuracy, impacted the Sentry. One caved in the front of his helmet scrambling his thinking, and the other punched him in the chest. He collapsed, fell down the steps, and stopped when his body rolled against the Corporal's legs.

"What is the meaning of this?" a woman demanded from the doorway.

Sabaia looked up and saluted, "Ma'am, we were just improving your security."

"Improving how? I thought the warriors were doing a respectable job," Jeta stated. "Who are you?"

"Ma'am, we are the advance unit for the Queen's Shield-Bearers. Under the command of Captain Breuci."

"You're the volunteers who went to Ivanaj with Altin and Battle Commander Sisera?"

"Yes, ma'am."

"I was told you died in a raid by a Labeatae war band."

"My Queen, that is an exaggeration."

"I can see that but…"

The scraping of marching feet broke the Queen's concentration. She watched silently as the courtyard in front of her house filled with a Company of men in bright colored armor.

"Queen Jeta," Captain Breuci announced as he marched to the foot of the steps, "may I present your Shield-Bearers."

"Elite soldiers, like King Philip's?" she inquired. "But how? You were all killed. Captain Mergim reported the incident."

"Mergim has a lot of explaining to do," Alerio said as he marched to stand beside Altin. "My Queen, your Shields are as competent as any Macedonian unit."

On the road below the courtyard, armored men gathered. Once they had fifty or so, Prince Agron paced to a position in front of them.

"Release my mother, reprobates," he challenged. "Come down and fight me."

"Sir, that's impossible," Sergeant Edon responded from the back of the formation.

"Impossible? How can you say that?" Agron demanded. "March off the hill and do battle."

"Prince Agron, it's impossible for the Queen's Shield-Bearers to fight the man they are sworn to protect."

The Prince looked puzzled until his mother strolled down the steps and walked proudly between the ranks. She stopped at the rear of the courtyard and waved at her son.

"Agron, do come up," she called down. "There is someone you should promote."

"Promote?" Agron asked. "Never mind, I'll come up and you can explain."

Four bodyguard joined him as he made his way up the drive.

"Shields, brace," Sergeant Edon ordered. "Present, spears."

Fifty-seven poles lowered to the top of shields as the Prince reached the courtyard.

Agron ran his eyes over the uniformed Company.

"I don't recognize their region of origin," he admitted.

"That's because they are from your house, my son," Jeta said while linking her arm in his.

"But they're unproven," Agron advised as he and his mother walked to Captain Altin Breuci.

"Then we'll have to think of a test," she said. "But the Battle Commander can't be involved. This has to be Illyrian against Illyrian."

"Prince Agron. Queen Jeta," Altin greeted them with a salute. "May I suggest a trial by combat."

***

The test was scheduled for two days after the Shields arrived in the city. And almost as if the Prince's street festival had returned, the city came alive. Wine and beer flowed, and food vendors claimed the corners of intersections. But unlike the birthday celebration, this street party hovered around the path leading up to the fort. As a result, the streets below the hill were crowded with people. And while no one wore masks, some of the revelers still threw off their inhibitions.

"You could have offered to duel Mergim," Alerio said to Altin, "and avoided all this."

People on the street bumped their shoulders as they marched alongside the columns.

"It wouldn't have given the Shields an opportunity to gain respect," the Captain replied. "Sergeant Edon. Keep our columns straight."

"Yes, sir," the NCO answered before scolding the Shields.

Ahead of the main group, Corporal Sabaia and a squad marched in a vee formation to clear the street. In theory, it sounded like a good idea. Except for the women who wanted to touch a Shield-Bearer as they marched by.

"This would have been easier if Queen Jeta hadn't bragged to everyone about her Shields," Altin noted.

Disrupting the orderly columns, women and girls dashed into the ranks and wrapped their arms around the necks of the Shields.

"Sergeant Edon…"

"I know, sir. Keep the columns straight," the NCO acknowledged. Then loudly, he instructed. "Put down the women and march. And women, please release the Shields and let them march."

Giggles and laughter came from the formation and Altin ignored the sounds as he marched stiffly down the street.

"This must have been what it was like when the Silver Shields entered a city after one of King Alexander's victories," Hektor exclaimed.

From the rear of the Shields, he and Pharos had a splendid view of the antics.

"I bet behind the Silver Shields were a couple of slaves pushing a cart," the big man grumbled.

"We're not slaves," Hector reminded him.

"But we are pushing this cursed cart."

When the shield formation turned off the street and onto the path to the fort, the women got set down and the Shields began the hike to the top. At the rear, the Greek youth and the big Illyrian bent their backs and pushed harder.

***

King Pleuratus the Second, and his advisors huddled inside the pavilion. Queen Jeta and a few Chieftains talked near the front and Prince Agron stood with several military Captains between the King and Queen. Off to one side, Warlord Caden Rian and his Lieutenant Enda scanned the first participant to arrive. Servants carrying and passing out beverages meandered through the rest of those gathered to watch the contest.

"Captain Breuci, good luck to you and to the Shields," Alerio said while saluting.

"It's been an honor training with you, General Sisera," Altin stated.

"That's the last time you'll have to call me that," Alerio reminded him. "But I know the men are ready and so is their Captain."

Alerio took a last look over the ranks of the Shields. Their bright armor cleaned and oiled, their iron helmets buffed, their shields repaired, and the poles in their hand selected to eliminate knots that might cause weak spots in the wood. Almost in sync, their pale salmon-colored cloaks blew in the morning breeze with Alerio's red Legion cape. He saluted one last time, turned, and marched away from the Shield-Bearers.

Alerio reached the pavilion just as the crowd let out a cheer. The King's phalanx lumbered from a barracks. Locked in a tight formation, they shuffled to keep their ranks close. Above their heads, the blunt ends of shafts showed they obeyed the rules. The poles weren't safe by any means. They could inflict damage, but the lack of sharp steel reduced the chance of slicing through shields or armor and into flesh.

Beside the sixty-four-man phalanx, Captain Mergim marched with a confident swagger.

"Battle Commander, come over here," the Queen instructed.

Alerio moved forward then stood outside a ring of visiting Chieftains for a moment. A hand pushed him from behind.

"Get in there and tell a few lies," Gazmend told him. "That way the Lords will know you're as dishonest as they are."

Jeta reached across the group, took the old man's hands, and drew him to her side.

"You are a curmudgeon," she teased. "Don't listen to him, Sisera. Whenever we make Gazmend leave his valley, he gets out of sorts."

"Didn't make me," the old Chieftain countered. "I came to watch the Shields. They trained in my region and got their first taste of blood defending my farmers. Least I can do is show my support."

Alerio glanced to the back of the tent looking for Gazmend's usual escort of old men. To his surprise, Ballaios stood with a foot on a bench along with a couple of fit looking warriors. By the expression on the warden's face, Alerio could tell he wasn't happy to be out of his mountain valley either.

A marshal assigned by the King rode to Mergim and indicated a direction. Then he galloped to Breuci and pointed to a position facing the phalanx. The direction wasn't lost on the pavilion crowd.

It'd be difficult for the Queen's Shield-Bearers to make a good impression for Jeta with their backs to her and the people in the pavilion. And, if the drill ran as expected, Captain Mergim and his eight ranks would easily slice through the men in the brightly colored armor and emerge to glorious applause by King Pleuratus, his Chieftains, and their parties.

"I warned you, Sisera," Gazmend grumbled. "They're all liars and cheats."

"Believe me, my Lord," Alerio said with a wink, "Captain Breuci is aware of it."

No one had noticed that under the Legion cloak, Battle Commander Sisera wore his combat gear rather than his ceremonial armor.

Chapter 21 - Martial Discord

Eight columns wide and set in ranks eight deep, created a solid block of soldiers. The phalanx marched to the far end of the drill field and stumbled. Turning proved awkward because of the tight spacing of the men. Finally, the formation aligned to face the tent, halted, and waited with sixty-four poles raised to the sky.

On one side of the pavilion, a Chieftain boasted, "All the King's phalanx needs to do to embarrass these famed Shield-Bearers is to march through their defensive line. Once the last rank pushes aside the Shield-Boys, Altin Breuci and his volunteers will be exposed for what they are, incompetents. And it will be proof that they're of no use to their Queen or King. I'm taking bets on Captain Mergim's command."

Compounding the insult, the Lord, without saying his name, included the Battle Commander by pointing at him. That could only be the result of comments made by Mergim concerning General Sisera.

Alerio jerked and started to respond but a hand on his arm stopped him.

"The Chieftain is Mergim's uncle," Jeta told him. "He's upholding his family's pride. It's best to let him have his say."

"Yes, ma'am," Alerio allowed.

Coins were pulled from purses, and the tent came alive with the bustling of people placing bets. Most were stacked for the phalanx, but a few tossed coins on the pile backing the Shields.

***

Across the drill field, the Queen's Shield-Bearers marched along the boundary to a spot halfway to the pavilion. In columns of seven, they performed a crisp right turn and started across the field.

The observers in the pavilion weren't sure what to expect. A clustered attack by the Shields or even a phalanx seemed the obvious choices to stopping the bull horns of the King's phalanx. When a double line of men dropped out of the marching columns far from the center of the field, the observers were puzzled. Then another two ranks stopped, followed by two more halting farther on, until the Shield-Bearers stretched across the drill field like staggered steps.

"Shields. Left face," Sergeant Edon instructed. The men snapped to the left, placing their backs to the pavilion. Then the NCO called out. "Come abreast with Seventh Squad, forward march."

In several paces the Shields collapsed the steps until they stood in two ranks, forming a defensive barrier. But two ranks against a dynamic phalanx was so thin that all betting stopped. At the conclusion of the movement, fifty-six poles raised in the air. As if posts in a loose picket fence, they faced the hammerhead of the phalanx.

"King's phalanx, forward," Captain Mergim ordered.

His Rank Leaders picked up and repeated the command. In response, the unstoppable mass of the formation shuffled forward.

The cloaks of the Shields waved in the breeze as they waited for the phalanx to reach their lines.

***

As if the ram on a ship-of-war, the phalanx bore down on the defensive pickets. At fifteen feet, the soldiers in the first four rows lowered their spears. Although blunt, the shafts projecting forward presented thirty-two rods aimed at just sixteen Shields and their Captain. In fifteen heartbeats, they would…

"First and Second Squads, lateral out," Captain Breuci directed.

As the two squads jogged from the center of the impact zone, the viewers in the pavilion gasped. The Shields had relinquished the middle of the field, admitting defeat.

But Captain Breuci wasn't finished. Lifting his arms from his sides, Altin ordered, "Flanks, fold inward, march."

The squads on the left and right wheeled inward, closing in on the sides of the phalanx. After issuing the order, Breuci jogged to the First and Second Squads.

"Spears," Sergeant Edon bellowed from the left. On the other side of the folding wings, Corporal Sabaia repeated, "Spears."

Double rows of poles jabbed into the sides of the phalanx. The soldiers, tucked in close to the men in front to provide pushing power, were punched into the men marching besides them. Thrown into chaos, the soldiers attempted to bring their long spears and shields around. But the tight formation hampered their movements. At the front, the fourth rank felt the touch from behind lift. They froze.

The third rank recognized the absence and they stopped. Then the second and, finally, the forward rank paused and looked back to see where the rest of the phalanx had gone.

"First Squad. Second Squad," Captain Breuci exclaimed. "Get back in the fight."

General Alerio Sisera had asked if Monunis from the first and Arvin from the second were fast. Now, the reason for his question became clear. The squad leaders raced to the front of the phalanx setting a blistering pace for their squads.

As if the Shield-Bearers had dropped from the sky, the vicious pokes by the poles that destroyed the integrity of the phalanx, visited ruin on the first two ranks of Captain Mergim's command.

In the pavilion, Lords shouted curses at the collapse of the phalanx. A few, including Chieftain Gazmend, and his warden countered by cheering.

Queen Jeta hid her face behind her hand to prevent anyone from seeing her gloat. But her eyes glistened with tears of joy. At last, she had an elite force to protect her son. One loyal to Agron with a worthy Captain, who would follow the Prince's directions.

The soldiers, still on their feet, were slowly collecting into groups facing outboard. As they formed up, the Rank Leaders relayed an order.

"Spearheads, use your spearheads," Captain Mergim bellowed.

From the center of the phalanx, the interior men flipped their spears around, revealing steel heads. Narrower in their leaf shape than the spears of the Shields, the spearheads were designed to stab an enemy, then withdraw smoothly to rejoin the heaving spears of the phalanx. The presence of the deadly tips changed the contest.

"Steel," two Shield-Bearers yelled when they saw the metal tips.

All along their double lines, the Shields alerted each other to the danger.

Sergeant Edon on the left side put his hands to his mouth and shouted, "Steel."

After hearing the warning, Pharos and Hektor wheeled the cart to Captain Breuci.

"Third and Fifth Squads, you are on containment," Altin instructed.

The sight of steel spearheads brought the uproar in the pavilion to a fever pitch.

"I should order the guards in before someone gets hurt," King Pleuratus offered.

"Those are two elite and highly agitated units, sir," a Chieftain observed. "If you send in warriors, you'll get men killed. And even then, I'm not sure if they could get control."

***

Sixty-four soldiers, some armed with spears against fifty-six Shields all with wooden poles, gave an advantage to the phalanx. Then Third and Fifth Squads ran to the cart while tossing away their sticks. As they passed the cart, Pharos threw spears to them.

Once fully armed, the sixteen men formed a two-rank containment line between the pavilion and the fighting.

"Fall back," Breuci commanded the remainder of the Shields.

Peeling off from the sides of the phalanx, the squads covered each other's withdrawal. Soon, two lines of Shields reached the containment line and reformed into a defensive formation two shields deep.

"Lock your shields," Sergeant Edon and Corporal Sabaia instructed. "No one gets through until we get new orders."

In rushes, the soldiers attempted to break the shield wall. But like the warriors of Labeatae in the mountains, each wave was repelled. Stopped by the interlocking shields, the soldiers suffered punishment from the ruthless hammering of the poles. After several attacks, the soldiers fell back and scowled at the Shields.

Captain Altin Breuci made an exaggerated sweep of his head as if checking on each of his Shields individually. Then he performed a sharp about-face and marched to the front of the pavilion.

"My Queen, the battle is yours," he declared. "Your Shield-Bearers can hold the enemy at bay, or release them, as you see fit."

"Prince Agron should issue the decision," Jeta suggested.

The Prince was dazed at the speed at which the Shields had broken the phalanx. While he knew the test against the phalanx was Altin's idea, he wasn't aware the Shields practiced the maneuvers before they left Ivanaj.

Out on the drill field, soldiers waited on the far side of the shield wall. A few, angry at the defeat, attempted to push their way through. They were beaten down by the poles of the second rank.

Also stuck behind the shields and stalking among his soldiers, Captain Mergim beat his fists against his hips. His fury barely contained.

"Warlord Rian, what do you think," Agron asked the Celtic commander, "should I allow them to pass?"

"Prince, it's never a clever idea to give a crushed enemy a chance for one last strike," the Warlord remarked. "Let them come through a narrow funnel for control."

"Captain Breuci. Form a tunnel of shields as a way through," Agron directed.

"Right away, my Prince."

Altin marched to the shield wall and spoke with Edon. A moment later, the Sergeant pulled back two lines of Shields until they formed a passageway through the wall.

Everyone expected Mergim and his Rank Leaders to come through first. Instead of the NCOs, soldiers of the phalanx filed between the shields. Even if they wanted revenge, none had an opening between the tightly locked shields to extract retribution.

"Come Sisera," Gazmend encouraged, "let's go congratulate Captain Breuci on the victory."

Alerio glanced at the Queen for permission. With the battle between Illyrian forces concluded, she waved him towards the drill field.

"Lord Gazmend, it'll be my pleasure," Alerio said.

Keeping his arm bent, Alerio allowed the ancient Chieftain to lean on his forearm. They marched out of the pavilion a little faster than Gazmend's old legs would have allowed.

***

Being angry about the humiliation, the soldiers stomped to the passageway. Coming through in uneven groups caused the entrance to clog. Pushing and shoving added to the confusion further aggravating the situation on the other side of the Shields.

"Captain Breuci, congratulations," Gazmend greeted Altin. He released Alerio's arm and took the Captain's hands in his. "You've made my region very proud."

A new round of yelling from the tunnel told of another issue. Alerio and Altin ignored it.

Then Sergeant Edon shouted, "Captain, duck."

Altin squatted dragging Gazmend to the ground. While Breuci and the old man blindly followed the advice, Alerio dropped to a knee and spun to get his eyes on the problem.

Captain Mergim with his legs spread wide and his left arm back for balance, had his right arm high overhead from where he released a spear. The missile itself arched into the sky.

Alerio caught a glimpse of the shaft as it tilted over. Then the spear became a single point of steel falling back to earth. Gazmend grunted. By the time Alerio rotated and looked down, the old man lay pinned to the dirt.

Without thinking, Alerio pulled the shaft from Gazmend's chest. Snapping around, he launched the spear in an almost flat trajectory. It flew, arrow like, to Mergim. The steel spearhead entered the front of his throat.

Mergim's Rank Leaders, seeing their Captain jolted off his feet, pulled their swords and charged Alerio.

"Defend the General," Corporal Sabaia instructed.

Six Shields pulled out of the shield wall and ran to intercept the eight NCOs from the phalanx. They blocked five.

***

Alerio came up on one leg. The other he rocked back while drawing his gladius. The first Rank Leader caught a foot in his mid-section and the second a blade through his forehead. The third forced Alerio to fall back and roll away to avoid the tip of a sica.

After two tumbles, Alerio came up on his feet in a guard position. But the fight was over. Altin Breuci stood over the downed Rank Leader, but he wasn't still. The Shield-Bearer Captain was kicking the wound in the side of the phalanx Sergeant.

"We won, you animals," he said with one final kick. Then he threatened. "Rank Leaders, get your people off my drill field before I follow my heart and release my Shields."

Ballaios raced by Altin and Alerio. He dropped to his knees and scooped the old man off the ground.

"We should have stayed in our valley," the warden cried as he carried Gazmend's body to the pavilion.

***

The Shield-Bearers adjusted to a defensive posture around their Captain and Alerio. Glaring, they lunged at any soldier who wandered too close. Soon after setting the semi-circle, a hole opened, and Queen Jeta entered the safety zone.

"Battle Commander Sisera, you need to leave Shkodër," she informed Alerio. "Mergim has a powerful family, and the Rank Leader you killed is the son of an important Chieftain. Captain Breuci, assign men to escort Sisera to the docks. And put him on a fast raider out of Illyrian territory."

"Yes, my Queen," Altin confirmed. "About the Shields, ma'am?"

"The Queen's Shield-Bearers, Captain Breuci," she corrected before walking to the defensive ring. Glancing back, she added. "Come see me later, Captain. We'll dine and talk about your future."

***

Alerio and Hektor jogged along the street in the center of the formation. Around them, First and Second Squads maintained the pace and kept the street clear.

"I miss the street festival," Hektor noted. Then he added. "Sir, you didn't get a trade agreement or safe passage for your transports."

"They aren't my merchant vessels," Alerio replied, "they belong to my father, Senator Maximus."

The formation reached the river embankment, hustled down to the shoreline, and located Epulon's ship. Alerio and Hektor scrambled aboard just as a mob appeared at the top of the bank.

"My Chieftain wants words with General Sisera," a big warrior proclaimed. "Send him up to me."

Arvin and Monunis formed their squads into a double line.

"We can't do that," Arvin shouted back. "The General has already launched."

"What are you talking about?" the warrior demanded. "He's standing right there."

"Right where?" Monunis asked. "I don't see him."

Neither squad leader had turned to look at Alerio or the ship. But their antics gave Epulon's oarsmen a chance to rush on board while the soldiers pushed the raider vessel into the river.

At the top of the bank, someone handed the big man a spear. After checking the balance, he reared back, and launched the shaft. It flew up, curved over, and dropped towards the retreating ship.

With sixty oarsmen and fifty fighters on the deck, the weapon was about to kill someone. Probably not Alerio or Hektor but certainly one of the crewmen.

Alerio picked up a cask of water, hopped forward, then back, and jerked from side to side, before figuring the spears trajectory. Finally, he lunged and held the barrel over an oarsman's head.

244

The spear split the barrel, the staves came apart, and water cascaded over the rowers. Dug into a piece of hardwood, the spearpoint fell harmlessly to the rowing bench. Then the shaft arched over and hit a wet rower.

"Better than the point," the oarsman declared while wiping the water from his head.

"Stroke, stroke," Captain Epulon called to the rowers. "The excitement is over people. Stroke, stroke."

The raider caught the current and between the smooth strokes of the oars and the flow of the Buna River, they left the city behind. Twenty-five miles later, the ship reached the mouth of the river and rowed onto the Adriatic Sea and away from Illyria.

Act 8

Chapter 22 – Transit Messina

Three days later, a merchant ship rowed out of the main current, bounced through the counter flow along the banks, and stroked into the harbor of Messina.

"We should be home in few days, sir," Hektor offered. "From the looks of it, you'll have no trouble finding a ride."

Alerio studied the ships at Messina. In addition to the Legion warships riding anchor in the middle of the harbor, others rested on the beach alongside Syracuse ships-of-war and the biremes favored by the Sons of Mars. In addition to the military vessels, several merchant ships were tied to the piers. After taking in the sight, Alerio decided there were too many vessels in the harbor.

"I'm not sure any of these are leaving for Ostia," he speculated. "This looks like the waypoint of a campaign."

The transport rowed to a docking spot and sailors jumped to the pier. After they tied off the vessel, Alerio walked to the Captain.

"Thank you for the ride," he commented. "I don't think I could have spent another day in that place."

"Few honest citizens want to live in an Illyrian pirate community," the skipper commiserated. "Imagine my surprise when you showed up on the beach."

"Imagine my surprise when an honest merchant beached to trade with pirates," Alerio replied.

"They have excellent goods to trade," the Captain said in his defense.

Alerio studied the skipper to see if he was blessed of Coalemus. Either the man was touched by the God of Stupid or he was simply oblivious to the honest merchant remark. Having nothing else to say to the skipper, Alerio handed over a handful of Bronze and went to meet Hektor on the dock.

"Where to now, sir?"

"They must have a port master, we'll start there."

After Hektor hired for a handcart, he loaded their bags, and the two walked down the pier to the warehouses. At the divide between the buildings, they left the dock and strolled into Massina.

War had been bad for most of the cities on the Island of Sicilia. But for the former Sons of Mars stronghold, war had been more than kind. As a military transit for Legion warships, Messina had new buildings and taller defensive walls.

"Tribune, where is the port master's office?" Alerio asked a passing staff officer.

At first it seemed the officer would ignore Alerio. But a shadow crossed his face, and he turned in a huff.

"Why are you addressing me?" he demanded. "Do I look like your friendly neighborhood oracle?"

Alerio had a long history of dealing with disagreeable staff officers. Any other time or on a different day, he would walk away. But Alerio had his fill of running and cowering in Illyria. Plus, it was bad form for a Battle Commander to knuckle under to a staff officer.

"Let me put it this way," Alerio said calmly while stepping forward and putting his nose a finger's width from the officer's snout. "I asked a question and I require a reply."

"Colonel Sisera, there's a Centurion with an escort heading this way," Hektor warned.

The staff officer must have missed Alerio's rank because he smiled and sneered, "We'll see who is answering questions now."

Alerio traveled in a linen shirt, rough woolen pants, and a wide brimmed felt petasos. The only things Legion in his wardrobe were the dagger on his hip and the hobnailed boots on his feet. The approaching officer and his escorts had no way of recognizing Alerio as a senior officer. When they arrived, the two Legionary guards stepped to their officer's sides but kept their spears on their shoulders.

"Is there a problem, sir?" the Centurion inquired.

His inflection was one of exhaustion while his faced showed disinterest.

"This miscreant assaulted me," the Tribune complained. "I want him held for punishment."

"Sir, you know Consul Cotta has ordered us to board for Lipari," the Centurion pointed out. "We don't have time to deal with civilians."

"Must I remind you that Consul Cotta is my cousin," the staff officer bragged. "You will take this vagabond into custody."

"Tribune Pecuniola, where would I take him?" the combat officer pleaded.

In the brief interval while the staff officer conjured up an answer, Alerio interrupted.

"How about the port master's office?" he offered.

248

"That's not going to…"

"Tribune Pecuniola, silence your mouth before you find yourself on the punishment post," Alerio growled. Then to the infantry officer, he reported. "I apologize for wasting your time, Centurion. I'm Colonel Alerio Carvilius Sisera of the Central Legion."

"Yes, sir," the Centurion allowed.

"Now, if you'll point me to the port master's office, I'll be on my way."

"No, sir, you'll be coming with me," the Centurion stated.

"Didn't you hear, I'm a Battle Commander," Alerio said again.

"Yes, sir, and I believe you," the infantry officer told Alerio. "And that's why I'm taking you to headquarters. You see, sir. Consul Cotta fired Colonel Quintus Cassius three days ago. Ever since, he's been sacrificing to Sancus and asking the God of Oaths and Honesty for an experienced Battle Commander."

"And here I am," Alerio whined.

"Yes, sir, here you are," the Centurion stated. "Please come this way."

Hektor and the escorts followed with the baggage, as Alerio and the infantry officer headed deeper into the city.

"That's the port master's office," the Centurion stated, directing Alerio's attention to a small building across the street from the warehouses.

"So it is," Alerio replied as they marched by the entrance. "Good to know for future reference."

※※※

Two blocks into Massina, they saw men run from a building and scatter. Alerio reached for his dagger.

"That's the headquarters building for Geminus Legion South," the Centurion told him. "You've nothing to fear, yet, Colonel."

While no physical attack followed the scramble, a verbal tirade rolled from the open windows.

"And that, sir, is Consul Cotta," the Centurion warned. "Consul Geminus is marching south of Palermo."

"Who are you with, Centurion?"

"Geminus Legion South, sir. We've been assigned to Consul Cotta," the infantry officer told him. "A third of Cotta Legion East is shipwrecked on Lipari or lost at sea. And their Battle Commander, Quintus Cassius, has been relieved of command."

"And that's where I come in?" Alerio questioned.

"Maybe, sir."

They reached the doorway, and the rant became words. And the words rolled out like thunder.

"Four Legions. One stalled at Himera with an unruly cavalry Centurion. My partner sweeping south of Palermo and out of touch," Consul General Cotta bellowed. "And most of my premier Legion is lost to the sea or stranded on Lipari. Is there no one around me competent enough to take command? Must I do everything myself?"

The two escorts extended their arms to stop Hektor.

"You don't want to go in there," they cautioned.

While Hektor and the Legionaries stopped, Alerio and the Centurion marched into the full force of Consul/General Cotta's fury.

***

A fierce man of average height with a permanent scowl on his face paced the floor. Turning to the doorway, he glared at the intruders.

"What is the meaning of this, Centurion?" Cotta demanded. "Aren't you supposed to be organizing the surviving Centuries of Legion East?"

"I am, ah, or rather was, sir," the infantry officer stammered.

"Well, which is it?" Cotta snapped. "Are you doing it? Have done it? Or have no intention of following my orders?"

"Sir..." the Centurion began when Alerio placed his hand on the infantry officer's shoulder.

"That will be all, Centurion," Alerio instructed while stepping in front of him. "You're dismissed."

"He's what?" Cotta barked. "Who are you to undermine my orders?"

"Colonel Alerio Carvilius Sisera of the Central Legion," Alerio announced while saluting. "I was in transit from Illyria, and I commandeered the Centurion to bring me here."

Aurelius Cotta swept a hand at the infantry officer, dismissing him. Then he strutted to Alerio and studied the out of uniform Battle Commander.

"I know your father, Spurius Maximus," Cotta remarked. "And I remember your reports to the Senate. Very impressive. But, as much as Spurius and I fight over politics, I don't know about sending his only son on a suicide mission. That would open too wide a gulf between us."

Alerio thought about refusing an operation that started with the notion of self-annihilation. He could walk away. There wasn't a Senate commission authorizing his position.

251

But, then again, someone would be assigned or selected to lead the mission.

"You have part of a Legion trapped on Lipari," Alerio repeated what he heard from the Centurion and during the Consul's tirade. "You either want someone to go in and help Cotta Legion East fight their way to the beach for extraction. Or, you need a Battle Commander to organize the survivors for an attack. Probably assisting Geminus Legion South when you assault the island."

"Very astute of you, Colonel," Cotta acknowledged. "Come look at the map and give me the benefit of your experience."

"Lipari Island has a history of breaking Roman hearts, Consul," Alerio advised. They crossed the room to a map table. Alerio examined the details, moved a hand over the mass representing the island, and stated. "Need I remind you, General Cotta, that eight years ago, Consul Cornelius Scipio lost seventeen warships at Lipari, and was taken captive?"

"I'm fully aware of the island's history, Colonel. As well as its traitorous inhabitants," Cotta added. "I asked for your opinion."

"Let me bring your Legion East to a beach," Alerio described. "The Navy can come in on a single wave and take them off the beach. We'll be gone before Qart Hadasht commanders know we're in the neighborhood."

"An excellent plan, Colonel Sisera," Cotta agreed. "But I don't want to simply escape with Roman lives. I want to punish the islanders."

Alerio and Aurelius Cotta locked eyes across the map table. One burned with a thirst for glory, while the other's eyes were soft with homesickness. Either mission presented an even chance of death. But, of the two commanders, only one had a personal relationship with the Goddess of Death.

Alerio broke the spell and spoke first, "Memento mori."

"What do you mean by that?" Cotta inquired.

"It means I need three days on the island to organize the counterattack," Alerio replied. "Plus, three more for traveling."

Cotta nodded his head in agreement with Alerio's timeline. Then he asked, "What else do you need?"

"Milon Frigian," Alerio replied. "The Sons of Mars' Captain knows the waters around the island. If anyone can get me, supplies, and an issue of javelins in undetected, it's him."

"I know most of the Sons' Captains. Why haven't I heard of Frigian?" Cotta commented. Then he blinked and inquired. "Why javelins?"

"If you haven't heard of Milon, it's because he doesn't care to meet you, sir," Alerio explained. "As far as javelins, when a man goes overboard, he can only take some of his gear. If he's a strong swimmer, he'll put his gladius on his shield and drag it to shore. If a little weaker, he'll put a spear on the shield because it partially floats. But no one, not a fish or a sinker, chooses to take his issue of heavy javelins for a swim."

"How many javelins?"

"That depends, Consul, on how many men are stranded on the island."

***

A few moments later, Hektor put his hands on his hips.

"You, sir, cannot go wandering around the alleyways of Messina without an escort," the youth declared.

"I can't go to Lipari until I do," Alerio said justifying his choice. "Besides, I need you to go to the Legion surgery and pull a bundle of medical supplies. We'll need it when we get to the island."

"Can you trust the information, Colonel?"

"Witnesses, according to the Consul, say ten Centuries made it to shore," Alerio replied. "Sadly, the loss of eleven warships means a lot of good men never made it to the beach."

"I'll take what I can carry. But treating eight hundred infantrymen is impossible."

"Take what you can," Alerio said as he walked away. "I expect most of the injuries will be to their pride."

At the first lane, he took a left, and scanned ahead. Brick and wooded walls formed the sides of an empty passageway. On the street, he went farther north before entering the next alley. He spotted a couple of locals at the far end. They looked tough enough, so Alerio slowed his pace.

"Nice hat, Latian," one said as he pushed off the wall. "That would look good in my collection."

"Might be a good idea," Alerio remarked while he pulled the hat off his head, "because even a fine hat like this can't help your girlfriend."

"Help her with what?"

"Her looks. She's ugly."

The thug drew back his fist and swung at Alerio. Using the hat to obscure the man's vision, Alerio ducked and slid his foot between the man's legs. With a grip on the thug's

254

arm, Alerio swung his weight. The man tripped and slammed into the brick wall. Alerio let go, dropped to a knee, spun, and punched the second man in the groin. Both dropped to the ground.

"I'm looking for Milon Frigian," Alerio told them.

He strolled from the alley, turned north again, and walked until he came to another lane. By the time he reached the far end, eight men stood on the street. Two were obviously in pain from the previous encounter.

"Good, you made excellent progress," Alerio remarked. "I'm looking for Milon Frigian."

"Never heard of him," one replied.

"How about you?" Alerio questioned a large man.

"Like he said, never heard of him."

"Then, I have no use for you," Alerio commented.

As if the eight men weren't there to beat on him, Alerio turned around and marched back the way he came. They chased after him but, being hemmed in by the walls of the lane, the first two moved shoulder to shoulder. None of them saw Alerio pull the Legion and Golden Valley daggers.

In a low voice, Alerio began to sing as he turned to face the first two.

Let all who grieve
chant the Sons of Mars Elegy
An empty bench
An idle oar
Our brother has passed
He'll row no more

With a dip, Alerio dropped to his right as if favoring the arm. The lead pair brought their blades up to defend against the slim dagger. Slashing from the left, the Legion dagger caught them off guard. They jerked back, scrambling away from the blade. In the narrow confines of the alley, they fell into the pair behind them.

Alerio sang as he backed away.

Walk me through Messina dears
A final view of the town I fear
Of the beautiful harbor at sunrise

The four in the lead pushed to their feet. Some of their confidence had been lost in the fall to the ground. But they shook like mangy animals to get the dirt off and that invigorated them. Then in the back of the mob, one heard Alerio and added his voice to the song.

And the high Citadel at sunset
As I recall good days of cheer
Let all who grieve
Chant the Sons of Mars Elegy

"How do you know that chant, Latian?" the singer questioned Alerio.

"It took you long enough to ask," Alerio replied. "My name is Captain Alerio Sisera of the Messina Militia. And I need to see Milon Frigian."

"There's no Messina Militia," the big man noted.

The singer pushed his way to the front and gawked at Alerio.

"There was a militia and, great Sterculius," he swore to the God of Manure, "Captain Sisera. Thank you for your restraint."

Chapter 23 – Moonlight Over Lipari

"Usually, Alerio Sisera, when you come looking for me there's more blood," Milon Frigian observed.

"Usually, it takes more than a song to find you," Alerio responded.

The two men gripped wrists and hugged.

"Are you escaping again?" Frigian inquired. "Or have you come to take me up on the offer to join the Sons of Mars?"

"Neither, but I do require a ride," Alerio told him. "I need to get to Lipari Island with some supplies."

"The marooned Legion," Frigian said before Alerio could finish. "The Legionaries have claimed a small plateau. So far, Qart Hadasht command has left them there to starve. After all, why waste soldiers when hunger will soon have them surrendering?"

"Can you get me there?" Alerio asked.

"My friend, I am a daring pirate and a cunning smuggler," Frigian exclaimed. "There's no place I can't reach. But Lipari is a main base for the Empire. You'd be safer commanding a Sons' bireme."

"I'll leave that to you," Alerio told him. "When can we leave?"

"Before dawn," Milon Frigian replied. "That will give us an evening for drinking and telling lies."

"I am a Colonel in the Republic's Legion," Alerio boasted, "I never lie."

"There's the first one and we haven't had a drink yet," Milon shouted.

Around them, the small pub exploded with calls for pitchers and mugs. The proprietor of the establishment grabbed one of his servers and pressed coins into her hand.

"Get to the cheesemaker and see if he has buttermilk," he directed. "Frigian's taking his ship into Empire waters. Some of the crew will require something else besides beer or wine tonight."

***

In the dark of early morning, Hektor, an NCO, and four Legionaries carrying supplies marched onto the dock.

"Are you sure about this?" the Optio questioned.

"Sergeant, the Colonel's note was pretty clear about the location," Hektor replied. "And being here before dawn."

"Well, we're certainly here before sunrise," the NCO acknowledged.

From the dark, a long ship with two banks of oars slid alongside the dock.

"Good morning, Hector," Alerio greeted the youth.

He jumped from the deck and marched to the NCO.

"Optio, did you requisition everything I asked for?"

"Sir, the quartermaster had questions about the number of wineskins," the NCO replied. "But General Cotta's aide set him straight."

"Vino and weapons, Sergeant," Alerio advised. "It's all a good infantryman needs."

"We also brought the dried beef, sir."

"Also, a requirement," Alerio added. "Pass the supplies to the crew."

Hektor stepped forward but Alerio rested a hand on the youth's shoulder.

"I need you to stay in Messina," he informed the Greek. "If I don't make it back, you're the only one who can tell my story."

"It's an excuse I'm becoming accustomed to hearing," Hektor complained. "But it doesn't get easier. I should be with you."

"You can claim space on the transports with the Centuries of Legion East. You're the valet for their Battle Commander. Even if none of them know me."

"Then I'll see you on Lipari, Colonel Sisera."

"Yes, you will."

Alerio stepped onto the bireme and Captain Frigian instructed, "Ready all. Stroke, stroke."

One hundred and twenty rowers dipped their oars into the water and the pirate ship vanished back into the night.

On the dock, Hektor stood staring at the black water until the NCO commented, "Sisera is either the bravest or craziest officer I've ever heard of."

"Colonel," Hektor corrected as he turned from the water. "It's Colonel Sisera. And yes, Optio, he is both of those."

***

The bireme picked up the current outside the harbor and rode the main flow into the narrows. Once through the Massina strait, they entered the Tyrrhenian Sea. With the sail unrolled, the ship cruised along the northern shore of Sicilia. At midday, they beached at Spadafora.

"Rest, everyone," Milon instructed. "We launch with the offshore breeze."

Cookfires were lit and bedrolls unpacked. They stayed on the beach until the land cooled. Around midnight the breeze blew out over the water and Milon ordered the launch. Soon afterwards, the bireme rowed northwest and out onto the open sea.

"When will we reach the island?" Alerio asked.

"With the rising sun, Vulcano Island will appear on our left," Milon replied. "Or, on our right. Or not at all, if my navigation is way off."

"Does that happen often?"

"So far, not to anyone's detriment," Milon Frigian explained. "But this far out to sea, it will only happen once."

***

Vulcano Island grew from the horizon. A mound reflecting the light of the rising sun, the island was a pleasing sight to the crew.

"You pulled it off again, Captain," a crewmen complimented Milon. "For a spell last night, I started to reach for my buttermilk."

"Settle your stomach, big man. We've sail together for years," Milton reflected. "Do you think I'd let you down, now?

"There's always a first time, Captain."

It took all morning and part of the afternoon to sail around the tip of Vulcano and up the west side of the island.

"The next island is Lipari," Milon pointed to a brown shape in the distance. "We'll put you ashore tonight at Cala Fico cove. The coastline is rocky, and it's a tough landing area, but it'll keep you away from patrols."

"How tough?" Alerio questioned.

Milon Frigian ignored the question as he ordered the ship to beach near a village. Seeing the bireme, the residents came out to trade.

"We're not always pirates or smugglers," Milon said to Alerio as he waved to the people. "Sometimes, we're just traders."

"Because they have important goods," Alerio asked.

"No Colonel. Because sometimes, we need safe harbors and friendly beaches," he responded. "Lentia village is one of them."

***

Late in the afternoon, two Qart Hadasht ships-of-war slid by on the horizon.

"It's going to be hard to dodge them," Alerio pointed out.

"Not at all," Milon assured him, "they beach at dusk. That's when we launch. And by morning, we'll be back in the same place, standing here waving at them."

They passed the day chatting with the villagers. Intrinsically Alerio understood their lack of sophistication. But spending time with people who had no idea there was a war between the Empire and the Republic, or that Illyria even existed, demonstrated the isolation of most people.

As promised, the bireme slipped into the water at dusk, and the oarsmen stroked away from Vulcano Island. Six miles to the north, the ship eased into a cove at Lipari Island.

"All I can see are black cliffs," Alerio observed.

From the water to the knobby tops backlit by the stars, the walls seemed impenetrable.

"That's Cala Fico for you," Milon confirmed.

"Then how am I going…"

The bow of the ship bumped into a spot below a gap, a rope flew up and lodged in the break. Then a sailor scrambled from the deck and vanished over the wall of rock.

"We'll hoist your supplies and then you'll climb up," Milton explained as the first bundle was raised up the cliff face. "On the backside, the land rises steeply but is scalable."

"And how do I locate the Legion?"

"Walk east, stay on the contour of the hills until you reach flatland," Milon described. "By then they'll find you or an Empire patrol will."

"It doesn't sound like you have much confidence in me," Alerio mentioned.

"None whatsoever," the pirate Captain confirmed. "This is a suicide mission."

Alerio gripped the rope, looked at Milon Frigian's shadowy face and said, "I've heard that before. I'll see you in Messina."

Raising his legs up, Alerio swung from the deck to the rock. Once he had contact, the Legion officer walked and pulled his way to the top. Marked by the moonlight, he counted four bundles resting on the grass.

"Thank you," Alerio told the crewman.

"Don't be here in the morning, sir. The Empire patrols along the coast."

After delivering the warning, the Son of Mars lifted the rope from the notch and threw it out over the water. With the evidence of their stop gone, the pirate dove off the cliff. Alerio heard him splash down, the whisper of Milon calling to his rowers, and the slap of oars before the night fell silence.

"Don't be here in the morning," Alerio repeated the warning of the crewman.

He stacked the bundles by twos on flat rails, secured them with lines, and slung the extra rope over his shoulders. Then, acting like a draft animal, Alerio pulled the supplies away from the cliff top.

***

Legionaries run, climb, and carry heavy loads. They persevere against adversity and overcome obstacles.

"Legionaries run, climb, and carry heavy loads," Alerio grunted as he struggled against the ropes.

Repeating the mantra with each step, he towed the bundles up from the cliff top, around a bend with uncertain footing, and up a steeper grade. Just as the bundles started to get the better of him, a voice called from the dark.

"Is someone there?"

Between the sweat in his eyes, the thumping of his heart, and the exhaustion that begged him to lay down and nap, Colonel Sisera didn't care who asked. If it were the Empire or the Republic challenging him, he would gladly relinquish the load. Mostly because he didn't have the stamina to fight.

From the darkness above, two people held a conversation.

"Optio, I heard something down the hill."

"Did you verbally challenge them?"

"I asked who was there."

"And did you expand your chest to make it a bigger target while you exposed your position?"

"I, I…"

Alerio stood straighter and smiled. Only a Legion NCO could string together a lesson disguised as humiliation to teach an infantryman how to stay alive.

"Optio, I have supplies," Alerio spoke into the dark.

"And who are you?"

"Colonel Alerio Sisera, newly assigned to Cotta Legion East."

"You and your staff can come ahead," the NCO instructed. "Slowly, one at a time."

"That won't be hard. There's only me."

"Just you?" the NCO grumbled. "A lot of good that'll do us."

"I'll pretend I didn't hear that," Alerio shot back. "Now, get a work detail down here and collect these bundles. I didn't drag them all the way from Cala Fico cove to leave them for an Empire patrol."

"Yes, sir," the Sergeant responded.

Clearly, he had gotten control of his emotions.

***

Sunrise gave Alerio an idea of how the Legionaries prevented the Empire from flushing them out. Between three hills around the plateau, they constructed dirt barriers on the approaches. It would be a bloody fight to assault over the mounds. Higher up the grades were sentry positions. It was one of these Alerio stumbled upon in the dark.

"Food's scarce, Colonel," a young Centurion named Galba Vitulus explained. "But there are two springs with fresh water nearby, so we aren't thirsty."

"You organized all this?" Alerio questioned.

"I did when we first scrambled ashore, Colonel," Galba Vitulus responded. "After our Third Maniple rowed away with the command staff, and the surviving ships with the Second followed, our warships, the ones hauling the First Maniple got trapped between the beach and the Qart Hadasht ships-of-war."

Galba's words came out in a long string, displaying his nervousness. Alerio wanted to tell the young infantry officer to relax. With a Battle Commander in charge, most of the weight of responsibility was lifted from the junior officer's shoulders.

"How many officers made it to shore?" Alerio asked. He didn't remark about the survivors being inexperienced First Maniple infantrymen.

"Just me, sir," Galba replied. "It was just me and four hundred Legionaries. So, I relinquished command to my senior Optios."

This was the first sign of internal trouble in a tough situation. Alerio taught that an officer should ask the opinions of his NCOs. But opinions were all. The final decisions had to remain with the officer.

"Who is this?" a big NCO demanded as he approached.

Stacked beside the infantry officer's camp, were the bundles Alerio brought. With disdain for his officer, the Sergeant placed a foot on one stack and leered. Then, he grinned at Alerio.

"I pulled those packages from the cliffs," Alerio explained as he stood. "They are heavy, meaning I had a rough night."

"Things are tough all over," the NCO mocked.

Two more NCOs strolled up and flanked the big man.

"Colonel Sisera, this is Optio Nexus," Galba said apologetically. "He's in charge of the command committee."

Alerio walked around the bundles, forcing Nexus to take his foot down so he could turn.

"Thank you for that Sergeant."

"Thank you for what?"

"For…" Alerio swung from below his waist, driving the fist up and into the NCO's chin. The force rocked his head, and the Optio flew back, bounced off the bundles, and collapsed on the ground. "For presenting your chin."

The flanking NCOs half drew their gladii. But the tips of a Legion dagger and a gladius were already resting against the skin of their necks.

"Centurion Vitulus, how's the ground around here?" Alerio asked.

"For what, Colonel?" the young officer inquired.

"For digging graves," Alerio replied. "I'm thinking three but there might be more before I establish who is in command."

"Who are you to come here and take control?" one of the NCOs questioned.

"I am Colonel Alerio Carvilius Sisera, and I'm your new Battle Commander," Alerio replied. "I've fought from Messina to the walls of Qart Hadasht alongside good men. My personal deity is Nenia the Goddess of Death, and my father is Senator Spurius Maximus. But, at this instance, there's something more important for you to consider."

"What?"

"Will I kill you slowly to set an example or fast so I can get on with my day."

"You make it sound as if there's no third option."

"I'm confused," Alerio admitted. "You three disrespected me, failed to offer military courtesy, or to call me by my title. As far as I'm concerned, you three are useless to me. And dangerous to this command."

"You can't come here and inflict your Legion nonsense on us," Nexus growled. He sat up and rubbed his bruised chin.

Alerio shifted his blades to a high angle. With pressure on the NCO's collarbones, he forced them to their knees. Once they were down, he kicked Nexus in the side of his head. Designed to protect a Legionary's feet, hobnailed boots could also deliver damage to an enemy. The big NCO's head bounced off his shoulder before his body crumpled to the ground.

"Galba, seeing as this is your Maniple, I need you to pronounce death sentences for these three rogue NCOs," Alerio instructed.

Colonel Sisera may have assumed most of the responsibilities, but a junior infantry officer needed seasoning. And making difficult decisions was one test of leadership.

Shaking, the young infantry officer braced at attention.

"I am Centurion Galba Mamilius Vitulus, a citizen of Rome," he declared, "and I'm the officer in charge of First Maniple, Cotta Legion East. My father is Senator Quintus Mamilius Vitulus. After considering the charges, I sentence…"

"Please, sir. Please, mercy," the two NCOs begged. "We were only doing what we thought best for the survivors."

Galba looked into Alerio's eyes for any sign of pity.

"The charges and punishment are fitting for the crimes," Alerio assured the infantry officer. "I'm ready to carry out your command."

"The sentence is death."

The gladius and dagger pierced the skin of their necks. After twisting the blades, Alerio withdrew the weapons and the NCOs fell to the ground, bleeding, and dying.

"And Nexus?" Alerio asked while cleaning his blades.

"We don't have trees suitable for crosses," Galba responded. "He'll have to be splayed on the branches of a midsized tree as an example."

"Are there any other sea lawyers in the command?"

"No Colonel. The rest of the NCOs will respect your position," Galba assured him.

"And your commands, Centurion Vitulus. Now, walk me around and introduce me to the men."

Chapter 24 – Run for Your Life

The trail tracked along the shoreline almost at the level of the tide. Between the beaches, the path rose to the tops of rocky cliffs before falling back to sea level. In single file, a unit of mercenaries hiked off the beach and climbed the grade. They didn't see the eyes spying on them from the tree line.

"Close the backdoor," Alerio whispered when the rear of the patrol reached the highest point on the trail.

An Optio acting as the Century's officer waved a signal to Centurion Vitulus. Shortly after, the infantry officer and thirty men slipped from the foliage, came to their feet, and jogged after the patrol.

"I guess we should collect some armor and weapons," Alerio remarked. "Maybe they'll have grain."

"That would be nice, sir," the Century's Sergeant offered.

The rear assault team had almost reached the last of the mercenaries when Alerio slashed the air with his arm.

"Let's go find out," he said. "Attack."

Colonel Sisera and another thirty men crashed from the trees. Coming from the right front of the patrol, they were seen immediately.

Responding to the assault, the Captain of the mercenaries waved his men forward to form a defensive line. But just as he called them forward, he noticed the Legionaries coming over the hill from behind. Caught between two unexpected forces, he jerked from front to back, and from back to front.

As they jogged, the acting Centurion remarked, "He's confused, Colonel."

"An unsure commander is a defeated commander," Alerio replied. "How many in this patrol?"

"I figure about forty," the Sergeant responded. "That's forty more Legionaries we can equip, sir."

"I'm afraid the next patrol will be a few hundred soldiers," Alerio commented as he drew his gladius. "However, we are accomplishing one thing."

"Sir?" the NCO asked.

"We're drawing their reserves off from Lipari city," Alerio remarked.

Then as he, the acting officer, and the Sergeant slowed up behind the fast-forming two rank formation, the Optio directed. "Assault line, tighten those shields."

Three times the inexperienced Legionaries had set ambushes and assaulted a patrol. Each time, they took food, weapons, and armor. But each time, the number of infantrymen without armor were outnumbered by the armed mercenaries. Of the sixty in the assault force, only thirty-five had chest pieces, helmets, shields, and steel tipped spears.

Given a chance, the armored Empire troops could have cut through the Legionaries. But they didn't get a chance.

"Second rank," Alerio bellowed. "Throw one javelin. Throw."

Fifteen of the iron tipped missiles flew into the clustered soldiers. And fifteen mercenaries fell back either wounded or trying to remove the long iron shafts and tips from their shields.

One soldier gripped the javelin's iron and bent the shaft back and forth. Seeing the abuse visited on the weapon, a Legionary ran forward and slashed him with his gladius.

"Don't be damaging our javelins," the Legionary scolded. Then quickly, he walked backwards until he rejoined the assault line.

"I want to see that infantryman when this is over," Alerio told the acting infantry officer.

"Yes, sir," the NCO responded.

He gritted his teeth in fear for Legionary Paco. Battle Commander Sisera had proven three times that he was a strict disciplinarian. There was no telling what he would do to an infantryman who broke the shield wall of an assault line.

***

Shortly after the hostilities ceased, Galba Vitulus marched to Alerio and saluted.

"Forty-four more spears, thirty quality knives, forty-four chest pieces, helmets, and shields," Galba reported. "Sir, we now have seventy-seven fully equipped infantrymen."

"Almost a full Century," Alerio acknowledged. "Congratulations Centurion Vitulus and welcome back to the Legion."

"Welcome back, sir?"

"Up to this point we've been raiders and marauders," Alerio explained. "Tomorrow, we march on Lipari as infantrymen. Even if most of us lack war gear."

"Sir, what if General Cotta gets held up?" Galba inquired.

"You mean if the fleet doesn't arrive? If no additional Maniples hit the beach and attack from seaward?"

"Yes, sir," the infantry officer confirmed.

"Then we'll take the city and the spoils for ourselves," Alerio exclaimed. "Pass out the rest of the dried beef and the wineskins. Tonight, we feast and sacrifice to Jupiter's winged enforcers. Because tomorrow, we come out of hiding and we fight."

***

Later that evening, Galba Vitulus stood on a hill and addressed the four hundred men of the First Maniple.

"I sacrifice to the God Zelos and ask him for enthusiasm for the coming battle," he prayed while sprinkling wine on the ground. Then before shaking more droplets of the precious liquid, he stated. "I sacrifice to the Goddess Bia and ask her for the strength to press the attack. And lastly, I sacrifice to the God Kratos and ask him for the might to wield our weapons until the last soldier falls and we stand triumphant."

At the end of asking for assistance from the Gods, the young infantry officer took a stream of vino, then performed a series of salutes directed at his infantrymen. Cheering accompanied Galba as he marched off the hill.

"Thank you, Colonel Sisera," he acknowledged upon reaching the officers' campsite, "for the opportunity to lead the sacrament."

"Your father is a Senator and you're a nobleman," Alerio questioned, "why aren't you a Tribune?"

"I've been tutored since childhood on military tactics. And instructed in the use of a shield and a gladius since I could handle the weight," Galba replied. "Being a messenger for command didn't work for me. I wanted to be closer to the action."

Alerio looked around at the makeshift campsites of the Legionaries. Thrown together from anything the men managed to salvage, steal, or scavenge, the area resembled a slum rather than a military bivouac.

"I don't think this is what you had in mind," Alerio offered.

"In a way, sir," Galba countered, "it's better. Other than the problem with Sergeant Nexus. But thanks to you, I've had more command responsibilities than a First Maniple Centurion could ever hope for."

Alerio studied the smiling infantry officer before remarking, "Your father should be proud. And Centurion, I'd have you in my command any day."

"And I'd be honored to serve under you, Battle Commander."

***

Before sunrise, fires blazed around the survivors' camp. Everything combustible was piled in five great stacks. And, as if points on a star, they blazed, sending smoke to the stars in the dark sky. From the small plateau, the bonfires would be invigorating. From the hills, with a view of the pattern, they would be awe inspiring. But there was no one in either location to appreciate the display.

The only eyes available to witness the fires were the Empire watchers on far off knolls. And from that distance, they couldn't tell the Legion camp was deserted.

***

Two and a half miles of traversing gorges and hiking down dales, placed the four hundred Legionaries in the forest above Lipari city. At the crest of a finger of highland, Alerio and Galba looked down from a three-hundred-foot perch.

"The fires were an innovative idea, Colonel," Galba mentioned. "They'll keep the Empire from realizing we've moved."

"There's that as well," Alerio commented.

They scanned the empty streets and the shadowy houses of the sleeping town. But mostly, the two Legion officers studied the night fires inside the headquarters stockade. Each fire marked a major sentry post and a threat. Beside offices for the Empire commanders, the fort housed a quick reaction force and the Qart Hadasht armory for Lipari. The force represented a danger to the understrength Maniple while the armory presented an opportunity. As if moths drawn to a flame, the eyes of the Legion officers were drawn to the stockade.

Galba inhaled sharply when a question occurred to him.

"Colonel, you said, there's that as well, when I remarked about our bonfires," Galba questioned. "Sir, is there another reason we burned our camp?"

"The primary reason was to assure full commitment from our infantrymen," Alerio told him. "The fires destroyed all their belongings. With nowhere to go and no possessions to return to, they'll be forced to win this battle."

The five NCOs, acting as Centurions, moved to the edge of the heights.

"The men are staged," one informed Alerio.

Another warned, "It'll be daylight soon, sirs."

"Centurion Vitulus. It's your command. Orders?" Alerio inquired.

They had five Centuries of inexperienced infantryman. But only one fully equipped, and that unit was short by three men. If they had been experienced Legionaries when the warships sank, they would have floated their shields to shore with whatever they could bring. As it stood, all the armor, helmets, shields, and spears in the Maniple were taken from mercenary patrols.

The patched together command staff waited for the young infantry officer.

Finally, with a quiver in his voice, Centurion Galba Vitulus instructed, "Let's go surrender."

***

The gate sentry lounged against the beam of the barrier. To his sleepy eyes, the figures coming down the street were tricks of the moonlight. Then he blinked to clear his vision which revealed columns of men moving towards the stockade. Panic set in and he began to cry out. But his mind still couldn't comprehend the large troop movement. Then he recognized the Empire issued helmets, and the tribal symbols favored by different mercenary groups on the shields.

"A busy night," a soldier proclaimed. He and another lifted the barrier and stepped aside.

"You can't bring them in here," the gate sentry grumbled.

But the leading edge of the columns had reached the entrance to the stockade.

"Look, we took a hundred and sixty of the Latians prisoners," the soldier complained. "There's no way, we can guard them in the dark, in an open field."

Caught without directions, the sentry watched as the men poured through the portal.

After glancing at the interior of the fort, he directed, "I understand your problem. Let's put them against the animal pens. My Lieutenant will be awake soon. He'll know what to do with the prisoners."

As they spoke, lines of shields, boxing in the detainees, passed his post. At least that's how it appeared to the sentry. If he could see the other side, his impression would be completely different. On that side, only a few armored mercenaries guarded the Legionaries.

From deep in the center of the detainees, Second Century's acting officer questioned, "Are you sure about this, sir?"

"We're going to be outnumbered no matter where we begin our attack," Alerio whispered. "It's better to fight for war gear first."

"If we can get to their armory before they wake up," the NCO said.

Nervous and worried, he had repeated Alerio's instructions. The Battle Commander wasn't displeased that the NCO used the 'get to their armory before they wake up' as his refrain.

"It's not if, Optio," Alerio corrected, "it's when we take their armory. Send out my miscreant."

The two Centuries of unarmored Legionaries and the seventy-seven men with seized armor, shields, and spears had entered the compound and remained together. Around them, Empire sentries watched their progress. Because the gate sentry hadn't issued a warning and the prisoners were under guard, the sentries at the posts didn't raise an alarm.

When the columns turned away from the barracks and headquarters building and moved towards the animal pens, a dark figure sprung from the columns.

Paco slammed into the dirt. Rapidly crawled under a wagon and hid behind a wheel. Armed only with a Legion dagger, he felt naked without his armor and shield.

"That's the last time I leave the ranks and break the shield wall," he whined. "I don't care how many javelins they destroy."

Across a short patch of open ground, a single sentry marched in front of the armory. Paco's job, the one Colonel Sisera volunteered him for, was to remove the sentry, silently, or to die trying. Then, even if gutted and bleeding, he was to open the door for the armory and stage weapons for the unarmored Centuries. Or Colonel Sisera would hunt him down in the afterlife and put him on eternal latrine duty.

"I should have remained in the ranks," Legionary Paco scolded himself.

***

Centurion Vitulus and the other one hundred and sixty-three Legionaries travelled in small units. Each took a separate route, but all had specific orders if confronted. They were to surrender. Most of the Empire forces were billeted throughout Lipari. Any confrontation would draw soldiers into the streets.

Those not taken prisoner, would make their way to the alleys outside the stockade gate. Once there, they would wait for one of three outcomes.

***

The Legionary moved up beside the wheel and tensed. When the sentry turned his back, Paco scrambled out from under the cart's bed. Staying low, he used his hands and feet to scurry across the open ground. Once in the shadow at the corner of the building, he flattened and made himself a small mound of dark on the soil.

The guard reached the corner of the building and stopped. Breathing shallowly, Paco remained still, below his line of sight. After waving at the sentries with campfires, and being ignored by them, the armory guard turned to make another round.

The other sentries watched the main gate or the walls but rarely glanced at the armory or the interior of the fort. Their campfires put up waves of heat creating a blurry curtain between them and the entrance to the armory. It was this placement that gave Battle Commander Sisera the idea to turn Paco into an assassin-raider.

"Never again will I leave the ranks," Paco swore as he tightened his grip on the dagger.

Then in a burst of activity, the Legionary jumped up, reached around, and slashed the sentry's throat. With the same motion, he grab the critically wounded man's shoulder and spun him. Paco ignored the blood gushing into his face and down his chest while he rolled with the sentry to the side of the building.

"Never again," he whined while pushing the body away.

After looking to see if anyone witnessed the killing, he rose. Walking bent rather than crawling, he crossed to the door, untied the rope, and stepped into the armory. By feel, Paco located stacks of shields and removed the bindings. Next, he felt for bundles of spears. In the next few moments, he carried armloads of spears and staged them to one side of the doorway. Then he shifted shields to the other side of the door. So far, there had been no shouts or challenges from the sentries. That was about to change.

***

From the mob of Legionaries, Alerio watched the door open and close. Sliding through the formation, he sidled up to the NCO in charge of the second Century.

"Have you been watching?" he asked.

"Yes, sir. Paco got inside," the acting Centurion replied. "We can go whenever you say, Colonel."

"Once your men have shields and spears, you need to control the barracks," Alerio reminded the NCO. "Contain them with everything you have. Good luck to you. Go."

From the milling throng of prisoners, eighty men raced for the armory. As they broke free, the seventy-seven armored ones separated and dashed at the sentry posts.

Seeing the prisoners break free, the sentries shouted warnings. Then the armored Legionaries were on them. Although silenced quickly, they had sounded the alarm, awakening the reaction force and the Empire officers.

The final eighty infantrymen sprinted to the headquarters building. Now standing alone at the animal pens, Alerio Sisera prayed.

"Nenia Dea, Goddess of Death, take me and all the souls you can harvest from the mercenaries of the Empire. But if

I've pleased you over the years, spare the Legionaries. There are already too few of them for this mission."

***

Centurion Vitulus saw two men knock the gate sentry to the ground and take command of the barrier.

"It's started, seal the approach," he told four runners.

They left the infantry officer, two crossing to the other side of the street. At each alleyway one would stop to say, "It's started, seal the street."

As he delivered the message, the second messenger leaped to the next alley. In moments, every Legionary outside the stockade had the command.

Soon afterward, a patrol of mercenaries strolled from the center of the city towards the compound. Relaxed at the end of their shift, the five had their spears on their shoulders and their shield straps loosen. Both put them at a disadvantage when twenty Legionaries with a mixture of cooking knives, daggers, and sharpened sticks emerged for the alleyways.

And no matter how frantically the patrol leader called for reinforcements, no one came from the fort to help them.

***

At the headquarters building, the eighty unarmored and mostly unarmed Legionaries located two entrances. Forming lines on each side of the walkways, they listened as the cries of the sentry posts faded one by one. As silence descended momentarily, an NCO at each entrance kicked the door open and bellowed.

"We are overrun. Retreat, retreat. The reserves are holding the gate open for you," they screamed. "Retreat, retreat."

The men lining the walkways repeated the warning. At the main gate, Legionaries in Empire helmets, and armor and holding mercenary shields stood in lines as if on a ceremonial detail.

Duty Lieutenants and Captains, still half asleep, burst from the headquarters building.

They picked up the cry, "We are overrun. Retreat, retreat. The reserves are holding the gate open for you."

Seeing the passageway through the gate lined with shields and secure, the Empire commanders continued to shout instructions as they raced out of the stockade and escaped down the street.

At the barracks, Legionaries motioned with their spears and shields as squads from the quick reaction force burst from the garrison.

"We are overrun. Retreat, retreat. We'll hold the gate for you, retreat, retreat."

The Sergeants for the Mercenary Companies ran from the barracks and into moonlit chaos. But the sight of their own shields and spears gave authenticity to the cries. They ran for the gate adding their voices, "We are overrun. Retreat, retreat. We are holding the gate. Rally on the street."

But when they reached the street, Latian voices bellowed from every alleyway. No doubt, they were surrounded. To save their men, the Sergeants led the soldiers of the quick reaction force up the street and away from the overrun stockade.

In a dark alleyway just off the street, an Optio inquired, "Orders, sir?"

"We don't have to run for the hills," Galba Vitulus noted. "Or rush in and join the fight. Happily, that leaves option three. We march in and take control of the headquarters compound."

"Absolutely the best of the three, sir," the Legion NCO agreed.

Act 9

Chapter 25 – From the Apex of Victory

The weak rays of the rising sun were blotted out by smoke from a mess of cookfires. All around the compound, Legionaries roasted meat and boiled grains and vegetables. Those not on kitchen duty manned the sentry posts including twenty armored men at the gate.

"There is one disadvantage to our success," Galba mentioned to Alerio.

"What's that Centurion?"

"We can't see the harbor from inside the stockade," Galba told him.

"I have an idea," Alerio declared. Then he shouted. "Paco. Legionary Paco, where are you?"

Overseeing the distribution from the armory, Paco had the time to secure a good fitting set of armor, a new shield, a properly sized helmet, and a finely crafted spear. He jogged up and saluted.

"You called for me, Colonel?"

"Lose the spear and shield and take off the armor, Legionary Paco," Alerio ordered. "I have a job for you."

"But, sir," the miscreant started to protest. Then he caught sight of Galba wrapping his fingers around his throat and mimicking choking himself. Understanding his Centurion, Paco changed his response. "Yes, sir. What's the mission?"

***

Already missing the feast and suffering from leaving the aroma of sizzling pork behind, Legionary Paco slipped from the compound. Two streets later, he almost walked into an Empire barricade. But he managed to circumvent it by backing away. After bypassing another group of mercenaries, he reached the outskirts of Lipari.

Once free of open streets and roads, the Legionary jogged to a rise and climbed until he had a bird's eye view of the town and the harbor. He stacked twigs and dried wood, then sat and watched the smoke from the stockade. Although too far away to smell the cooking meat, he inhaled and dreamed of fresh roasted pork.

The morning drifted by while Paco gnawed on odd pieces of Colonel Sisera's dried beef.

"Never again will I leave an assault line," he grumbled as he chewed.

Late in the morning, he gawked as warships rowed into the harbor. He waited to be sure, then with shaking hands, Paco pulled out a flint and a piece of steel. In moments, flames leaped from the wood. Almost smothering the fledgling fire with a handful of green leaves, Paco produced a plume of smoke.

The smoke relayed a message to Battle Commander Sisera. He in turn passed the message to the men in the compound. They cheered at the arrival of Consul/General Cotta, the fleet, and Legions of Republic infantrymen.

Alerio found a stack of firewood and sat on it.

"Orders, Colonel?" Galba asked.

"Leave twenty men here to defend the stockade," he instructed. "Take the rest and support the landing."

"What about you, sir."

"Centurion Vitulus, while you are off chasing glory," Alerio replied, "I'm going to sit here and relish our small victory."

***

An initial compliment of Geminus Legion South and Cotta Legion East splashed ashore and fought on the beach. By the second wave of Legionaries, the Empire forces began to retreat from the shoreline.

"General, you'll have the city by early afternoon," an aid informed Cotta.

"So soon? I thought this would be a nastier fight."

"Reports from the First Maniple and Second Maniple say the mercenaries are short on spears," the Tribune replied. "No one knows why, but without the weapons, they can't keep our Legionaries off their shields."

"Any word from Colonel Sisera?" Cotta inquired. "He should get the news from me."

"Not yet, we have skirmisher squads out searching for him," the staff officer explained. "If he's alive, General, we'll find him."

"We better find Sisera alive," Cotta uttered. "I've only met Aquila Carvilius a couple of times socially. I don't want to add losing a son to her problems."

"If he's in Lipari, we'll find him, sir."

***

Decanus Nino cursed. His lightly armored Veles should be near the beach with the heavy infantry. Instead, the nine men of his squad jogged through the streets looking for a Colonel.

"If a Battle Commander is stupid enough to go strolling around a city in the middle of a battle," the squad leader complained, "he probably shouldn't be allowed away from his nurses."

"What did you say Nino?" one of his skirmishers inquired.

"Nothing, keep your eyes peeled for…"

Nino and his men halted in the middle of an intersection. On two sides, columns of Empire soldiers marched towards them. Then, the other cross street quickly filled with more Qart Hadasht mercenaries. Looking back for an escape route, Nino saw another unit coming from the rear.

"What did we do?" his pivot man asked.

"Form a circle," Nino directed. "They may take us, but the Velites will make them pay for the privilege."

In the center of the intersection, the ten light infantrymen put their backs to each other and snugged their shoulders together.

"What I wouldn't give for a few javelins," one skirmisher stated.

"You and me both," Nino concurred. Looking around, he encouraged the squad. "Keep it tight."

Formed into a ring of midsized shields and spears, they waited for the first Company of mercenaries to come and butcher them. Then from one of the streets a voice commented.

"That's a very pretty defensive formation, you have there, squad leader," Galba Vitulus observed. "But we've been tracking those mercenaries for five blocks. And they belong to Cotta Legion East, First Maniple. You can have the leftovers. For now, move out of our way."

"What do we do?" a skirmisher asked.

"We're as good as dead anyway," Nino admitted. "Let's move aside and see what happens."

The armor, shields, helmets, and spears might have been Empire designed. But, the coordination of the three-rank assault line was pure Republic. On two streets, the Maniple formations began the Legion cadence of left, stomp, left, stomp as they closed the distance to the real Empire soldiers.

Nino leaned his head against the wall and let out his breath.

"What's your name, Decanus, and why are you in the middle of Lipari with a squad of light infantrymen?" a young man asked.

His tone held a hint of impatience and there were three older men standing close enough to act as bodyguards or advisors.

"Lance Corporal Nino, sir," he answered with the honorific just in case the man was a staff officer. "We're searching for a Battle Commander Sisera."

"The Colonel is at the headquarters stockade," Galba informed him. Turning to one of the older Legionaries, he instructed. "Send a squad to guide Decanus Nino to the compound and to keep him out of trouble."

"We Velites can take care of ourselves," Nino boasted. "You can keep your protection."

"You really do like living dangerously," one of the older men warned. Then to Galba, he said. "Centurion Vitulus, I'm sure it's the close call that has the squad leader rattled."

During a battle, the last person a Legionary wanted to disrespect was an infantry officer. Other than facing the enemy, insulting a Centurion was the fastest way to get dead.

"Sir, I apologize," Nino begged.

"Get him out of here," Galba ordered. Then, the young officer turned away, quickly scanned the battle line, and bellowed. "Optio, straighten your left side. If your squad leader is too weak, find another who knows how to fight. And someone send word around the block. It's time to close the backdoor."

Nino walked away with the NCO.

"You guys are First Maniple," he remarked. "I thought your officers were supposed to be more forgiving than experienced Centurions."

"We've been cut off and, thanks to Colonel Sisera, we survived," the Corporal told him. "There's nothing forgiving about our situation. So, there's no pity allowed."

"I guess the Battle Commander isn't that old," Nino said.

"What?" the NCO asked.

"Nothing Corporal, just a thought," Nino stated.

As the two squads patrolled towards the compound, Nino noticed bodies on the streets. At another intersection, the corpses of dead mercenaries stretched in unbroken lines from a crumpled barricade to the next cross street.

Crushed by stomping and cut by blades held low, the wounds told him two things. Legion heavy infantrymen had done the assaulting, and no surrender had been accepted, therefore no prisoners had been taken.

Nino changed his mind. He was no longer sure he wanted to meet the Colonel who taught this Maniple how to survive.

***

The fighting for Lipari took a unique turn at midday. Three hundred mercenaries marched through the Legion lines. Consul Cotta at first thought they were prisoners.

"If they're surrendering in droves, we must be close to winning," the Consul proclaimed. "Find out who took them, I want to reward the Centurion and his Tribune."

The unguarded Empire mercenaries, stripped off their armor, pulled out rations, and prepared meals. Shortly after the cookfires began heating their pots, the aid returned.

"General, those aren't mercenaries," he explained. "Those are the survivors of your First Maniple, East. Commanded by a Centurion named Galba Vitulus."

"Vitulus. I know that name. He's Quintus Vitulus' son," Cotta pondered the reward for rescuing a Senator's prodigy. "Who freed them?"

"Well, Consul, here's the circumstance. Centurion Vitulus and his Maniple were taking the city street by street. He terrified the Empire commanders so much, they refused to surrender when confronted by our Legions. Vitulus and his Legionaries were prolonging the battle for Lipari. A Senior Tribune begged the Centurion to retire his Maniple."

"An impressive young man," Cotta allowed. "Any word from Colonel Sisera?"

"Sisera sent word that he will come to you once the Qart Hadasht armory is secured."

"And who might I ask captured the armory?"

"This morning before daylight, Colonel Sisera and Centurion Vitulus took control of the headquarters stockade," the aid reported. "I've asked the Senior Centurion of Legion East to task a Century to relieve Colonel Sisera and secure the rest of the Empire spears."

"I guess that explains the spear shortage," Cotta mentioned. "Check with the priests. I want to know the highest honor I can use to reward Centurion Vitulus. With a decorated son, there's no way Senator Vitulus will vote against my triumphant parade."

"Yes, sir," the aid acknowledged. "What about Battle Commander Sisera? Should I ask about a medal for him?"

"Don't bother," Consul Cotta told him. "Colonel Sisera's military career is all but over."

***

Alerio felt good. The injuries to the First Maniple amounted to a few cuts and twisted ankles. For an inexperienced Maniple, the lack of seriously wounded and dead was a miracle. Their survival rate along with their accomplishments gave Alerio a boost to his pride.

"Colonel Sisera to see Consul Cotta," he told the infantrymen of First Century.

Cotta had commandeered a villa with a view of the harbor. While he waited to enter, Alerio breathed the sea tinted air and felt his muscles relax. With Lipari taken and the survivors reunited with the Legion, Alerio could continue his journey home.

"Please come in, Battle Commander," the aid invited.

***

They crossed a great room, strolled down a long hallway, and entered a sitting room with a balcony overlooking the sea.

"General, Colonel Sisera reporting."

Aurelius Cotta sat at a desk with scrolls and pieces of parchment scattered over the top.

"Sit down Alerio. A drink?"

"No thank you, Consul. It seems Galba and I have become celebrities of a sort," Alerio commented. "The infantry officers from the first wave of the landing force want to force vino on us."

"It's the spears and I don't blame them," Cotta offered while searching among the scrolls and correspondences. "Here it is. I am sorry this took so long to reach you."

Taking the parchment, Alerio smoothed it over his leg, and read the missive.

Alerio Carvilius Sisera, Colonel of the Legion, Citizen of the Republic, and Son of Spurius Carvilius Maximus

Alerio,

I trust this note finds you in good health with vigor to boost your spirits.

It is with a breaking heart that I must inform you that General Maximus has taken ill. You may have noticed his frailty before you left. After a brief summer illness, he seemed to recover but then fell into a stupor.

We know he loves you but little else. Not whether he will survive. Or even if he will last long enough for you to get home. In case I haven't been clear, you are needed in Rome as soon as possible.

Aquila Carvilius Maximus, loving wife of Senator Spurius Maximus, and your mother

Lady Aquila

***

Alerio's joy from the victory seeped away with each word. He let the parchment dangle from his fingers.

"We received the letter after you were dropped on the island," Cotta informed him. "I've had people searching for you all day to deliver it."

"General, I formerly request to be separated from Cotta Legion East," Alerio stated. "And, with your permission, to leave on the next warship off Lipari."

"I can't spare a quinquereme. The waters are swimming with Qart Hadasht ships-of-war, and I need my five-bankers," Cotta advised.

"I understand, sir," Alerio said. His heart sank at the thought of not speaking with General Maximus one last time.

Consul Cotta stood and reached his hand across the desk. Then he explained, "I've tasked a trireme with taking you all the way to Rome. She has a navigator who studied the Egyptian art of traveling by the stars. They're ready to launch as soon as you get to the beach."

Alerio gripped the extended wrist and shook it.

"I don't know how to thank you, Consul."

"One day, you may be in the Senate. On that day, I'll tell you how to thank me."

"I'm afraid there's not much chance of that, sir. I'm no politician."

"Safe travels, Battle Commander Sisera."

Alerio saluted the Consul, turned about, and marched from the room. Once in the hallway, he raced for the exit to the villa. Seeing the Consul's aid, he grabbed the Tribune by the shoulders and asked, "Has anyone seen Hektor Nicanor."

"He's on *Theia's Horizon*."

"He's what?" a confused Alerio demanded.

"Your three-banker is named *Theia's Horizon*," the staff officer explained. "Named for the Goddess of Sight. She's beached to the left and waiting for you."

Alerio restrained himself as he passed through the guard post of First Century. Then, he sprinted for the beach, the warship, and home.

Chapter 26 – Blessing of Nenia Dea

Commerce on the Tiber moved aside as *Theia's Horizon* rowed up the big blonde. Partially because with one hundred seventy oars dipping and rising from the water, the rowers on the warship threatened to club any boatman who drifted close to the sideboards. But mostly, because of the bronze ram streaming just below the surface of the river.

"I need to make another offering," Alerio announced.

"Sir, you've made a sacrifice to the Goddess Nenia twice a day, every day since we left Lipari," Hektor reminded him. "You'll be at the villa by this afternoon."

"As long as the Goddess of Death is here with me," Alerio explained, "she's not at Villa Maximus, taking Spurius' soul."

"Bread on the water, or wine?" Hektor inquired.

"Neither. This close, it must be something special," Alerio stated as he drew his Legion dagger. He hovered the blade above his arm. "Nenia, take this offering and give him this day, if that's agreeable with you."

Then he plunged the tip through the skin of his forearm. Blood boiled to the surface and Alerio held his arm out over the aft rail of the ship.

"A blood sacrifice, sir?"

"Actually, two offerings," Alerio clarified. "The blood for Nenia and the pain to honor the Goddess Bia, Maximus' personal deity."

The droplets fell into the pale water of the Tiber. Caught in the swirls created by the hull of the warship, they were quickly whisked away.

"I'll get the vinegar and a bandage," Hektor proposed.

Alerio didn't reply. He stood on the steering deck staring upriver towards home. Visions of his adopted father drifted in and out of his thoughts.

When they first met, Spurius Maximus was a Senator, a little beyond his physical prime but at the peak of his mental powers. And Alerio was a wet, exhausted Lance Corporal from a trapped Legion with a bag full of politically sensitive letters.

He could have asked for a large reward at the time. But the Senator advised him to hold the favor until there was a prize worthy of it. Alerio never got around to claiming the reward. Instead, the Senator and his wife, a childless couple, adopted Alerio and made him a nobleman. Other than the Senator's friendship, it was the greatest reward of all.

Looking down, Alerio was surprised to see Hektor tying off the bandage.

"Does it hurt," the Greek asked.

"Only when I think about losing him."

***

At Rome, sailors tossed lines to dockworkers. As they reeled in the ropes, *Theia's Horizon* drifted to the pier. Before the sideboards reached the structure, Alerio jumped off the warship and sprinted for the street.

"Do you know Villa Maximus?" he asked a carriage driver.

"No, sir. Can't say that I do," the coachman admitted.

"It's east of the Forum. I'll show you," Alerio instructed as he climbed into the coach.

The vibration of the carriage on the paved street should have felt comforting. But Alerio was troubled. He'd never hailed a coach where the driver didn't know the homes of powerful Senators. Yet, this coachman had no idea where Villa Maximus was located. Then worry about his adopted father overtook the idea and Alerio forgot about the issue.

***

As he had for years, Alerio bowed to the statue of Bia when he arrived at Villa Maximus.

"Goddess, thank you for the drive and strength of purpose," he prayed before rushing to the front door.

It opened and a servant stared for a moment before Belen elbowed him aside.

"Am I too late?" Alerio asked.

The Senator's secretary threw the door open and bowed.

"I believe General Maximus has been waiting for you, Master Sisera," Belen ventured. "The doctor can't think of any other reason that he's held on this long."

Alerio dashed through the doorway and sprinted across the great room to the hallway. At the end of the corridor, his adopted mother stood outside a bedroom door. He broke stride and approached her slowly.

"I came as soon as I could."

Lady Aquila turned and reached out with both arms. Alerio leaned into a fierce hug.

"He's in so much pain, but he waited for you," she whispered. Then with strength Alerio didn't know she possessed, Aquila turned him and pushed him into the bedroom. Behind him, she wept and said, "Tell my General, he can go."

***

His emaciated form was almost lost in the blankets. And other than a jerky rising and falling of his chest, he was as still as a corpse. But when Alerio approached, Spurius Maximus opened his eyes.

"Battle Commander Sisera, I'm afraid Algea is winning this skirmish," Maximus rasped.

"General, the Goddess of Pain doesn't know your strength," Alerio told him while kneeling beside the bed. Reaching out, Alerio wrapped Maximus' hand in both of his. "I'm told you've been holding out until reinforcements arrived."

"I've rallied the Legionaries and staked a claim to the high ground," Maximus groaned. "But my hold is tenuous."

"I am not worthy to fill your boots, sir, but I'll stand with you."

"You are more than capable, my son. It's good to see you again."

"And you father. Can I get you anything?"

"A twenty-year-old body and a future," Maximus replied. He coughed and his chest rattled. It took several beats before he continued. "There are things you need to know. When I pass, the ravens will gather and circle…"

The air expelled from his lungs in a great woosh and the body already thin, flattened as the old campaigner died.

"Thank you, Nenia," Alerio uttered to the Goddess of Death. Then loudly, he called out, "Lady Aquila, I require your shoulder."

Instantly, Aquila was beside him. Still on his knees and holding Maximus' hand, Alerio buried his face in his mother's shoulder. They both cried at the passing of former General and Senator Spurius Carvilius Maximus.

Chapter 27 – The Circling of Ravens

Alerio was exhausted and disheartened when he walked through the door.

"Belen, you were right," he complained, "I should have allowed you to hire additional mourners for the temple trek."

"Sir, I'm glad you're back because…"

"I assumed a great man like the Senator would have more than a handful. But the turn out wasn't stellar," Alerio continued without listening to the stress in the secretary's voice. "It was disappointing."

"Colonel Alerio Sisera, sir," Belen pleaded.

"I'm sorry. Is there a problem with the funeral feast?" Alerio inquired.

"There is nothing wrong with the feast," Belen assured him. "But there is a priest from the Temple of Jupiter with Lady Aquila."

"That's fitting. Bia is one of the God's winged enforcers and the Goddess was…" Alerio remarked as he walked into the great room. Then he stopped and glared. A stranger lounged near the door to the patio. "Who are you, sir?"

"My name is Laudatus. I know it's indelicate at this time, but there is a bill due."

Alerio faced Belen and asked, "Is this the problem?"

"No sir, and neither is the man waiting in your study or the one on the patio," the secretary commented. "My concern is the priest."

"How many visitors do we have?"

"Four, sir," Belen responded. "I suggest, strongly, that you begin with the priest."

"Master Laudatus, if you'll excuse me for a brief period," Alerio stated. "I'm sure we can sort this out later."

He walked through the door. On the patio, a Chief from the Samnites Tribe jumped to his feet.

"And you are, sir?" Alerio inquired.

"Gavia. And I must speak with the Senator's heir," the Chief insisted.

"Please stay right there," Alerio begged. "I'll return shortly. Belen, see that the Chief has a beverage."

After confirming the order, Belen guided Alerio across the patio, through a row of hedges, and into a garden. The secretary indicated Lady Aquila sitting with a robed priest in the shade of a gazebo. Glancing at the disturbance, the Lady waved to Alerio.

"Ah, my son, was there a good turnout for the funeral parade?" she asked.

"We could have used another beverage donkey," Alerio lied.

"That's to be expected when a great man dies," she offered. Then with a gracious turn of her hand, she introduced the priest. "This is Cleric Savium from the Temple of Jupiter. He was just complimenting us on the statue of Bia in the front. I told him the Goddess was Spurius' personal deity."

"General Maximus was a man of strong will who exemplified Bia's virtues," Alerio added. As he talked, the priest shifted his hand to cover several coins. When the hand moved, the tabletop was empty. Alerio sat on the bench opposite from the cleric. "Are you here to officiate at the feast?"

"Oh, no, I am here simply to pay my respects," the priest replied. "The Senator was well known at the Temple of Jupiter. For years, he was one of our biggest donors and once a leading depositor."

Alerio understood the dwindling donations, the Senator had curtailed his travel to temples in recent years. But the remark about Spurius Maximus' deposits troubled him.

"His estate, I'm sure, has deposits at the temple," Alerio said.

"Very little, I fear," the priest advised. "I should be going. Again, Lady Aquila, my condolences. And Master Sisera, if you feel the need for counsel, please avail yourself of the services at the Temple of Jupiter."

While Aquila stood with the priest, Alerio remained seated. He would need to have Belen check the balance sheets.

"It was nice of him to stop by," Aquila remarked. When Alerio didn't respond, she said again. "It was nice of him…"

"How much did you give the Priest, mother?" Alerio asked.

"You're just like Spurius, always worried about my gifts to the temples. He had Belen policing me and I don't know how many times Spurius inserted himself in my conversations with priests."

But she was talking to an empty bench. Alerio had already sprinted through the row of hedges.

***

On the patio, Chief Gavia lifted a glass of wine in salute when Alerio ran by. Inside the great room, Laudatus braced as he prepared to layout his case, but Alerio didn't stop to listen.

"Belen, who is in the Senator's study?" Alerio called out when he reached the corridor.

Hektor stuck his head out of a doorway.

"It was a lawyer names Ignazio," the youth answered. "Belen is out checking on the food preparations. Is there a problem, Colonel?"

"When did the lawyer leave?"

"Just a short while ago," Hektor answered. "He had a stack of papers for you to sign. But said he'd come back when it wasn't so chaotic."

The house hadn't been hectic when Alerio arrived. The use of chaotic was a slip of the tongue. A more apt description for after the lawyer's departure.

"Take a horse and ride north," Alerio ordered. "I'm riding south. I want that lawyer."

The Greek youth and Alerio had been through enough that Hektor didn't question the instructions. They both raced through the house to the stables. Alerio guided Phobos from a stall, shoved a bit into the stallion's mouth and tossed the bridle over his head.

***

At the front of the villa several carriages pulled up and guests for the funeral feast stepped down.

"Lady DeMarco, it's good to see you again," Lucius Metellus greeted her.

"Senator, a good afternoon to you," Gabriella responded. "Alerio will be pleased you came."

"Spurius Maximus was a worthy opponent in the Senate," Metellus told her. Then another man stepped down from his coach, Lucius introduced him. "And this is Senator Quintus Vitulus."

"I really shouldn't be here," Vitulus offered. "Spurius and I fought more than we held civil discourse."

"Nonsense," Lucius Metellus disagreed. "We all debate strongly at times. Today we are here…"

Two horses galloped from the stables, cut around the pedestrians and weaved through the coaches before vanishing down the drive. At the boulevard, they split, one racing north and the other heading south.

"Wasn't that Alerio Sisera?" Lucius Metellus asked.

"I'm sure my husband will be back shortly," Gabriella remarked, "with a reason for rushing off. Shall we go in?"

She indicated the open front door, while peering in confusion at the boulevard.

***

Using the habits of an enemy to predict his next move or to set an ambush was a proven tactic. Knowing Belen would panic when Lady Aquila began shoving coins at the priest, and that the secretary would channel Alerio to the transaction, left Maximus' study and the Temple chits unguarded. Add in a lawyer with a relationship to Spurius Maximus and it became, as the Senator had predicted, a circling of ravens picking at a carcass.

He kneed Phobos and the big horse responded. They flew by coaches and carriages. Alerio holding on tightly while looking into passenger compartments, searching for Ignazio in each transport. Finally, on the road to the docks, he spotted the lawyer.

It took muscle to slow the stallion and turn the beast back to block the carriage horse.

"Your passenger robbed my villa," Alerio explained to the coachman. While sliding off the horse's back, he urged. "Master Ignazio, step down and face me."

"I don't know who this man is," the lawyer declared.

"Should I call the city guard?" the driver asked.

"No, no. I'll handle this," Ignazio stated.

He dropped from the carriage with a knife in his hand.

"Do you know who I am and what I do?" Alerio questioned the lawyer. "Because if you really want to fight, I'll gladly slice you into tiny pieces and feed them to you."

"I, I know who you are Colonel Sisera," Ignazio admitted. He dropped the knife. "It was the priest. He said he'd protect me."

"It seems Cleric Savium is not only a thief, but a liar to boot. Where are the temple chits?"

The driver got an extra fee for hauling the Temple chits back to Villa Maximus. Standing on the roadside, Ignazio sweated and feared for his life until Colonel Sisera and the carriage turned off the road and headed for the boulevard.

***

From the great room to the feasting room, to the patio and garden, Villa Maximus hosted acquaintances of the late Senator Spurius Maximus. While they drank wine and talked memories of the departed, down the hallway and passed the guard at the entrance, Alerio sat at Maximus' desk.

"Tell me Master Laudatus why bring this to me today?" Alerio asked.

"The word in my trading circle is with Master Maximus gone, you'll default on his loans," the merchant described. "No offense, but you are a military man. And if you're killed in battle, the estate will go to the Republic. And we won't get paid."

"Are you aware that I am a full partner in the Noric ore trade," Alerio listed, "and in the travertine quarry? Both are separate from the estate."

"We, or rather I, wasn't aware that you were a man of business," Laudatus stated. "This of course puts things in a different light."

"Let me see the voucher," Alerio requested. After examining the parchment, he made Laudatus an offer. "I can hand you temple chits and scrub this bill from my books, but we will never do business again. Or, you can retain the invoice and tell everyone, you trust me to fulfill the family's obligations. For that, you will be first in line for our business. What do you say to that?"

A smile spread across the merchant's face, and he extended his arm.

"Master Alerio Sisera, it's a pleasure doing business with you," he gushed as he gripped wrists with one hand and took back the bill with the other. "I will report to my trading group that our investments are in capable hands. Good day, sir."

The man scurried from the office and Alerio dropped his head to the chairback, pursed his lips, and blew out hard. He hadn't had a chance to review the accounts, but he knew if the Laudatus had taken the chits, the Maximus estate would have been cash strapped. Short until Alerio rode around the capital collecting on coins owed to the estate. It would have looked bad and confirmed the trading group's first impression of Alerio.

"Civi, find Hektor and have him bring the Samnites Chief to the office," Alerio called to the villa's head of security.

"They want you, Colonel, at the feast," Civi informed Alerio.

"Tell Lady Aquila and Lady DeMarco just one more meeting," Alerio promised.

Moments later, a very intoxicated Gavia staggered into the officer.

"Chief, you appear to be drunk."

"I am celebrating the life of my friend," he explained.

"We can conduct our business later," Alerio offered. "Perhaps when you are clear headed."

Gavia strolled along the walls of Maximus' office. As he moved, he caressed first, then ran his hands over the broken weapons and shields mounted on the walls.

"My people are warriors," Gavia stated. "We are so tribal that we fight each other when there's no one else around to fight."

Former Optio Civi Affatus appeared in the doorway. He made a fist, extended the thumb, then jerked it in the direction of the feasting hall.

"I've had the honor of tangling with Samnites," Alerio remarked. "It was a painful experience."

"You are like the General," Gavia said. He touched the last trophy then fumbled with a pouch before extracting a piece of parchment. "He also liked to fight when he was younger."

"I imagine so, but why are we talking?"

"He also enjoyed rewarding people," Gavia said.

"That is so true," Alerio confirmed.

"He rewarded me with a mountain of timberland on the east coast of the Republic," Gavia exclaimed. "I won't tell you why, but it came with a prerequisite. When he died, his son would receive a share of the profits from the sale of timber."

Gavia placed a temple chit on the desk, but Alerio ignored it.

"Can I take my share in lumber?" he asked. "Say, enough to build a couple of fast attack ships. Warships capable of guarding my trade routes against Illyrian pirates?"

"That would be easier for me than bringing you coins," Gavia said. Then he burped and his stomach rumbled. "Can we go to the feast, I'm growing hungry."

Act 10

Chapter 28 – Old Fears, New Possibilities

The priest from the Temple of Athena gave a speech about the General. Although it had been years since he commanded a Legion, and despite his other accomplishments, Spurius Maximus loved the title of General.

"And so, Athena the Goddess of Good Counsel and Heroic Endeavors blesses the man who personified her qualities in life," the priest said concluding his sermon.

Belen and Hektor signaled the waitstaff. Soon after, platters of beef and vegetables, stacks of flatbread, and bowls of grain arrived in the feasting hall.

"Have you thought about your future Alerio," Senator Metellus inquired.

"My options are open," Alerio replied. "Right now, I need to consolidate the family holdings and double check the accounting."

"Surely you have a Greek for that," Senator Vitulus remarked. "Have you considered politics? Maybe even claiming your father's seat?"

"Quintus, unfortunately Alerio is a year too young and can't take his father's position," Metellus informed him.

"Then the seat will go to another family," Vitulus warned. "You could still serve on a Senator's staff, Alerio, and learn the procedures. Then you'll be ready to assume a minor seat when you turn thirty-two."

"For all of the battles and duels I've fought, Senators," Alerio explained, "none gave me pause as much as political discord and the bitter rivalry between factions. I am simply not a political warrior."

"That Greek playwright Euripides said, *things do not look the same when viewed from far or near*," Metellus pointed out. "You would soon learn, Alerio, up close there is less disrespect in the Senate than you might suspect."

"Are you a philosopher now?" Vitulus questioned.

"If you'll excuse me, gentlemen," Alerio said, "I have to mingle or suffer the anger of the Ladies."

"Totally understandable," Metellus allowed.

Alerio walked away feeling as if he escaped a preplanned attack.

***

In the morning, Lucius Metellus and Quintus Vitulus stared at the empty seat as if Spurius Maximus would amble in and begin dictating proposals.

"I didn't always like his politics," Metellus noted. "But he was fair. I'm afraid someone of Cotta's ilk will get the seat."

"That would throw off the entire balance of the Senate," Vitulus remarked.

A gavel pounded and the presiding officer called the chamber to order. Lucius Metellus went to his section and Quintus Vitulus moved back to his. Although friends outside the Senate, in the chamber they were rivals.

"We have a missive from Lipari," the President announced. "Consul Cotta boldly led two Legions in the attack and has claimed Lipari and the neighboring islands for the Republic. He requests a triumphant parade upon his return."

Although a few cheered, more Senators called out 'no' to the ego-based spectacle.

"Please hold your voices until the vote," the President urged. "Further, Consul Cotta asks the Senate to vote on his recommendation for the awarding of a Gold Crown. As the commendation states, the medal goes to a Centurion who kills an enemy in single combat or for holding his ground until the end of a battle."

Groans rose from sections around the chamber. Here was a case of Cotta rewarding someone to prop up his faction.

"Prior to the battle and during intense fighting, First Maniple infantry officer and Cotta Legion East standout Centurion Galba Mamilius Vitulus surpassed the requirements for the Gold Crown. Written details to follow."

Quintus Vitulus could barely catch his breath for all the backslapping and congratulations. He finally had an opportunity to seek the eyes of his friend.

Lucius Metellus shook his head yes, twice. They would approve Cotta's parade through Rome and endorse the medal for Quintus' son. But then they would have to strategize about a new Senator to maintain the equilibrium of the political body.

***

The bright sun of the morning created shadows in alleyways and where tall buildings bordered the boulevard. Bands of lightness than darkness made the day flicker.

Traveling in a small convoy was Alerio, Civi Affatus, and another household guard on horseback. Hektor drove a small cart. They turned onto the forum and a short while later, began the climb up Capitoline Hill. At the Temple of Jupiter, the caravan halted and Alerio dismounted.

His hobnailed boots echoed on the tiles and the sunlight that streamed into the temple reflected off Battle Commander Sisera's ceremonial armor.

"Colonel, welcome to the Temple of Jupiter," a priest greeted him. "How can the Sky Father help you?"

"I am Alerio Carvilius Sisera," his voice boomed throughout the building. "A Priest from your temple attempted to cheat Spurius Maximus' widow on the day of his funeral. If he were in my command, I would execute him. But he is not. I and my family have lost faith in the Temple of Jupiter. Therefore, I am withdrawing all funds from this accursed temple."

Panic among the high priest sent them running to negotiate with the Battle Commander. Because, they didn't have the coins in reserve to pay out all of Spurius Maximus' accounts.

Chapter 29 - Gabriella Carvilius DeMarco Sisera

As he had done for the last four days, Alerio sat gazing at the sky.

"Husband of mine, I have something to say," Gabriella announced. She came up behind the chair and rested her hand lightly on top of his head. Then, as she walked around to face him, she allowed her fingertips to trail over the scar and down his cheek. "You need to come to a decision."

"You, too?" he said with a sigh.

"Not too," she shot back, "Me, your wife, the mother of your children, and the woman who keeps the hearth lit while you're away, is not a 'you too,' ever."

With a sheepish look on his face, the Legion officer sat straighter and gazed at the gold flecks in her brown eyes.

"I apologize, wife of mine," he stated. "You're right, I do need to choose."

"I'm not finished," Gabriella declared. After Alerio nodded, she continued. "If you want to be a farmer, I'm all for it. Growing food is a valued career. Raising our family on the country estate will be pleasant and having you home every evening a treat. As I said, farming is a worthy occupation. But does it match your temperament?"

"That's what I…"

She rested a finger on his lips to stop him from talking.

"You're a fighter my dear, but I'm not sure if battling vermin, drought, and storms are enough enemies for you," she explained. "We can stay in Rome, and you can pursue commerce or battle in the political arena. Or do both, like Senator Maximus. But you can't sit here ignoring those who call on you and refusing invitations."

"I'm just considering my options," Alerio pleaded.

They both turned at the sound of approaching footsteps. Hektor Nicanor stopped, shrugged his shoulders, and held out his hands as a sign of surrender.

"Senators Lucius Metellus and Quintus Vitulus are here to see you, Colonel," the Greek youth reported. "Senator Vitulus said they wouldn't leave until you spoke with them. So, I put both in your office."

Alerio gripped the chair and closed his eyes. Tension flowed through his muscles, sending a shudder down his body. While Hektor stepped away, Gabriella leaned close to her husband's face.

"What's the quote," she remarked, "you can ignore politics?"

"Just because you do not take an interest in politics doesn't mean politics won't take an interest in you," Alerio answered. "It was said two hundred years ago by Pericles, a Greek statesman and General."

"Is it any less true today?" she questioned.

"It's as true today, if not more so."

"Then Alerio Carvilius Sisera, stand up, gear up, and stiffen up," Gabriella instructed, "because Battle Commander, the arena of politics is taking an interest in you."

The End

A note from J. Clifton Slater

Savage Birthright is the 18th book in the *Clay Warrior Stories* series. Thank you for reading the novels and affording me the opportunity to research and write the tales.

My goal in every book is to find holes in history and write stories around them. Or to create origins, as I've done in *Savage Birthright,* for coming events by offering plausible, if not fantastical, explanations.

King Agron of Illyria

In 250 B.C., two years after the fictitious events in *Savage Birthright*, King Pleuratus II suddenly died. Agron of Illyria fought his way to the crown and then, as King Agron, took his army and united the southern and western Illyrian tribes. Reportedly, his military tactics used heavily armored but mobile lines of soldiers reminiscent of Legion's Maniples.

King Pleuratus II

During a time of peace and prosperity, as one ancient writer claimed, Pleuratus II built an army and a navy. We can only surmise that he was preparing to defend his kingdom against a known threat.

King Pleuratus II, ruled from 260 – 250 B.C. We have almost no other information about the Ardiaean ruler. To build this story, I made Agron 10 when his father became King and gave Pleuratus the job of Chieftain of a fishing fleet before rising to be King. Also, I created Jeta, the Kings' wife and Agron's mother.

History before Story

Why is the difference between story and history important? Because events don't happen suddenly. They have origins. In 231 B.C. when King Agron died, his 2nd wife Teuta became Queen and the regent for Agron's one year old son. Queen Teuta was ferocious and faced down the expanding Roman Republic while holding her kingdom together. Although a good tale, this wasn't her story. *Savage Birthright* was an attempt to tell some of the history before the unification of the Illyrian tribes.

The God Boa

To the Illyrians, the God Boa was the Divine Snake. Signifying potency, fertility, and ancestors, the cult of the serpent went back to the mythology of the founding of Illyria. In the mythology, Cadmus failed to rescue his sister from Zeus and couldn't return home. On the advice of the Oracle of Delphi, he followed a special cow and built the city of Thebes where she lay down exhausted. When he sent men-at-arms to find fresh water for a sacrifice, they were killed by a dragon or a large serpent. Enraged, Cadmus slayed the snake.

Unfortunately for Cadmus, the dead serpent was Ares' dragon. The Greek God of War took his revenge years later in Illyria. He turned Cadmus into a serpent. Other Gods seeing Cadmus' wife in distress at losing her husband transformed her into a serpent so the two could be together. In mythology and in real life, snakes became important to the tribes making up Illyria.

Agron's Tactics

King Agron fought his army in small units composed of heavily armored but fast-moving soldiers. It proved successful against the tightly packed phalanxes and tribal melees of his enemies. Although in the story, Alerio teaches Agron's soldiers the tactics, history offers no proof that the King borrowed the Maniple formation from the Legions.

Illyrian Ships

Using sixty oarsmen on a two-banker raiding ships, the Illyrians swarmed transports allowing no time for the crew of the merchant vessel to put up a fight. And, although the Illyrians had no ram or ability to participate in a sea battle, the raiders weren't opposed to attacking a Greek, Roman, or Carthaginian ship-of-war if they had a numerical advantage. For their navies, the more prosperous Illyrian tribes had ships with rams, like other sea powers of the era.

Celts vs. Gauls

The tribes who spread across Europe, Asia Minor, and the British Isles from south central Europe were called Celts and Gauls. Historians would name the wars with tribes north of Italy in 220 A.D. as the Gallic Wars. However, they used the term Celtic Britons for those on the British Isles. But, Gauls were a group of Celtic peoples, therefore, the designations can be used interchangeably.

Modern Map and Story

When researching for the Clay Warrior Stories books, I look at geography, coast lines, land elevations, ancient ruins, and anything of interest in a location. Since 1997, Shkodër, Albania has been the location of the Venice Art Mask Factory. In the factory, craftsmen design the decorative masks made famous by Carnival in Venice, Italy. After reading about the factory, I had to include masks in *Savage Birthright*.

Ancient Dyes

To create a peach-colored dye, ground chestnut husks were used in ancient times. However, peaches were from China so no one in Europe in 252 B.C. would know the color peach. The Adriatic Sea did have salmon, and on the color palette, peach and salmon are close. Therefore, Jeta's Shield-

Bearers have capes and armor colored pale salmon rather than peach.

Poison Control

Warning: Hydrogen cyanide is a poison compound made from the stone pits of certain fruits. The potassium from bone meal and salt Hektor used are not antidotes for cyanide poisoning. Although, charcoal has been used for centuries to absorb toxins from victims of poisoning. Hektor needed a quick antidote, so I took liberties.

A battle that could happen

The battle in *Savage Birthright* in the mountains between the villages of Ducaj and Boge, Albania was purely fictitious. After the death of Queen Teuta in 227 B.C., Agron's dynasty fell. History shows the Ardiaei no longer controlled the area around Lake Shkodra or King Pleuratus' capital city of Shkodër. The Labeatae tribe moved in when she died. I took that fact to mean there existed animosity between the two tribes from long ago. Given the history that followed, I felt it was a battle that could happen.

Consuls in the Clay Warrior Stories are historical figures

Gaius Aurelius Cotta was Consul in 252 B.C. and again in 248 B.C. Three stories demonstrate his authoritarian style of leadership. When Tribune Quintus Cassius went against orders and engaged the Carthaginian fleet off the coast of Lipari Island the Tribune lost ships and Legionaries and sailors. Consul Cotta stripped Quintus of command and took his rank of Tribune for disobeying orders. During the same campaign, a fire destroyed a Legion camp. He demoted a relative, who was in command of the stockade, from a senior officer to an infantryman. And lastly, Cotta fought with his unit commanders over tactics. In one instance, the cavalry of a Legion refused Cotta's orders. I don't know what happened, but I'm sure it didn't go well for the Centurion of Cavalry. Hopefully, I captured Consul Gaius Cotta's personality in this story.

***

I appreciate emails and reading your comments. If you enjoyed *Savage Birthright*, consider leaving a written review on Amazon. Every review helps other readers find the stories.

If you have comments e-mail me.

E-mail: GalacticCouncilRealm@gmail.com

To get the latest information about my books, visit my website. There you can sign up for the newsletter and read blogs about ancient history.

Website: www.JCliftonSlater.com

Facebook: Galactic Council Realm and Clay Warrior Stories

I am J. Clifton Slater and I write military adventure both future and ancient. Until we once again step forward and take our place in a Legion's assault line, Alerio and I salute you and wish you good health and vigor. Euge! Bravo!

***

Other books by J. Clifton Slater

Historical Adventure – *Clay Warrior Stories series*

#1 Clay Legionary	#2 Spilled Blood
#3 Bloody Water	#4 Reluctant Siege
#5 Brutal Diplomacy	#6 Fortune Reigns
#7 Fatal Obligation	#8 Infinite Courage

#9 Deceptive Valor   #10 Neptune's Fury
#11 Unjust Sacrifice   #12 Muted Implications
#13 Death Caller   #14 Rome's Tribune
#15 Deranged Sovereignty
#16 Uncertain Honor   #17 Tribune's Oath
#18 Savage Birthright   #19 Abject Authority

Novels of the 2nd Punic War - *A Legion Archer series*
#1 Journey from Exile   #2 Pity the Rebellious
#3 Heritage of Threat   #4 A Legion Legacy

Military Science Fiction - *Call Sign Warlock series*
#1 Op File Revenge   #2 Op File Treason
#3 Op File Sanction

Military Science Fiction – *Galactic Council Realm series*
#1 On Station   #2 On Duty
#3 On Guard   #4 On Point

Printed in Great Britain
by Amazon